THE ETERNAL

THE ETERNAL

THE WAR OF SOULS
BOOK THREE

CHRIS A. JACKSON

This, the third in the War of Souls, is for all of those fighting to preserve our world from fascism. I began this trilogy during the 45th presidential term of our country, initially as a thought experiment as to why things had gone the way they had. I never dreamed any of this would progress further that that first horrific four years. Now, we face harder, deeper challenges, these to the very fabric the Founders of this nation wove to protect us from tyranny. In this reality, money and propaganda have done what the Nephilim orchestrated in this work of fiction.

But know this, my dear friends.

There is hope.

1

GAME CHANGER

I step out of the late-model SUV onto a parking lot hot enough to fry a steak. The blinding heat triggers a flash memory. *Riding a camel, wrists bound with golden chains, the trophy of a Bedouin warlord seventeen hundred years before God sent his son to die among humans. He's not an unkind master considering some I've had before.* I shudder, blink away the unwelcome recollection, and focus on the here and now; Wichita Falls in summer isn't exactly the Sahara, but it's close. It's hard to believe that we were near here three months ago in a sub-zero Arctic bomb cyclone. Even at only nine a.m., I can see heat waves rising off the pavement.

"*Fuck*, it's hot!" Gippy grumbles, fingering his collar.

"Could be worse," I quip, trying to keep the mood light. "Could be raining." After the monsoons of Central America, the dry heat seems less stifling. We're dry for the first time in weeks.

"Wait for it," he growls with a nod to dark clouds looming north of the city.

He's not wrong; the Midwest is in tornado season, and we've already driven through several torrential storms. This world seems to only have two weather patterns anymore: winter storms and summer storms. The miles and the days from Panama to here are a blur, as are most road trips after the fact. We took our time and kept away from our previous route south as much as possible, which wasn't easy with so few roads open in Central America. We've also changed vehicles and identities half a dozen times. I'm a blonde again, and Caucasian if my makeup doesn't melt in the heat, dressed demurely in a high-necked, drab dress with frills at the collar and cuffs, circa 1850. The light little bonnet looks silly but shields my ears from cameras and the blistering sun. The skirt has slits in the sides and is poofy enough to hide the Glock strapped to one thigh and three magazines to the other.

Gippy's wearing a shirt and tie. He and Canción are outfitted as orthodox Christian missionaries, right down to straw hats and Bibles. The books conceal pistols, of course. He's handling the heat, but he's a child of the tropics; his lips are chapped to the point of bleeding.

Chaki's a problem, silent, sullen, and resentful at our every attempt to help her but cooperating with information whenever we ask. The mental trauma of being possessed for so long has left her a mess. I've helped her as much as she'll let me, but even that has caused resentment. She doesn't like the intrusion, and I can't force her to accept my help. Her memories are burgeoning thunderstorms full of agony. She and Gippy have settled into a smoldering hate-hate relationship that I can feel like a space-heater, especially in the confines of a car. He's still dealing with the trauma of what he went through, and may never recover all that he's lost or come to grips with all the things the incubus did with him. But we're alive and now only days from home, or our *new* home, anyway. Jeri and Hank have set up house in Charlotte, North Carolina, and we'll join them soon.

Personally, I'm dying for some downtime among those I love, but first, it's time for a little family reunion, or union, I guess, since Canción has never met his father.

"Gip, why don't you two grab something cold to drink. We'll get a room." The funky little motel/restaurant isn't much but has anonymity written all over it.

"Sure. Come on, chica, I'm buyin'."

Chaki follows him without a word.

On our way to the office, I spot a two-door Ford Econolectric parked near room seven, Emil's. Canción stares at it, so I nudge him. "Come on. You do the talking, remember?" He's become our front man, simply because NAFAS doesn't have his face on their network yet.

"I remember." His eyes remain fixed on the car. "I just... don't know what I'm going to say."

"Say, 'We need a room for four.'" I nudge him again as he glares at me. "Don't worry. I imagine Emil's thinking about the same thing right now. You two will get along fine. I promise." I know they will because Emil can get along with anyone, even a son he never knew he had. He's one of the kindest men I've ever known. How ironic that a priest who harbored the fallen angel of destruction sired the great-grandson of God.

Canción gets us a double, paying cash, and we move our gear from the SUV into the musty room. The air conditioning is struggling, but even thirty degrees feels like a gust of cool air. I've lived in so much worse that it's palatial. I text Emil that we're here and give him our room number. When I texted him that we'd found his son and Cora had survived, he insisted on a meeting, and Wichita Falls wasn't too far out of our way or his. I haven't told him many details of what happened in Central America yet, or much about his son. I'll let that come out in its own good time.

Canción freezes at a knock on the door, clearly terrified by the prospect of meeting his father.

I smile at his discomfort and head for the door, checking just to make sure it's Emil before I open it. He looks very different clean-shaven with his hair long, but I recognize his eyes. I open the door to find Sister Janice with him, the two of them decked out like retro-1970 hippies, right down to tie-dye shirts, beads, and the scent of patchouli.

"Emil!" I embrace him unabashedly, feeling his joy and apprehension, and he returns it. "You look well!"

"I am. Uh, *we* are." He releases me, his eyes fixing on Canción. I feel his heart swelling with love and longing. "And you must be Canción."

He advances with a hand extended. "Good *lord*, you look like your mother!"

"All but her eyes." Canción shakes Emil's hand and tries to smile, but his nervousness is overwhelming his good manners. "She always told me I had your eyes."

"I suppose you do at that." Emil barks a laugh. "I never imagined... Sorry, I'm just flabbergasted. I never dreamed I had a son, and when I learned, the chances of ever actually meeting you were so remote... I never truly hoped this day would come, and here it is."

"Mother left me a journal," Canción stammers. "She told me about you, how sorry she was that she had to leave, but..." He sighs, and I feel his sorrow resurging, but with a core of determination as well. "She loved you very much but knew she couldn't stay."

Emil's smile is agonizing. "I understand."

The mixture of pain and love emanating from him is so intense I feel like I'm being torn in half; the urge to help somehow beating against my heart in waves, but I know I can't. I wonder if Canción can. We're the same in our innate desire to assuage pain, and he's learned to curb his impulses, but I worry that he won't be able to keep from stripping away Emil's emotional agony.

"Why don't we let these two get acquainted," Janice suggests, and I realize I'm staring at the two men, tears pooling in my eyes.

"Good idea." I force my attention away from the glow of their emotions and turn to the door, then turn back, unable to at least offer a gentle reminder. "We'll be in the restaurant. Canción, please remember what we talked about."

"I will," he assures me, and I feel the truth in it. "We'll be fine."

"And thank you, Empa, for..." Emil nods to Canción. "Well, for everything."

"We'll talk later. Join us when you're ready." I follow Janice out into the blinding heat, the emotional barrage snapping off as the door closes behind us. I can breathe. On our way across the scorching parking lot, I fill her in on a couple of necessary details, namely Chaki and Gippy. She knows the basics, but not the details. "Chaki's not violent, but she's not coping well either. We can't trust her or let her go; she knows too much. But she seems to be trying to help us. Gippy seems to be dealing with his own trauma, but he's... quiet about it. I'm afraid of what it might have done to him."

"I can't imagine." Janice sighs, no stranger to working with traumatized people, especially women. "I'm still having trouble accepting the existence of demons and... well, your kind, if you know what I mean. It's changed my whole outlook, and not in a bad way."

"I'm glad for you." And I am, for she's a much happier person than the dour nun I first met at St. Luther's. While she had faith, she'd considered herself beneath the notice of God, or unworthy of saving. She's just about the only person I know who took the news of the War of Souls as an affirmation of her faith rather than looming Armageddon. Our struggle gave her hope, as it did me. "Just don't mention too many details about yourself or Emil around Chaki. What she doesn't know can't hurt us if things go badly."

"Of course." Janice is pragmatic, if anything, and one of the strongest women I know.

We find Gippy and Chaki sitting in a corner booth nursing sodas. His face lights up at the sight of Janice, and he stands to embrace her. I feel a flash of mixed emotions from Chaki, resentment, disgust, anger, as the other two exchange warm greetings. I sit and gauge her, but her eyes snap to mine, and her features harden.

"Stay out of my head."

"I'm not in your head," I assure her, but I see she doesn't believe me. The harder I try to temper her fear of me, the more afraid she becomes. I shrug. "Fine, but try not to look like you hate the whole world, please."

"Why not? What's the world ever done for me?" Bitterness radiates from her like heat from a furnace.

Her point is spot on, at least from her perspective, and maybe the root of her entire tortured life, but I decide this isn't the time or place to discuss it and scan the restaurant as I wait for Janice and Gippy to sit. *See everything, readiness is a constant state...* We've drawn a little attention, but nothing untoward. There are no police, and the wait staff looks too tired and overworked to pay much attention. The place is remarkably busy for mid-morning, which is good, for the more faces there are, the more invisible we are. Yet another lesson Gippy has taught me.

Gippy and Janice sit, still beaming at each other. She's gushing, astounded by how much he's changed in only a year or so.

"I just can't get over it! You look like a completely different man!"

"The company I keep, Sis. And you lookin' like you traded the habit for tie-dye. It's a good look!"

"Thanks." She actually blushes, which I find adorable; hardly the hardened bride of Christ I knew in Cincinnati. "We opened a shop; incense and oils, natural soaps, candles. We have to look the part."

"Sorry we threw a wrench into your lives," I say.

"No matter." Janice seems to notice Chaki for the first time and holds out a hand across the table. "I'm Janice."

Chaki stares at her hand for a moment, then shakes it perfunctorily. "Chaki." She doesn't offer anything more, but Janice ignores the slight.

We're delivered from the uncomfortable silence by a waiter, and we order drinks and a plate of nachos for the table.

"Two more will be joining us in a bit," I explain.

He nods and hurries off, and I'm surprised again how busy the place is.

"A lot of business here for this hour." I'm not just making conversation, and Gippy picks up on my observation.

"I wondered why too. Waitress said this is the *lunch* break. This time of year, everyone rushes to get work done before the weather hits." He shows me his phone, the weather app displaying a deep red and purple blob to the north, heading southeast. Several red polygons delineate tornado warnings, but we're out of the zone. "Dodgin' twisters puts a cramp on the daily routine, I guess."

"That certainly explains the bustle," I agree.

"'Tis the season." Janice sighs. "The growing season's short, and this is still the breadbasket of North America."

"Fools scrabbling for scraps in a burning house," Chaki mutters in Spanish, evidently in a mood today.

The food and two tall Styrofoam cups of iced tea—or something that's supposed to be tea, but probably isn't—are delivered. I sip mine and bemoan the rich black coffee of Boquete and Cartagena. We nibble and talk about nothing important until Emil and Canción arrive, both of them wearing sheepish smiles.

Gippy stands to embrace Emil, and Canción sits beside Janice, introducing himself. She stammers and blushes, clearly taken by his beauty and literally angelic voice. The conversation resumes, and we touch on a few details of our recent foray into Central America, nothing Chaki doesn't already know or might induce someone to call the police if overheard. Nobody mentions Canción's abilities, for that's something we can't afford to have strangers overhear. The food's decent, and the warmth of the company of people I love bolsters my good mood. When the meal winds down, I suggest that Emil and I go for a walk to chat while the others relax in our room.

The storms have swept by to the north, a black freight train of destruction that is life and death in Tornado Alley, which now stretches from the Rockies to the Appalachians, and Hudson's Bay to the Gulf of Mexico. The badly needed rain brings life to crops, but hail and winds can flatten fields as well, life and death incarnate. Emil and I stroll down side streets, and I fill him in on his son.

"Canción is like no mortal I've ever known, Emil. He's truly the grandson of both Heaven and Hell." I keep my voice low as I speak, and sweep the streets with my gaze constantly for police, cameras, or stalkers, a habit that has kept me alive for millennia.

"You mean the Nephilim that... we banished." He looks worried. "You're not saying he's evil, are you? He seems so... caring."

"He's the grandson of Israfal and Azkeel, the angels of music and destruction, but he was raised by Cora, and a loving and caring environment has made him a loving and caring young man, but what he can do..." I shake my head. "Frankly, it frightens me, and you need to know all of it."

"What he can *do?*" He looks even more worried.

"He has the ability to absorb negative emotions, or maybe emotions in general. He grew up taking away people's fear, anxiety, and anger without anyone knowing. Cora didn't even realize what he could do until the very day they were separated, forced to flee from the Nephilim. When we ran up against demons and Nephilim in Cartagena, we discovered that he could... absorb them as well."

"*Absorb?*" He's skeptical. "You mean exorcise them? Send them to Hell?"

"No, I mean take their... essences or *souls* into himself and destroy them utterly." I shake my head. "The... residual energy of these emotions and destroyed souls is... formidable. He can expel that energy in a pulse of sound that's devastating. He saved our lives with his gift, but..."

"But it frightens you." His brows knit as he meets my gaze. "Why?"

"Two reasons. First, because he grew up doing this before Cora knew about the ability, and when he absorbs and expels other people's anger, hate, or fear, he does the same to his own. Until we met, he did it often. He said he couldn't stand to see people in pain. And he did it without people's consent or even their knowledge."

"That's..." He glances back the way we've come. "That wouldn't be healthy for a child."

"I know, but he seems reasonably stable, though he's headstrong and has a temper. No worse than many young men I've met, though, and he's had some hard knocks. Taking other people's painful emotions is dangerous, both for them *and* him. He did it to me when we first met, and I just about walked away for good. He took my grief like shucking an oyster from the shell, and I felt... violated." I take a deep breath and let it out slowly, steadying my calm, burying the memory. "When the woman he was living with in Los Brisas found out that he'd done the same to her, she slapped the hell out of him. She was terrified of him. Their relationship collapsed, and he didn't understand why. It took some explaining, but he's learned to curb the impulse somewhat."

Emil remains silent for a few steps, deep in thought, trying to take it all in. He's a psychologist by training and would know even better than I how deleting anyone's emotions wouldn't be healthy in the long term. Then he looks at me and asks, "And the second reason?"

"That's even more troublesome, and something I've *not* talked to him about." I stop, and Emil turns to face me, clearly worried. I've thought a lot about how to tell him this, or if I even should, but he needs to know the danger. "Destroying a soul, even if it's a demon's or Nephilim's, is... unprecedented. I'm not certain that he couldn't do the same to *my* soul, or *positive* emotions. If he'd been raised by Nephilim instead of Cora, he could have turned out to be... something else entirely. A weapon for Hell instead of Heaven. Gippy told me they wanted to capture me to... make more like Canción, but to corrupt them at birth."

Emil's eyes widen. "Jesus, Mary, and Joseph..."

I smile through his horror. "Don't worry about Canción. He's a good man. He saved Gippy from possession; something that would have taken days of exorcism, he did in the blink of an eye. He did the same to the succubus that possessed Chaki, and two Nephilim. With what he can do, we could *seriously* tip the scales in our favor."

"You mean destroy the Nephilim instead of banishing them." He frowns. "I'm not sure how I feel about that, Empa. To destroy the soul of the grandchild of God..."

"I know, but consider, Emil: God made him what he is for a *reason*. Of that, I'm certain."

He nods, still troubled. "God's plan..."

"Right, but putting Canción's gift to use will take careful planning. They know of him, though not much more than his origin and a vague idea of what he can do." I grin openly and grip his arm, lowering my voice even further. "And they don't know Cora's alive!"

I haven't yet filled him in on the details of Cora's masterful disappearance after destroying the NAFAS task force sent to murder her. "She had tunnels under their hacienda, and napalm that she detonated once she was in the clear. She staged her own death right down to the gravestone. Even Canción thought she was gone. When she turned up later, the people of Boquete literally took her secret to the grave."

"But that was eight years ago. Why wouldn't she seek Canción out?"

"It would have been too dangerous. She went into deep hiding, and the jungles of Central America are the perfect place to disappear; totally off grid, impassable, but with enough resources to survive." I shrug and we resume walking. "My biggest question is, why didn't she follow through with her research into Laurence Caldwell? Maybe she did, and was caught infiltrating the records at Our Lady of Healing. Maybe she was the one who deleted the record before I got there. Either way, she never went after Martin Pederson."

"Maybe she couldn't find him?" he asks.

"Possible, but he wasn't that hard to track down, and Cora's relentless." I shrug helplessly. "She might have figured the Church of the Coming Dark was too hard a nut to crack."

"Any ideas how to find her?" He hesitates, then adds, "I mean, if she's still alive."

His hope shines like a beacon, and I hate to crush it, but he needs to know the truth. "Some, but we'd have to hack into Our Lady of Healing's database to leave her an encrypted message, and doing that might raise some red flags. After what happened in New York, Nephilim might be investigating our backtrail."

He nods. "If she does try to track down Pederson, *she* might find *you?*"

That hits me like a hammer, and my steps falter. "What?"

"You and Gippy created quite a stir in Manhattan, and there are even a few blurry pictures of you both on their websites." He huffs a laugh. "They've labeled you 'religious terrorists.'"

"Not the first time." I've seen the pictures and thanked God that they're not better resolution. I've also read some chatter about the attack in Cartagena. NAFAS is trying to link the two, but they have no photos of us there, and our spin that NAFAS soldiers assassinated Bishop Vargas is getting some traction and causing some international consternation. Officially, NAFAS is denying approval of the incursion, labeling the conveniently dead task force commander a rogue chasing religious terrorists without authorization. I wonder if Cora might spot the news and look into it, fearing for Canción, but there isn't any solid evidence of me in Cartagena.

Emil interrupts my musing. "The Church of the Coming Dark's

blog sites are still active, you know. If Cora's looking for Pederson, she'll probably search there and might spot your picture. You could drop some breadcrumbs there for her to find. It would be easier than hacking Our Lady's database and shouldn't cause a stir. Just another comment on a thread."

"That's... not a bad idea, Emil. Thank you!" Frankly, I'm embarrassed that I didn't think of it first.

He smiles that disarming smile that makes him such a good psychologist. "Glad to be of help."

The Nephilim, Son of Samyaza, Fallen Angel of Pride, stood at the expansive windows of his penthouse office/residence, glaring down at the Los Angeles waterfront from eight hundred meters above the street. The view from the Grand Hope Tower was the best on the west coast of the continent, a panorama from the mountains to the raging Pacific Ocean.

Grand Hope... The irony of the name struck him every time he thought of it. Occupying the former site of the New Hope Park, the skyscraper took up an entire city block, a bastion of steel and glass, the tallest building in North America and center of the state-sponsored news, entertainment, and propaganda conglomerate, Transmedia. As CEO, the Nephilim personally wielded the power to sway the hearts and minds of more than a billion humans, and sway them he had, sowing despair, hate, bigotry, and dissent wherever he could. He was also senior among the Nephilim, his father the foremost Grigori, second only to Lucifer.

His watch vibrated against his wrist; it was time.

The Son of Samyaza turned from the view, shot the cuffs of his custom-tailored suit, and sat at his desk. The chair—a marvel of modern technology and ergonomic comfort—conformed perfectly to his shape and slid forward to the edge of his desk. One touch of an armrest control brought up an arc of nine monitors from the smooth surface of his desk. They were blank save for the central lowest that displayed names of the adult Nephilim still on Earth; currently 167 of them, including their locations and positions. Six had been banished permanently to Hell, and twenty were too young to be active in the network. Two others, the sons of Samsaveel and Eartael, were freshly respawned, their hosts killed in Cartagena, and still no one knew exactly what had happened.

The climate apocalypse had worked in their favor globally, sowing despair, poverty, starvation, and destroying the hope of humans everywhere, but it also played hell with communications, which was the Son of Samyaza's business; his stranglehold on the human race.

He tapped on the icon that would simultaneously open sat-com links to every Nephilim in his network. The monitors blinked on in a cascade of stern faces from every continent on Earth. He waited until all but a few had connected—there were always a few last-minute dropouts, usually due to weather—and called them all to order.

"Reports." He sat back and listened as senior Nephilim gave reports on their current projects. The war between India and Pakistan was going well, with hundreds of millions of refugees fleeing the now-nuclear exchange. The Russo-Chinese union was progressing with a few hiccups. Australian droughts were being exacerbated by carefully orchestrated wildfires, as were those in Canada, Siberia, and the Amazon. Finally, the Son of Batraal, Senior Chief Investigator for the NAFAS Secret Service, gave his report on the Central American mission.

"We have a serious problem." That focused the attention of every Nephilim present, for they all knew the mission had been to remove the last of the Ageless, the one responsible for the recent banishment of several of their number permanently to Hell. "The Sons of Samsaveel and Ertael have not respawned into new hosts."

The Son of Samyaza felt the cold hand of dread on the back of his neck. "Explain how that's possible." He fought for control, but there was a tone of something he didn't like in his voice. Fear. Something he hadn't experienced in millennia.

"We're unsure, but the identities of their host corpses were confirmed. They died in the monastery of La Popa, the Son of

Samsaveel apparently from gunshot wounds and blunt force trauma of an unknown type. The Son of Ertael had a needle puncture in one thigh, high levels of ketamine in his blood, and two Taser wounds in his torso, but no other injuries. Cause of his death is unknown. Reports through our demonic network indicate that the two did not respawn into new hosts and were *not* banished. The Father of Lies was unaware of the deaths of their hosts and didn't cast their souls back to Earth."

This elicited a number of incredulous curses in many dead languages from the assembled Nephilim.

The Son of Batraal raised a hand for attention and continued. "Three demons also associated with the mission have gone missing."

"Missing?" The Daughter of Penemue, currently the prime minister of Egypt, curled her lip in a sneer of disgust. "*Define* missing."

"Not on Earth, not in Hell." The Son of Batraal scowled right back. "One of the demons, a dybbuk, went missing before the attack on La Popa. The human host returned after an assignment empty. It was hypothesized by the Son of Samsaveel that the last Ageless had found the offspring of the Daughter of Israfal, and that the young man had some... power. We don't know if the demon was somehow captured or utterly destroyed, but they weren't exorcised. The same may have happened to the succubus, incubus, and the two Nephilim."

The meeting of Nephilim erupted into expletives and accusations, but the Son of Samyaza pressed a single key that made every monitor flash once. "Quiet! We need details."

"This is nonsense!" Another Nephilim snapped accusatively. "The get of the Seraphim and Gregori cannot procreate!"

"So we believed, but the Son of Ertael reported from Panama that they'd captured the companion of the Ageless, Empa, and coerced him into possession by the Incubus Ardat. The demon told them that his host and Empa had discovered some months ago that the Ageless Terpsichore had become pregnant while attending Brown University in Rhode Island two decades ago. She left and went into hiding, evidently in Panama. They were searching for Terpsichore and her *son*. Reportedly, the father was an autistic priest whom she met at

Brown University in 2052. The priest was possessed by the Son of Azkeel, who has been banished to Hell. Under direct questioning from the Father of Lies, the Son of Azkeel admitted that he knew of the potential offspring of an Ageless-Nephilim union."

"And you believe this... *creature* can destroy the souls of demons and Nephilim." It wasn't a question, but the Son of Samyaza had to make this hypothesis clear.

"That *is* the supposition," the Son of Batraal said. "There's no other feasible explanation. The anomaly can absorb negative emotions—fear, hate, anger—and destroy them. He may have done the same to the three missing demons and two of our cousins."

The other Nephilim were visibly shaken. Banishment was one thing, but to be completely destroyed was unthinkable. Fear among Nephilim was rare and horrible to witness, and the Son of Samyaza despised the seething core of it within himself. This was unprecedented and unacceptable.

"Find the anomaly and destroy it, Son of Batraal. The man is undoubtedly with the Ageless, Empa. Use *all* of your resources."

"We're already searching," he said, then added, "And the anomaly has a name: Canción."

"Canción?" *How appropriate*, the Son of Samyaza thought, *for the Ageless Terpsichore to have named her son 'Song.'* "Very well. Find this *Song*, and silence it forever!"

2

REUNION

I t's not much of a neighborhood," Gippy observed, though he'd
lived in much worse.

Track homes and multiplexes next to a former park had
been converted to mass slum housing. The huge oak trees that had
given the neighborhood its name were dead or dying, victims of the
unprecedented shifts in climate, blazing hot summers, and icy winters
never before seen in Charlotte, North Carolina. Many of the oaks had
been cut down for firewood, though the houses weren't built with
fireplaces. He spotted the retrofitted stovepipes of old cast-iron stoves
that had seen a resurgence in popularity. The streets were occupied by
a few parked cars, most of them immobile, rusted out, and bereft of
tires, headlights, or anything else that could be scavenged.

"Good camouflage," Empa remarked.

"Hank's got a good eye." Gippy agreed.

Hank had picked the place, looking for something as anonymous
and invisible as possible. Dilapidated neighborhoods like this one
were thick as fleas on dogs in this country. The rich could afford
better, and the poor couldn't afford to keep up the maintenance. With
Hank's status as a genuine NAFAS citizen and military veteran, the
purchase had been made without a hitch. He and Jeri had left the

Atlanta house in a hurry, packing only what couldn't be left behind: computers, weapons, backup drives, burner phones, and Jeri's disguise supplies. They couldn't leave anything incriminating and could never go back. In fact, they'd barely gotten out in time.

Gippy followed his phone's directions and piloted the SUV into a two-car driveway shaded by the denuded limbs of a massive dead tree not yet cut for fuel. The house needed a coat of paint but seemed sound, no broken windows or damaged siding.

The garage door opened without his prompting, which elicited a smile. "Jeri's watchin'."

"Home is where the people you love are," Empa said.

"True *that!*" He parked beside a late-model four-door Ford Tempo with visible rust but good tires and killed the engine. Before he could even open the car door, the garage door closed behind them, and the door into the house opened. Gippy got out and grinned at Jeri and Hank. "Hey, you two."

"Hey." As the passenger side door opened, Jeri took two steps and crashed into Empa hard enough to bruise, fists knotted in her hair, mouth devouring her.

Empa took the tumultuous greeting in stride, finally breaking the clinch. "Jeri, we have guests."

"Oh, right." She glanced at Canción, blinked, and blushed. "Sorry. Hi. I'm Jeri, this is Hank. Welcome home." Jeri then rounded the car and grabbed Gippy's hand before he could reach for the trunk lid. "Don't you *dare* start unpacking!"

"Jeri, I think we should—"

"And *I* think we should go to bed." She pulled his hand toward the door. "I haven't seen either of you in more than a month! I flipped a coin, and it came up heads. That's you. Come on." She dragged him past Empa, grinning at her. "You're tails. See you later."

"Jeri!" Gippy resisted her pull as she dragged him through the door and toward the stairs to the second floor. At a glance, the house was clean, plainly furnished, and spacious enough for everyone. He stumbled up the stairs, unable to break her grip without hurting her. "Jeri, we have to talk!"

"We'll talk after!" She pulled him to a door and opened it into a bedroom, dragging him through after her. The door slammed, and she whirled to grasp him by his shirt, kissing him deeply and gnawing on his lip.

When her fingers started working on the buttons of his shirt, he grasped her wrists and pulled them away. "Jeri, stop! We have to talk *first*! This is important!" He hadn't told her all that had happened to him, unwilling to discuss such personal details over the phone. Empa had sketched it out for her, but Jeri had to know the rest... and the worst.

"What's so important?" Jeri looked a little hurt, but her eyes had shifted from feverish lust to worry. "I ain't been laid in ten weeks, two days, and six hours! Talk fast!"

He took a deep breath, knowing this would be physically painful to say. "What happened to me... I don't know if you'll understand, but Chaki, when she was possessed and working with the naffies, she... tortured me with sex."

"What?" Her arms went limp in his grasp, her eyes widening. "How... you mean with whips and shit?"

"No, with..." He heaved a sigh and closed his eyes, shuddering with the memory. "It wasn't her, but the succubus, Duvara. What she did... She hurt me in ways I never knew were possible, drove me over the edge. I wanted to kill her with my bare hands, nearly *did*, and..." The memory sickened him, panic rising like sour vomit. "She cut me loose, and I... But she wouldn't let me..."

"Gip! Stop! You don't need to tell me." Tears pooled in her eyes now, pity and fear twisting her face into a mask he didn't know.

"I *do*! I need you to understand what it did to me." He heaved a breath and told her of that horrific moment, throttling Chaki with his bloody bare hands while she wouldn't let him pull out of her, the chasm of madness that had opened in his mind, then the filth that had invaded him. When he finished, tears were cascading down her cheeks. "Having that... *thing* in my head, sharing its thoughts, what it wanted to do to the entire *world*, nearly drove me insane."

"But... Canción destroyed it, right? He saved you." She gently caressed his cheeks with her fingertips. "You're *back*, Gip."

"Yeah, I'm back, but... I don't know if what happened changed me somehow. I don't know if I'll *ever* be able to think about sex without remembering that... *filth*." He realized that her fingertips were tracing the tracks of his tears. "Jer, I want to, but..."

"But you're afraid." She looked worried. "You don't have to be afraid of me, *ever*, Gip. You know that, right?"

"I know, but... It's not you, Jer. I'm afraid of *me*. I've had so many nightmares... I don't know if I trust myself."

"*I* trust you, Gip."

"You shouldn't." He dropped his eyes, shame and the horror of what he might do, what the demon had done.

"But I *do* trust you, Gip, and you know deep down that you're not going to hurt me, and I'm not going to hurt you. That's not who we are. We don't have to do this at all if you're not ready, but I think you should let me help you." She lifted his chin and kissed him tenderly. Her feverish lust was gone; only caring and longing remained.

"I don't know if you *can* help me, Jer," he whispered, dropping his gaze again, hating himself for saying it.

"Look at me, Gip."

He raised his eyes to hers and saw nothing but love there, nothing but trust.

"I want to help you, and I think I can, but you have to be ready and want me to try." She took his hands in hers and squeezed. "If we start, and you're uncomfortable or something, just tell me to stop, and I will. We'll go slow, at your speed, only what you want, but I know you can get through this with my help."

"*How* do you know?" he asked, hating the rising doubt.

"Because I know *you*, Gip." She smiled that sweet Jeri smile that he'd fallen in love with. "And this is *love*, not hate, not evil, but *good*. However long it takes, I'm going to erase everything that fucking demon did to you. I can do this, but you have to want me to try." She smiled again, and there was a hint of mischief in it now.

And he knew in his soul that he did want her to try, but the doubt still loomed. "Okay, yes, but you gotta understand... I'm *scared*, Jeri. What if I... can't?"

"Then we'll just have to work through it." She grinned, now full of her old mischief. "You know how I love a challenge." She slowly undid the buttons of his shirt, tracing the exposed skin with her fingertips, sending electric jolts through him. "Just relax and tell me what you need."

As Hank, Canción, and I unpack and get everyone settled, I fill Hank in on what really happened in Central America. He's a soldier and understands war like I do. He's also been surfing the media with a practiced eye and has news for me.

"The naffies are pitching Cartagena as a terrorist attack, and Las Brisas is sticking to the story that NAFAS military murdered a Catholic Bishop. Las Brisas managed to get some traction from the Catholic Church with pictures of the dead bishop riddled with bullets and the commander of the mission in NAFAS uniform. The Cardinal in Bogota's mounting an investigation and has the backing of the Colombian government and the Pope." Hank shrugs and makes a face. "Of course, NAFAS Media is on it like flies on shit. They're posting old pics of you and Gip in Manhattan, and of you in St. Louis with plenty of talking heads spinning tales about religious terrorism. They don't have any footage of you in Colombia, but one boat pilot's singing like a canary." He nods to Canción with a wry smile. "Thankfully, they've got no pictures of you, just a name."

"Lucky," Canción mutters, then looks to me. "So, we lay low and put out fishing lines for my mother?"

I nod. "That's the plan, and I have a solid strategy." I glance toward the kitchen where Chaki is raiding the fridge. "I want to keep this quiet, but Emil gave me a good idea, and you've pretty much confirmed its viability, Hank. The media is all over us, and I want to use that to our advantage. If Cora's alive and continuing her research, she'll end up looking for Martin Pederson. The recent blip in media coverage will draw her attention, and activity on the Coming Dark websites is up. If she sees any of the fuzzy pics of me, which seems likely, she'll know I went after Pederson and start really digging. I can leave some breadcrumbs for her to follow on website forums."

Canción frowns. "NAFAS will be watching their media as well, won't they?"

"Yes, which is why my breadcrumbs will be disguised and coded in a way only Cora will recognize."

"Give her the number of a burner phone, and we can route the signal through a VPN," Hank suggests.

I nod. "Yes, and we only check it once a day remotely. That should keep us safe."

"And if she finds it and contacts you?" Canción asks, and I hear the hope in his voice.

I smile and pat his arm. "Then we can set up a family reunion, but *carefully*. The last thing I want to do is put your mother in the crosshairs. She put a lot of work into disappearing."

He nods. "Yes, she did; even from me."

"To keep you *safe*," I remind him. He's still a little resentful of Cora's abandoning him, even though he knows why she did it. *Ah, youth...* Some lessons you just have to learn for yourself.

"And what about her?" Hank asks, with a nod to the kitchen.

"We watch her, keep her here, and take whatever information she can give us. Unfortunately, so far that's been slim. Demons aren't part of the Nephilim network. Their job is to corrupt humankind while Nephilim fight the war."

"The war we now have a chance to win," Hank adds with a grin to Canción. "Thanks to you."

"Right." The muscles of Canción's jaw bunch and relax. "No pressure."

A cockroach the size of a mouse skitters across the keys of my laptop.

I flick it aside with enough force to send it against the wall, but it takes wing and lands to glare at me.

I glare back. Years in the jungles of Central America after my staged death reacquainted me with these little monsters; at least the ones in Nashville don't bite. "Go ahead and fuck with me, bug."

Its antennae twitch—an insectoid "Fuck off!"—and it skitters away.

I've put out bait traps, but I think they've started snorting the stuff like cocaine. Squishing doesn't even deter them. I think they're plotting to kill me in my sleep. I've lived under far worse conditions—rats, scorpions, fleas, and other vermin—and survived, so this is just a minor inconvenience. I recall a slave ship crossing the Mediterranean, rowers chained to their benches, their feet raw from rat bites. That horror makes this tiny little flop house seem palatial by comparison; the roof doesn't leak, there's electricity, and the toilet down the hall works, even if I have to sit on a foldout daybed to work. Besides, the roaches give me something to talk to other than myself.

I have money to afford better, but this is good cover, and not having a roof over my head for more than seven years has given me perspective. Memories of fleeing into central Africa after the fall of civilization 3800 years ago kept me alive, even if it was a different jungle. Physical discomfort I can deal with, and I've learned to eat things that most humans would never consider food, but being alone for so long isn't good for me. I am, after all, a creature of music, and what good is music if there's nobody to share it with? That doesn't keep me from playing, of course, but I long for an audience, and roaches have no appreciation for music.

I finger the bamboo penny whistle I fashioned by hand while in the jungle and force myself not to pick it up. I've got work to do. I can hear the music from the club two floors down, which soothes me, even if it is techno. I tap my foot and open a link to yet another fringe site, hot on the trail of Martin Pederson.

Drugs, prison, crime, and finally, he landed in a cult, but the Church of the Coming Dark has fallen on hard times in the last year. Whoever's keeping up their websites isn't very good, and the backlog of old posts is hard to weed through without any proper date indexing. I have to scan the pages' source code to get dates, and my eyes grow bleary from reading HTML. Thankfully, as with most websites, they've never thrown anything away. I only have a few thousand pages to scan, and I'm more than halfway through.

Then I find it, and my fragile hope is instantly crushed. Martin Pederson is dead, murdered by religious terrorists less than a year ago. My search has come to an abrupt and heartbreaking end.

"Fuck!" I lurch up and pace my tiny room, feeling like a caged rat with nowhere to go. I reach for my hoodie and penny whistle, intending to go out. I've been posing as a street musician, begging for coins in out-of-the-way places, spreading the love of my music as best I can. Then my eye catches a few lines of code, and I freeze.

"J-pegs!" There are pictures.

I sit back down and pull up the actual page recounting the incident. Martin Pederson isn't looking too good, thin, aged, eyes sunken, skin blotchy, clothed in baggy robes with what appear to be bandages visible at his wrists and neck. They call him "The Prophet," and there are recordings of his diatribes on the looming end of mankind on Earth. It's all bullshit, of course, but I weed through it for anything that might give me a clue about the exorcism of Laurence Caldwell.

There's nothing coherent, just tacked-together conspiracy theories, and references to the climate crisis as "God's judgment." I'm getting discouraged again when I come to the event of Martin Pederson's death. Wars between religious fanatics are as old as religion itself, but this one is peculiar, more of a surgical strike to take out Pederson than all-out war. My well-founded suspicion flares, and I wonder if a Nephilim might be behind this. They've assassinated religious leaders before, but the Church of the Coming Dark sows despair, not hope, which is right out of Hell's playbook. Of course, if they suspected he had successfully exorcised a Nephilim, they might take him out to eliminate whatever he knew.

Evidently, the assassins posed as a pair of traveling musicians who bribed their way into a meeting with Pederson. A high priestess and several guards and acolytes were also killed, but Pederson was their target. There are crappy resolution pictures of the pair, a man and a woman with wild hair carrying guitar cases that were later found to contain weapons. I skim past the photos, for there are a lot of guesses about who might have been behind the attack. Then I come to a highlighted update inserted into the text.

"Perpetrators may also be responsible for assassinating a Catholic Bishop recently in Cartagena."

"Cartagena!" Worry explodes within me like a nova. The chances that anything to do with the only priest ever to have possibly exorcised a Nephilim and the drowned city are minuscule, unless the same people were hunting Canción. *But how could they even know about him?*

I click links and read voraciously. The sheer volume of articles, investigations, and political backlash of this incident—all current—feeds my suspicion. Since the virtual collapse of global trade, NAFAS generally doesn't take much interest in what's happening in other countries. Now the Colombians are accusing NAFAS of the assassination, and NAFAS is insisting they were pursuing international terrorists with the cooperation of the assassinated Catholic bishop. There are graphic photos of the murdered bishop, NAFAS soldiers, and a number of security personnel who tried to protect the bishop. There are even photos of two destroyed MRAPs, which look like they were hit by a freight train.

I examine the ruined vehicles with a critical eye and realize something's amiss. They aren't scorched or blown apart; they are crushed.

"What the fuck does that?" I've seen a lot of wrecked and bombed-out vehicles, and these have been knocked backward by a high-speed accident with something massive, but the road's too narrow and curvy to allow high speed, and there's no larger vehicle.

Throughout the articles, the continuing NAFAS manhunt for those responsible focuses on the same two terrorists who assassinated Martin Pederson, even though all they have are vague descriptions and no plausible connection.

"That makes zero sense!"

I scroll back to the images of the pair who murdered Martin Pederson. The woman's decked out like a 1990 punk rocker, purple hair in a wide mohawk with a bunch of odd jewelry and makeup. The guy—a mixed-race fellow with bleached white hair close on the sides, and even white eyebrows—sends a pang through me. I've been with a lot of musicians, and this man is straight out of the new wave of "rebel rock." I examine his face but draw a blank; cute but hard, I can see the defiance in his angular features. I try to zoom back out, but my fingers slip on the mouse pad, and I pan across the image. The woman's face is now enlarged on my screen, and my heart skips a beat.

"The fuck?"

I zoom in, but the image only blurs further. I save it, enhance it, and still can't be sure.

I pull up old news websites covering the pacification of the St. Louis uprising. Scanning through the vast library of photos, I find her, my dear cousin, Empa, her mouth gaping with rage, her hand gripping a rifle above her head. I split the screen and enlarge both photos. Between hair, makeup, and the very different expressions on the two, it's hard to tell, but I know my cousin when I see her.

"Sweet Jesus of Nazareth, Empa, what were you *thinking*?" My mind whirls. That she's even alive is astonishing after the catastrophe of St. Louis, but she obviously survived. What I can't figure out is why she would want to murder Martin Pederson. How she came to even know of his existence, however, blasts into my mind like a bullet. "She found it!"

The old laptop I left with Emil is the only way she could have found out about the exorcism of Caldwell, and digging into the clinical history, as I did, she would have found the record missing. Or did she delete the record herself? That seems unlikely, since it would have left a trace of her being there, and Empa is, above all else, careful. Also, if she'd deleted the record, she wouldn't need to track down Martin Pederson.

"So, you found Pederson, and somehow he died, and you had to shoot your way out of Manhattan." I don't know who the young man accompanying her was, but he doesn't look like a soldier. My curiosity burns, questions flicking through my mind like bullet points. Did she discover how the exorcism worked? Did she meet Emil? Did she learn of my pregnancy? Did she tell him? Then I remember the connection NAFAS investigators are pushing to the incident in Cartagena.

"Canción! She had to have known!" The trail of clues falls together like a row of perfectly placed dominos: stumble onto Emil, discover his unique possession, investigate, find my things, crack my code, learn both of Laurence Caldwell and my pregnancy, try to find Caldwell's medical record, find it missing, track down Pederson, the shit hits the fan, she escapes. Then, when things cool down, she tries to track me down. Empa is the most tenacious person I've ever met, but how she managed to find Canción, I have no idea. She obviously did, but it sounds as if she was followed by a NAFAS task force, and once again, the shit hit the fan.

"Please, please, please..." I flip through the articles, feverishly scanning for word of my son. There is nothing, only hints that the terrorists had local accomplices. Why she would kill a Catholic bishop, I have no idea. Maybe she was working with the bishop, and he was caught in the conflagration.

I find a Colombian article listing the casualties by name, and Canción's isn't there. "Thank God."

I scan more articles and find no clue what happened to the supposed terrorists. Manhunts are being conducted in Colombia and Central America, but no arrests have been made. Without any clues to link the two incidents, I return to the Church of the Coming Dark site and search forward by date. It's a long slog, for every page has a comments section where the devout espouse their beliefs. It's like reading the notes on the walls of an insane asylum. I'm flicking between pages and their source code, when I spot some images of musical riffs. I recognize a phrase from Bohemian Rhapsody, strange enough to draw my attention.

The poster's handle is "Beelzebub," which I also find strange. I read the post, but it's religious nonsense, how God has forsaken mankind and is wiping the Earth clean of our infestation, and Hell has a devil set aside for anyone foolish enough not to believe this truth. That seems to dovetail with the riff from Bohemian Rhapsody, but the musical notes trail into something else that doesn't quite make sense.

When I recognize my own cypher, an inarticulate cry of joy escapes my throat.

Snatching up paper and pen, I decode the message and jot down the translation. "Empathy + Music = Love," then ten digits. A phone number.

"Son of a... She knows I'm alive! She's looking for me!" I stand and pace again, trying to think it through. "Or this is a big fucking trap."

The more I think of it, the less that seems likely. Someone would have had to crack my cypher, know I'm alive, know Empa's alive, and know about Martin Pederson and why we were interested in him. Then they'd have to use *my* cypher to lay the trap. That's so convoluted even an AI wouldn't think of it.

I pick up my phone, make sure the encryption's engaged, and call the number. It's out of service. Not surprising if Empa's being careful, which she always is. I send a text instead. "Amadeus - 1776-7."

There's nothing to do but wait, so I turn off my phone and laptop, tuck everything into their hiding places, and go out to play some music. The heat is stifling, but evening's falling, so I can wear my hoodie without drawing much attention. I hunker in a disused doorway, place a cut-off juice bottle with a few coins in it by my knee, and play whatever comes into my mind. Six hours later, I've made seven NADs, spread a lot of love, and my ass is numb, but my nerves are calmer. I stagger back to my little roach motel and power up my phone.

My text has received a reply. "Musashi - 1633-41."

"Empa!" I grin and type "RUOK?"

The reply comes instantly. "Ichiban! Your Song lives with me."

I gasp, and my phone hits the floor hard enough to crack the screen. "Canción!"

3

LOVE AND PAIN

Boredom wore on Canción like a rough bow on poorly tuned violin strings. Sitting in this damned house was worse than being stuffed into a car for weeks. At least then he had the tension of constant vigilance to keep him occupied.

He appreciated what Empa was doing for him, but these people were strange. Hank seemed too old to have anything in common with everyone else, but spoke their language when it came to war. Gippy seemed to be in better spirits, grinning like an idiot every time the little nympho, Jeri, was in the room. That he and Empa were both in a relationship with Jeri shocked him at first, but they seemed okay with it. She blushed every time she met Canción's eyes, which almost made him laugh. Gippy had already warned him that Jeri was an addict. He was a new flavor of her drug, but he wasn't about to step into the middle of a polyamorous relationship.

Chaki was another problem; she was terrified of him, still a traumatized mess, and resentful that no one trusted her. Canción could see her pain as clearly as he could see the sun outside. She even shied away from Jeri's overtures of friendship, spending all of her time on her phone, helping Empa search for Cora. He longed to take away her pain but knew that would be a mistake. Her resentment would only return, intensified by his invasion of her privacy. All the years of hurting people when he thought he'd been helping them rode on his shoulders like a leaden weight, right alongside the pressure of being their "deliverance" or "chosen one." All the conflicting emotions he couldn't resolve or simply expunge left him feeling like running away, but he longed to see his mother, and these people were his doorway to her.

He spent time with Hank—who repressed a lot of pain and hid that with humor—to familiarize himself with the house, security, and the startling number of armaments they kept at the ready. Empa encouraged them all to carry weapons at all times, but all other firearms were kept in print-locked safes. Nobody trusted Chaki with a gun, and for good reason.

To pass the time and indulge his love of music, Canción ordered several musical instrument kits online. The flute and clarinet were assembled, and he was working on the guitar. Hank, of course, offered to help, but Canción declined. The feel of the tools, wood, and metal in his hands reminded him of his love of building things. He plucked the newly fitted D string, twisted the peg until it was close, and reached for the G.

"You're good with your hands," Hank commented, his own occupied with breaking down a compact pump shotgun, laying out every piece on a soft towel.

"I built houses," he said with a glance around. "Way better than this one."

"That don't surprise me," Hank said with a snort. "This is a piece of shit track home. The place we had in Atlanta was old, solid, deep cellar, thick walls. Surprised this one hasn't blown down yet. I'd kill for a deep cellar. Set up a gun range, dojo, training gym."

"If we're here long enough, I'll help you build one." He fitted the G string through the peg, tied it off with his thumb on the string to keep it in place, then twisted the nut. "It would take a while."

"And might draw too much attention." Hank shook his head. "Getting rid of the dirt and rock, bringing in construction materials, the noise. Best to find a house that already has one and renovate."

Canción nodded and threaded the B string. Once again, Hank was thinking like a soldier while he was thinking like a builder. He had to adjust his thinking; they were at war. Every action should be taken with safety and security in mind. He hadn't needed to think like that since their flight through the jungle after Cora blew up Casa Musica.

"Canción!" Empa stepped into the room, phone in hand, her face alight. "She found us."

He stood so quickly that the guitar hit the floor with a discordant, thrumming thump. He stepped over it, catching his foot on the unstrung B string, and nearly faceplanted. Recovering, he stumbled up to her, eyes fixed on the phone.

"You... spoke to her?"

"Yes. She's in Nashville." Empa chuckled. "I really should have guessed that. She's safe, so we switched to backup phones and I filled her in on what happened in Panama and Cartagena. I also texted Emil that we found her. We can arrange something, a reunion, but I want to be careful."

Canción's eyes never left the phone. "Is she... Can I talk to her?"

"Of course." She handed over her phone. "She's waiting for you to call, but you should take it in your room for privacy's sake."

He took the phone as if it might bite him, thanked her, and hurried to his room. The door slammed, and he sat on the bed, staring down at the shiny blank screen as if a ghost might rise from it at any moment. He unlocked it, pulled up the video phone app, and called the last contact, one that Empa had cunningly named "Muse." It rang once, and the screen flickered as the video link established.

Her hair was black, short, and unkempt, her eyes shaded by brown contacts, her skin hued darker with makeup, but it was her, and her smile lit his heart like a supernova in the night sky.

"Canción! My *God*, you're..." She barked a husky laugh. "...you're all grown up."

"Almost nine years," he said without knowing why. "You haven't changed at all, except for the hair and makeup."

She winced. "Yes, well, I never change, but I guess you know that now."

"I know."

Her brows drew in, lines forming between them. "Look, Canción, I wanted to say that I'm sorry I left you, but there was no other way."

"Don't." He heard the pain in his own voice and hated it, but that pang of abandonment still lingered. "I thought for a long time that you were dead, until only a few weeks ago, in fact. I'm trying to understand why you didn't make your way to Cartagena, but..." He gritted his teeth. "Maybe *you* could explain why?"

The lines between her eyes vanished, and her features hardened; her defensive face. "It wasn't safe, love. Very few people knew I was alive, and they were sworn to secrecy. I had to vanish completely. If I'd shown up in Cartagena, word would have spread. My music had gotten out; I was too well-known. That was my mistake, and I accept that."

He nodded, knowing she was probably right, but that old pain still stung. A few months ago, he would have expunged that smoldering anger, but Empa had told him that wasn't healthy. Learning to deal with emotions he was used to simply deleting wore on him. "Well, you sure blew the hell out of Casa Musica."

She winced again. "I had to make sure they thought I was dead."

"None of them survived to look for your corpse."

"I didn't know that until later." She sighed. "Look, Canción, I'd like to see you. Both you and your father, in fact. Empa and I will line it up, but we have to be—"

"Careful, yeah, she already said." He bridled his poorly disguised resentment and nodded. "I met Emil. He's an interesting man. I like him. I can see how you fell for him."

She smiled. "He's one of the best men I've ever known, which is another reason we have to be careful. I'd hate to put him in danger." Her smile fell suddenly. "That is, if he wants to meet me at all. He probably still hates me for leaving him."

"He doesn't hate you, Mom. He's still in love with you; says he always will be. He joined the priesthood, you know."

"Empa said, yes. It doesn't surprise me. He only ever wanted to help people in need." An awkward silence ensued, but she broke it quickly. "Empa also told me about your power, Canción, what you can do to demons and Nephilim. You must know that it's…"

"Unprecedented." He made a face, tired of being everyone's new hope. "Yeah, it's kind of hard to deal with sometimes. I don't know if I want that kind of pressure."

Her smile was more sardonic than sympathetic. "Sorry, love, but it's yours, and you're a game changer. You *must* realize this."

"Yeah, that's what Empa said." He snorted a laugh and shook his head. "She's kinda scary sometimes, you know."

"She's always been that way: intense, suspicious, guarded, a loner and a survivor. She's experienced more pain than any other living being in the history of mankind, Canción. She can't help it. She was made to heal the hurts of the Earth, and has tried, but she thinks she's failed." Cora shook her head. "She's not wrong; we *all* failed."

"Until now," he amended. "Now we have a chance."

She smiled sadly. "Yes, my love, but we can't do it without you on our side. You're just going to have to get used to that."

"I will… eventually, but I gotta say, I'm scared of it." *The truth*, he thought. *For the first time, I'm telling the truth.*

Cora smiled ruefully. "Oh, love, you'd have to be stark raving mad *not* to be terrified of this, but we have time to put together a solid strategy. Don't worry."

"Right, what do I have to worry about? Only an entire *government* looking for me. What could possibly go wrong?"

Chaki pretended to listen to the non-existent music playing over her earpieces, bobbing her head as she prowled around the kitchen, straining to overhear the conversation in the living room. Playing the willing accomplice wore on her very last nerve, but it was better than being treated like a prisoner. Not that she wasn't a prisoner, really, but pretending to help had given her a certain amount of freedom. Freedom to listen, plot, and plan the right time to act. They had ripped from her the only power she'd ever had, and she was going to get it back.

She hadn't yet learned enough to make her move. Information was her currency, and even the identity of Canción's father, the location of Empa's safe house, and that the Ageless, Terpsichore, had survived and was living in Nashville wasn't enough. She needed more for her value to skyrocket. If she could hand all three, Empa, Terpsichore, and Canción, to the Nephilim, she could regain her place, and maybe even her crown.

They're going to set up a family reunion... Perfect. All she needed was a time and location, then she'd be golden.

Chaki grabbed a soda from the fridge and went to her room. The window was barred, of course, but she could find another way to break out when the time came. There were knives in the kitchen, and that old geezer, Hank, was the weak link. A knife in the gut, open the gun locker with his fingerprint, grab the keys to a car, and she'd be on the road. All she would need was a phone that would actually make a call. The one Empa had given her was locked into passive mode; she could surf, but couldn't even leave a comment or take a picture.

She sat on the bed and kicked off her shoes, flexing her aching toes. She felt the itch like a building orgasm and opened the dresser drawer. The needle she'd stolen from a sewing kit came free of its crack in the corner of the drawer, and she crossed a foot over her knee. A box of tissues, and she was ready.

The needle slid beneath the polished nail of her big toe easily, drawing a silent gasp from her gaping mouth. *Yes!* The pain was exquisite, shuddering through her, spurring the memories of her grandeur, her dominion, her power. Duvara had been unrelenting in her torment, and Chaki had come to relish it, believing she would be one with the demon princess in Hell when the end came. But Duvara was gone, and Chaki had to make her own torment.

"I'll regain all I've lost," she hissed between clenched teeth as she withdrew the needle and plunged it in again, deeper this time. "I'll buy my way back into the fold and ride my next host right into the arms of Lucifer himself!"

4

A NET CAST WIDE

His earpiece pinged twice, and the Son of Batraal answered with a clench of his jaw. "Zhao."

"Latest analytics on the Colombia terrorist investigation are available, sir. Eyes-only authorization necessary."

"Transfer to my desk." He severed the connection as a window popped up on his desk's secure monitor.

<Retinal Scan Access – Eyes-Only> flashed in the window. The Nephilim blinked twice to activate the scan and held still while the system's AI verified his identity.

<Approved> the AI responded, then <Voice authorization code>

"Chief Investigator Horatio Zhao."

The screen flashed <Approved> and a larger window with the day's analytics of the investigation flashed up. There were hundreds of leads being followed. Most would turn out to be nothing, but AIs couldn't make decisions on which ones were actionable. While they were very good at data mining, they were shit for reasoning; that still required a human mind—or in this case an inhuman one.

The Son of Batraal began scanning the entries, each one supported by data that could be real or could be smoke. If the son of the fallen angel of shadows was good at one thing, it was seeing through obscurity. One after another he flagged as low probability; several others he requested further investigation before taking action; less than five percent of the entries caught his full attention and warranted action.

One in particular caught his eye: a cypher had been found in a post on one of the Church of the Coming Dark's websites, among thousands of comments. The username "Beelzebub" and a musical phrase from a well-known popular song a century ago didn't raise any flags, but the analytic program had spotted an anomaly in the music. After the familiar riff, the notes devolved into nonsense. The AI cracked the cypher in a matter of seconds and found a ten-digit number. A phone number. Chasing the rabbit, it discovered the phone had been purchased at a kiosk in Atlanta four months prior in cash. Tracing the number hit two roadblocks: the phone was encrypted, and the signal transferred through a VPN in a North African country that specialized in anonymity. The phone's GPS was off, and the user also turned the phone off when not in use; two sure signs of illicit activity. The AI was smart enough to know there was no chance of pressuring the server's owner into coughing up data, so it waited and monitored satellite networks for traffic to that number. Finally, it tracked the user to Charlotte, North Carolina, and narrowed down the satellite transmission to a four-block radius in a suburban neighborhood. After a number of text transmissions and a couple of calls, the phone went dark. Either the user had finished their illicit business, or they'd switched to another phone.

Probably just another religious troll, the Nephilim thought. They had been pitting religious sects against one another for millennia. Still, the code was suspicious enough to warrant putting some boots on the ground. He sent a command to the Charlotte Secret Service section office to deploy investigators. A house-to-house search would take time but might turn up something interesting.

Not long after he moved to the next entry, a black SUV with two NAFAS Secret Service officers in the front seat left an underground parking lot in downtown Charlotte, heading toward the suburban neighborhood of Grand Oaks.

"Don't like it, E," Gippy grumbles, shaking his head. "Just the two of you with no backup? Nah, you're puttin' all your huevos in one cup, just askin' to get kicked in the sack."

I snort a laugh at his mixed metaphor—*So Gippy*—but he's not wrong. "Okay, but you riding shotgun doesn't put *fewer* of our eggs in one place, and the naffies are looking for you and me together."

"Right, so you need..." His face scrunches up, and he looks at Hank. "What's that called when you got someone watchin' your team from far away?"

"Overwatch." Hank cocks an eyebrow at me. "Not a bad idea, Empa."

I frown. "Okay, but that leaves you and Jeri here watching over Chaki, and Gip without backup."

"So, take me along," Jeri suggests. "I ride shotgun with Gip, and Hank stays here to babysit."

I purse my lips, thinking it through. Gippy and Jeri teaming up is worrisome because they're in love, and people in love do stupid things to protect the ones they love. At the same time, she's going to need field experience at some point, and I'm in love with her, too, though I'm slightly less likely than Gippy to do something stupid to save Jeri's life. At least I think I am. I'm no stranger to being stupid. Then there's the option of Hank accompanying Gippy and Jeri staying to watch over Chaki. While the balance of that arrangement might be better, Jeri will balk; I can see it in her eyes. I don't want to fight that fight. There's no real relationship tension at stake; we got past that a long time ago. But Jeri thinks I'm sheltering her, which might lead to resentment.

I fix Gip with my most serious stare. "And if shit goes sideways?"

"We deal with it. Cool heads, hot lead, and badass bitch with a blade watchin' my back." He grins at Jeri. "You know I'm better with a long gun than a pistol, and Jeri's better with a blade than a gun. We're not a bad match-up."

"True…" I hadn't considered that and turn to Hank. "You okay with that arrangement?"

Hank shrugs. "No problems from me. I'd rather sit in a comfy couch watchin' webflix than in a kidney-bustin' car seat. I'll put an ankle bracelet on Chaki so she won't get lost."

I nod. We've talked about that before, and it's a solid precaution. Chaki won't like it, but she's the least of our worries. "Okay, so where do we have our reunion? We need someplace safe without much NAFAS presence."

Gippy grins. "I been thinkin' about that. Cora's in Nashville, we're in Charlotte, and Emil's way the fuck out west. How about the Osage reservation? They're good folks, and NAFAS doesn't have much of a presence there."

I consider, and it's another not-bad suggestion. I pull out my phone and search the map, looking for a likely spot. We need a town big enough for us to be invisible but small enough to keep NAFAS' eyes elsewhere. "Pawhuska seems a good choice. There are a couple of hotels in the downtown area."

"And don't forget the food," Gippy reminds me with a grin. "Best steak I ever had."

"Steak?" Jeri perks up like my hand is in her pants.

"That *is* true!" I swallow, my mouth watering at the thought of a twenty-ounce buffalo porterhouse, and switch to my messaging app. "I'll text Emil and Cora, and we'll set up a date. Sooner would be better than later, I think. Canción's getting antsy, and I can't blame him. If they're okay with it, we could be on the road tomorrow."

"Perfect." Gippy gets up and nudges Jeri. "We drive the Taurus; you take the SUV. We'll start packing."

"And I'll work on our disguises." Jeri grins. "You up for your Afro-Asian getup?"

"Maybe something both of us can wear." I start texting, trusting Jeri to make me not look like me. "They may have pics of me as an Afro-Asian, and you always put too much padding in my jeans."

Jeri pouts. "Aw, come on! I like you with a bootie!"

I give her my best evil eye. "Are you saying my ass is too skinny?"

She mirrors my evil eye, adding a wink. "Your ass is *sensational*, E, I just like watching you jiggle a little now and then."

"Stick with something that'll cover me up, but nothing I can't move in. And don't push Canción's over the edge. They don't have his face yet, so we don't need anything drastic."

"Sure, ruin all my fun." She follows Gippy out, and I finish my text. Hank's eying me, and I see a question in his eyes. "What?"

"Dunno. This whole thing feels rushed. Maybe you and Gip should lay low for a month or two before another road trip."

He's not exactly wrong but needs to hear my reasons. "I'd like nothing more, but I think we should get Cora, Canción, and Emil in the same room soon. They're a family, and they've all been through hell. They need to talk this through in person, not over the phone."

He nods. "I get that. Just watch your ass, E. NAFAS has a dragnet out for you and Gip, but they don't know Cora and Emil exist at this point. You don't want to blow *their* cover."

"You're absolutely right; that's the *last* thing I want." My phone vibrates. It's Cora. She's in. Less than ten seconds later it vibrates again, and Emil echoes her reply to the letter. "Okay, we're a go. Let's get this show on the road. Canción and I leave at first light, Gippy and Jeri thirty minutes behind. We'll coordinate GPS positions on the road."

"Ay-firmative." Hank gets up and heads for the garage. "I'm going grocery shopping. With no car while you're gone, we need supplies."

"Watch for tails on your way back, please," I remind him.

He waves off my concern. "Not my first rodeo, boss."

I reply to Cora and Emil, giving them our rough itinerary, then pull up my reservation app and make arrangements in Pawhuska, my mouth watering again at the thought of that twenty-ounce buffalo porterhouse.

5

A TRAIL OF SORROW

Drive slow and don't run any stoplights." Gippy closed the passenger door with a grin.

"Just keep track of us." Empa affixed the veil of her Hijab and checked her look in the mirror, tucking away a few strands of hair. With dark contacts, darker eyebrows, and the hood covering her ears and hair, facial recognition software wouldn't have a chance of IDing her.

"Gotcha locked in." Gippy showed her his phone, a red dot pulsing on the garage of the house.

"See you in Nashville," Jeri added, squeezing Gippy's arm.

"We'll be in touch." Empa's smile reached her eyes, and she toggled up the window.

Canción, who only wore Middle Eastern-style shirt and pants, and dark hair color to match Empa's disguise, started the SUV and tapped the garage door opener. Gippy and Jeri backed away and watched them leave, the garage door lowering to block them from view before they drove away. Jeri sighed, and Gippy jostled her arm.

"Come on, Jer. We'll see them tonight, and we still got work to do."

"Sure." She followed him into the house where their bags waited.

"At least we had *time* to pack. Not like when we had to bug out of Atlanta." She lifted a guitar case and a duffle. "I miss that house. This one is..."

"Better than anything I ever lived in before we met E." He lifted his own guitar case, another duffle, and followed her out to the Taurus. The trunk was big enough to stow it all with room to spare, and they weren't planning to be gone more than a couple of weeks. Still, they loaded two more duffels full of clothes, disguises, and emergency supplies, following Empa's axiom that it was better to overpack than come up short when the fertilizer hit the air conditioning. "Weird to think we was livin' on the street a year ago, ain't it?"

"Too weird." She slammed the lid and smiled up at him. "We got more than we ever had, but it comes with the cost of being in the middle of a fuckin' war."

"Worth it." He tousled her already professionally tousled hair and checked his phone. "Come on. They just got on the freeway. Let's say goodbye and hit the road."

"Ay-firmative."

He followed her into the house and found Hank in the kitchen still wearing a robe, pouring midnight black coffee into a thermos. "Somethin' for the road," he said with his always-ready grin.

"Excellent!" They'd already eaten and had their morning jolt of caffeine, but it was a long drive to Nashville, their first stop. The plan was to meet up with Cora there and drive separate cars for the second leg to Pawhuska. "Thanks for watchin' the ol' homestead, Hank."

"Ain't no thing, brother." Hank handed him the thermos and shook his hand.

"Cm'ere, you!" Jeri embraced the old soldier. "Take care of the crazy bitch for us."

"Easy as fallin' out of bed," he replied, patting her head affectionately. "Speakin' of which, she's still in her rack. I'll tag her ankle when she gets up."

"Careful with her, Hank," Gippy warned. "She's—" His phone vibrated a pulsing sequence that meant one of the security cameras had picked up something. All three of them pulled their phones simultaneously and saw the porch camera view. "Shit!" Two men in suits were coming up the walk toward the door, a dark SUV parked at the curb behind them.

"They don't look like Jehovah's Witnesses." Hank pulled a SIG from under his robe and checked the breech. "Get Chaki and get ready to run. I'll stall 'em."

"Go, Jer! I'll get her. Yer drivin!" Jeri's eyes widened, but she nodded once and dashed for the garage.

Gippy sprinted to Chaki's door and tried the handle, but it was locked. He didn't have time to knock, and it was just a flimsy latch anyway. His boot opened it without too much racket.

Chaki sat up in bed with her hair all over the place, blinking bleary eyes.

"We got trouble! Grab clothes and come on!" He kept his voice low but urgent.

"Wha..." She just stared at him.

"Come the fuck *on*!" He grabbed her arm, hauled her out of bed, and pushed her toward her dresser. "There's naffies at the door! Grab clothes! Now!"

Getting the message, she grabbed a double armload of clothes and staggered after him. He paused long enough at the hall gun safe to thumb it open and grab their ditch bag. He thought about taking up the SIG XM7 assault rifle and emptying the mag through the door, but Hank already stood there shouting questions through the intercom and waved them toward the garage. Gippy secured the gun safe, urged Chaki into a run, closed the garage door behind them, and stuffed her into the back seat of the Taurus.

"Get on the floor!" He dumped their ditch bag on top of her. The bag didn't have any weapons inside, just money, IDs, and medical supplies, so he wasn't worried she'd pull a gun and blow his brains out. "And put some pants on!"

He closed her door quietly before getting in the front. Jeri sat behind the wheel, engine running, a Mach-10 machine pistol in her lap. He pulled out his Glock and phone. The porch camera showed the two suited goons, one holding an ID up to the peephole, while the other stood with one hand under his coat.

"Wait," he told Jeri. "Hank might handle this."

"And if he can't?"

"Then fucking drive like Hell's on our asses, because it *will* be."

She nodded, bit her lip, and shifted the car into reverse.

Gippy watched his phone. Hank finally opened the front door and stepped back as the two goons surged into the entry hall. He switched the view to inside. The entry hall pickup had audio, and he could hear Hank arguing with the pair. One of the two men had him backed up against a wall with a hand on his chest, quick-firing questions, while the other looked around.

"You own this house?"

"Yes, free and clear."

"And your name?"

"Henry Walberg, and I'm a US Military vet. I've got rights!"

"News flash, old man, the US isn't even a *country* anymore, and your rights don't mean shit when it comes to national security."

"Oh, shit," Gippy hissed. "He called Hank 'old man.'"

"Isn't he?" Jeri asked. "Old, I mean?"

"Yeah, but you never, *ever* call—" But Hank was already on a tear.

"Who you callin' old, punk? I was serving in combat when you weren't even a bulge in your daddy's hip pocket! Where do you get off harassing honest, law-abiding citizens?"

"And whose are these?" the other intruder asked, lifting a pair of women's red underwear from the floor where Chaki had dropped them in their rush.

"None of your business!" Hank retorted.

"Everything's our business! Answer the question!" the other barked.

"Mine! They're mine! What of it? I'm allergic to cotton, and I like the way they feel! You gonna arrest me for wearin' fancy underwear?"

"Maybe, now shut the fuck up." The one holding Hank at bay nodded to his partner. "This is bullshit. Tear this shithole apart."

As the other officer moved out of view, the clatter of cupboard and closet doors audible over the pickup, Gippy watched Hank reach back under his robe.

"Shit, shit, shit! He's gonna—" Hank's SIG barked twice, and the officer staggered back, but even point blank, the pistol didn't penetrate the man's body armor. The third round, however, caught the man under the chin and painted the ceiling with a spray of bone, blood, and brain tissue. As Gippy opened his mouth to tell Jeri to go, the other man stepped out of the kitchen leveling a thick-muzzled machine pistol. "Go-go-go!"

As Jeri's foot flattened the accelerator to the floor, a burst of fire from the gun knocked Hank back against the wall. Gippy gritted his teeth as his friend slid down, leaving a trail of blood. His limp form lay there unmoving.

They smashed backward through the garage door, trailing torn aluminum and two tracks of smoking rubber on the driveway. Chaki's scream matched the tone of squealing tires as Jeri wheeled around onto the street and slammed the car into drive.

The front door opened, and the man who had gunned down Hank stepped out, the machine pistol leveled.

Gippy raised his pistol but didn't want to fire past Jeri. She evidently didn't need his help, however, and extended her left arm out the open driver's side window, Mach-10 in hand. She sprayed a full magazine from the Mach-10 in the general direction of the house and hammered the gas pedal. Gippy doubted she had hit the man, but at least it made him duck. Then he had an idea.

"Stop beside the black SUV!"

"Why?" She hammered the brakes to stop beside the larger vehicle.

"It's bullet proof, and I need to keep the fucker from chasing us!" He reached under the seat, feeling for the rack of four grenades: frag, flashbang, smoke, and incendiary. He pulled the last one, depressed the lever, and yanked the pin. Bullets pinged against the black SUV, but Gippy couldn't see the man through the tinted glass. While he reached across her to fling the bomb out the window, Jeri slapped another magazine into the Mach-10. *Good girl*, he thought as the grenade clattered and rolled under the SUV. "Now, go!"

Jeri floored it, emptying another magazine at the house without even looking where she was aiming.

The grenade detonated behind them, sending white phosphorus streaming out in all directions and setting the SUV on fire. Gippy glanced back. The gunman crouched in the doorway, gun in one hand, phone in the other. That was bad.

"He's calling for backup!" Gippy cringed at the noise and realized Chaki was still screaming. As far as he knew, no bullets had touched the car, so he doubted she'd been hit. He leaned over the seat and bellowed. "Shut up or I'll put a fucking bullet in your head!"

"She's *scared*, Gip!" Jeri said, though Chaki took the hint and shut up. "Give her a break."

"So am I, but screaming don't help and damages my calm!" He noticed Jeri's lower lip was bleeding. "Good job, by the way. You kicked ass!" In fact, for her first firefight, she'd done amazingly well.

"Thanks. Where to?"

"Just drive. We need to switch cars and put some distance between us and the house. He probably called in a description of this one, so they'll be looking for it. Stay off the main streets and look for something I can jack! I've gotta let E know that the shit just hit the fan."

"How fucked are we?" Jeri asked, her knuckles white on the wheel.

"All depends on who they were and who that guy's calling." He started texting. "If they're just cops, we should be okay. If they're military, we're in deep—"

An explosion lit up the early morning sky six blocks behind them.

"—shit!" He sent the text to Empa, knowing she'd forward it to everyone else. "*Really* deep!"

"*Jesus!*" Jeri swerved over to the curb and screeched to a stop behind a rusted-out Ford F-350, barely stopping in time to avoid hitting the massive bumper. "What the *fuck*, Gip?

"Drone strike. Someone panicked. Frag your phone and get our stuff into that truck." He got out and glanced around, but the street was still quiet. That wouldn't last as people started coming out to investigate the blast. He dropped his phone on the street and stomped on it three times. "I'll try to get this beast started. If they have eyes in the sky and spot this car, they'll send another missile." Luckily, they were parked under a massive oak that wasn't quite dead yet, which might block drone-borne cameras.

"Shit!" Jeri scrambled out of the car, flung open the back door, and dragged Chaki out. The terrified woman resisted, but Jeri persuaded her with one cold-hard fact. "We gotta go, Chak, or we're dead!"

The truck was miraculously unlocked, so Gippy flung open the driver's door. Then their luck ran out. "Fucking electronic ignition!"

"Is that bad?" Jeri hoisted Chaki into the back seat, shoving bags and clothes after her.

"Maybe not." After Cartagena, where they were momentarily foiled by a garage full of electronic ignitions and electric and hybrid vehicles, Gippy had delved deeply into the dark net for a better screw-driver. He'd found a hack but hadn't put it into practice yet. He dashed back for the Taurus' trunk. "Get the gear. This might take a minute."

"Sirens, Gip." She grabbed the guitar cases. "Dunno if we got a minute."

Distant wails filled the air, singing on Gippy's every nerve like static electricity. Rifling through his duffle, he found his spare phone and the highly illegal dongle. Booting up the phone, which seemed to take forever, he plugged in the dongle and waited. When the screen cleared, he pulled up the app and tapped in "Ford F-350."

The app displayed "Press Start."

Gippy flung his bag into the back of the truck and climbed into the driver's seat. Foot on the brake, he pressed the start button, but the dash only displayed "No Key Found." He waited and watched the app, which told him "Working."

"Come on, come on!" Technically, the app was simple. It listened for a ping from the vehicle and tried the few thousand codes assigned to that make and model of car. Once it transmitted the correct code, the car would think the phone was the key fob.

The app displayed, "Press Start."

Gippy pressed start again, and the dash displayed "No Key Found."

"Fuck, fuck, fuck!"

The passenger door slammed, and Jeri announced, "Good to go!"

"Working on it." Which was literally what the app told him, a small icon swirling like a yellow spiral of death as the drone that had blown their house to bits flew somewhere high overhead, looking for a steel-gray Ford Taurus.

The app flashed, "Press Start."

Gippy pressed start once again, and the big coal emulsion engine roared to life. "Fuck yeah! I *do* love technology!" He shifted in gear and drove away at a sedate pace.

"What now?" Jeri asked.

"We find a place to hide and figure out how they found us." He glanced into the back seat, but Chaki just met his accusative glare with wide-eyed terror. Okay, maybe not her, but there had to be a leak somewhere. "Deep breaths, everyone. We'll switch cars again as soon as we're in the clear. And your lip's bleeding, Jer."

"Fuck," She wiped it and frowned. "I think I tore out one of my piercings."

"Take the first exit you can." I take a few seconds to text our emergency code to Emil and Cora, then pull a multitool from the glove box and pry my phone open with shaking hands. *Steady spirit... Calm is strength... They're alive...*

"What happened?" Canción signals and moves to the right lane.

"I don't know yet, but we're made, or at least Gippy is, or maybe the house." I lever out the SIM card with pliers and crush it, then rip out the battery, trying to keep calm. *Steady spirit...* It's difficult with the thought of Gippy and Jeri in danger, but descending into dread would only make things worse. I check for any sign of anyone following us, and fling the pieces of shattered circuitry out the window. "I have a spare phone in my bag. I'll find out the details as soon as I can, but we've got to get off the freeway and find someplace to hole up." We're still on the outskirts of Charlotte's sprawl, which might be inside their search circle, but we have no choice. They'll be watching the interstates.

Canción takes an exit—*#13... I hope that's lucky*—onto a nondescript road and turns south. I try not to take the number as an omen of bad luck and reach to the back seat for my shoulder bag. An inside zipper pocket yields my backup phone, and I power it on. By the time it boots up, we're coming up to a crossroads, a four-lane highway through once bustling suburbia, now fallen to disrepair and despair. The countryside is a mosaic of struggling farmland and strip malls converted into slum housing. We pass a supermarket surrounded by a chain-link fence with barbed wire, armed guards standing at the only gate in; a rough neighborhood.

"Which way?" he asks as we stop at the non-functional stoplight.

"Left. I think we passed a small town. I'll find someplace we can get a room. Drive slowly and don't break any traffic laws." Canción hasn't been driving long, but we've put in a lot of miles from Central America. He's also a young man and tends to drive too fast. At least traffic is light.

I pull up a map app, but leave my GPS off. In the unlikely but real possibility that Gippy's been taken, they might crack his spare phone, which has the number for this one in it. He won't call me—our emergency protocol is for text only—so if my phone rings, I'll know we're in very deep shit.

I follow the interstate and find our exit and the nearest town. "Gastonia. There's a motel just off the main road."

"Won't checking in this early draw attention?"

"Maybe." He's thinking clearly, at least, which is good. Maybe more so than I am. I take a deep breath and let it out slowly, calming my hammering heart. "Find a diner, then. We'll kill time until midday."

"Not much around."

He's not wrong; some auto parts stores, a few specialty shops for farm supplies, incongruously, a stable advertising draft animals for rent, a corral full of mules guarded by rifle-carrying men with stern faces. Another supermarket, this one huge and also fenced and guarded. This doesn't bode well.

I spot a roadside bar with a parking lot full of motorcycles and a sign advertising "Good Food. Bad Beer. Open 24 hours." *Just my kind of dive.*

"There. Park around back, and whatever you do, don't hit any of the bikes."

"Really?" He slows and pulls in, squinting at the faded red paint and bars on the windows. "Looks dangerous, and we don't look like locals."

"It'll work for a few hours, and don't let biker bars fool you. Most bikers are just folks, not criminals." I remove my veil and shake out my hair. There won't be any cameras in a place like this, and a bare head will be less likely to draw racial profiling. "You take the lead, just like we practiced, and if anybody gives us a hard time, do your thing."

"My *thing*?" He pulls around back and kills the engine.

"Yes, your *thing*. Take their anger or whatever you can do to calm them down."

He half-glares at me. "I thought you said I shouldn't do that without consent."

"This is a special circumstance." I get out and move my Glock to the front of my belt, easily accessible through the slit in my baggy abaya. "We're passing through after driving all night, headed for Charlotte, stopping for breakfast."

"Okay." His long shirt covers his weapon and sunglasses hide his eyes.

We stroll around front, and I close my eyes tightly for a few seconds before Canción opens the door. It'll be darker inside, and the trick helps adjust my vision faster. The funky odor of sweat, leather, sour beer, greasy food, and motor oil wafts over me with tinny strains of country music from a sound system in dire need of repair. I open my eyes wide as the door closes behind us and scan the room. As biker bars go, this one is less of a dive than I expected. We draw stares, but nothing overtly malicious, and the regulars include enough women and people of color that I doubt we'll be hassled.

"Sit anywheres ya like," a woman says from behind the bar. "Be with ya in two shakes."

"Thank you," Canción says with a nod, leading me to a surprisingly unoccupied and clean corner table.

I get a few more stares than he does on the way, but not many. He *is* gorgeous, after all, and more than a few men nudge their female companions to tell them their eyes are straying too long. There are some chuckles and snide comments, but none directed toward us. We sit facing the room and the bartender brings two laminated menus, her swagger self-assured and her countenance neutral.

"You ain't the type we usually get in here." She hands the menus over.

"I imagine not," I say with a smile.

"We've been driving all night and saw your sign." Canción unfolds the mold-spotted menu. "What's good?"

"Ever-thing but the beer, sweety." She gives him her best smile, her hands on shapely hips. "Coffee?"

"Yes. Two, please." I examine my menu as she swaggers off, not hungry, but we have to order something. Canción's nervous, so I give him a nudge under the table. "Relax. We've got bigger worries than a bar full of bikers."

"Can you ping Gippy?"

"Not yet. They're probably busy." *Or dead*, I can't help but think. "He'll text me when he has a chance."

"And if he doesn't?" He's obviously thinking along the same lines as I am.

"Then we try to find out what happened to them." I pull up breaking news on my phone, and get nothing. It's too early. There's no TV in the bar, which I find refreshingly odd. Maybe the clientele knows that all the news is crap anyway, and professional sports have gone the way of the dodo.

Our waitress returns with two steaming cups. "What'll it be?"

"I'll have the 'Train Wreck' if the meat's not pork," I say. The menu describes the dish as 'Meat of the Day fried with onions and potatoes,' which could mean anything.

"Not pork, but I can't tell you if it's woodchuck or trash panda." She grins. "Catch as catch can 'round here, ya know."

"That's fine." I sip the coffee and force myself not to cringe. It tastes like burned dishwater.

"I'll have the same." Canción gives her a nod and smile that leaves her open-mouthed. "Thank you."

"My pleasure, sweety," she stammers, swaggering back to the kitchen to put our order in. A guy at the bar asks her if she needs to change her panties, and she tells him to fuck off, which draws a round of chuckles.

While we're waiting, my phone vibrates. My heart skips a beat as I see the text is from Jeri's backup phone. I pull it up and read with my teeth clenched.

"Two naffies showed up asking questions. Hank dead, house destroyed by drone strike. Gip, Chaki, and I got out. On the road. Don't know how they found us, but they didn't know anything. Didn't get a good look at Gip. Both naffies likely dead."

Hank... I see his ready grin, feel his enthusiasm for helping me, the baggage that weighed so heavily upon his soul. *So much pain... Steady spirit... Focus. See everything.* I text her, "Head east, no freeways, switch cars. Meet up in Spartanburg tomorrow. I'll text you where."

Moments later, I receive, "Okay. Love you. Xxooff."

I can't help but smile at her slightly pornographic addition to the old endearment, and show Canción the text.

He frowns. "How did they find us?"

"No way to know for sure, but it sounds like they were canvassing the area. If they suspected who they were looking for, there would have been a whole strike team instead of only two." I put my phone away. "We regroup and move on."

He sighs and nods. "How do you live like this?"

I blink at him and realize again just how young he is, younger than Gippy, in fact, and without the survival experience from living on the street. "Day to day, Canción. You survive day to day." I put my hand on his and squeeze. "We're safe for now."

He snorts a laugh. "In a bar surrounded by bikers?"

"Safer than in your mama's arms," I tell him with a nod around the room. "Naffies show up here, they'll end up in the blue-plate special."

He blinks at me wide-eyed, and I realize he thinks I'm serious. Then the food arrives, and I think my dark humor might not be too far off base. "Kidding," I assure him, thanking the waitress and picking up my fork. "Now eat. We've got time to kill and miles to go before we sleep."

6

———

BLIND FLIGHT

I read Empa's emergency code, and my heart rises to my throat. *Canción...* I drop my phone on the floor and crush it under my heel, banishing the visions of horror that are playing in my mind like discordant music. Whatever has happened is over and worrying won't change the outcome. I have to move immediately, for if they found Empa, they might find me as well, but I have no escape plan. I never plan. Every time I do, my plans turn to shit and everything ends up in flames.

The sound of screams, the smell of burning wood and flesh, the searing heat of flames on my skin.

I grab my shoulder bag and start stuffing things into it: money, laptop, my penny whistle, clothes, a backup pistol, snacks, and a few sundry items. The world might burn down around me, but at least I'll have clean underwear and my toothbrush. I scoop up the pieces of my shattered phone—I'll turn on my spare later, when I'm safe—and stuff them in the pocket of my hoodie. Lastly, I smear some carefully prepared grime on my face and hands and leave my roach motel for the street, with no idea where I'm going.

It's early, and the city's mostly quiet. I find a dumpster, deposit the shards of my phone in it, and move on. Long practice has taught me the stoop-shouldered gait of despair that the homeless perfected before the invention of the wheel. It tells the world that I have nothing worth stealing, a lie I've used for centuries. I walk aimlessly, but some dormant, unpanicked portion of my mind—the part that knows Nashville like the color of my own eyes in the mirror—takes me north across town, through Music Row. Even at this hour, some of the clubs are open, and the strains of tunes I've never heard before cool my blazing nerves. I try not to think, to dread what might come with the next text.

Is Canción dead? Have I killed him by following the trail of breadcrumbs Empa left for me?

My conscious mind isn't buying that for a second. *Stop blaming yourself, Terpsichore. You don't know what led the hounds of Hell to their door.*

I stagger past a row of homeless people huddled in the shelter of a soup kitchen's awning, the scents of urine and desperation wafting up like smoke. Block after block, I pretend to ignore my surroundings, feign despair—not hard at all right now—and pray to my father's mother that my pretense won't become genuine later.

Canción... my dear boy... my sweet song...

After wandering for an hour or so, my feet take me to a place I know from another life. I stare at the Losers' Bar and Grill like I'm looking into the face of an old friend. Behind me, the crappy little three-story walk up I lived in a century ago is still standing, but now beyond crappy. It's nearly falling down, but a hand-painted cardboard sign tacked to the door reads "room for rent." I shamble up and try the latch. It's unlocked.

Maybe God loves me after all.

I pull the sign down and enter. It smells worse than my previous hovel, but there's a door to my right with the word "office" painted on it. I knock. After a minute with no reply, I knock again, louder.

"The fuck?" The woman's reedy voice is clearly half asleep. Locks click and chains rattle. The door opens, and I'm staring at the barrel of a sawed-off shotgun. "Who the fuck are you?" The face above the weapon is only slightly more welcoming than the weapon, and the alcohol on her breath curls my eyebrows.

I show her the sign. "I wanna rent yer room."

"Well, shit-monkeys! Why didn't you say so?" She lowers the weapon and holds out a hand. "Fifty NADs a week, first two weeks in advance. I find out you're whoring up there and yer out on yer ass. No loud music either. I get enough of that from across the street."

"Fine." I rifle through my pockets for crumpled bills and hand her two fifties, which she takes without a word. The door starts to close, but I block it with my foot. "Which one?"

"Six. Upstairs and left." She looks down at my boot. "Move it or lose it."

Ironically, the same room I lived in before. "Key?"

"Fuck no, there ain't no key. You want locks, you put 'em in yourself! Now move your goddamn foot!"

I pull my foot back, and the door slams. I hear mumbling through the door and the clink of glass on glass. Climbing stairs so creaky that I worry they might collapse, I find number six and try the latch. It turns and I push the door open warily, one hand in the pocket of my hoodie resting on my pistol. The single room is much as I remember it, save for the woman and two young children huddled on the moldy mattress stuffed into one corner. The children are sleeping but the woman is awake, her eyes wide with fear.

Clearly, they're squatters, but I can't make myself evict them. I hold up both hands, empty and unthreatening, then place one finger to my lips. "Let them sleep."

She blinks at me, still fearful, and starts to move.

"Stay. There's room for everyone." I close the door behind me and move quietly to the moldy armchair in the other corner. I doff my bag, dig out my spare phone, and sit. She's still staring at me, but hasn't moved. I boot up the phone and text Empa's backup number. "New digs, no one following. Safe for now. Leak must have been on your end. Everyone safe?"

The reply comes quickly. "House caught in dragnet. They didn't know who they were looking for. Lost one man, but someone called in an airstrike. House gone, and we think the naffies with it. We're in the wind for now."

I bite my lip and ask the only question I truly care about. "Canción?"

"Safe and sound. I'll text you tomorrow. Maybe stick to our plan."

That surprises me. "With N on your trail? Think that's safe?"

"They probably don't know who lived in that house. All evidence destroyed. Nothing to point to us or our plans. May as well have our family reunion."

That seems cold to me, but I'm not going to look a gift horse in the mouth. "Okay. Txt tomorrow." I put my phone away and raise my eyes to find the woman and both children now staring at me wide-eyed.

I smile, finding it easier now that I know Canción's safe. They don't smile back, but I have one thing that might put them at ease. I pull my penny whistle from my bag and play softly whatever comes into my head. The youngest girl smiles, and the other's face goes slack with amazement. The woman is taken aback by the music I'm playing, but the tension in her shoulders slowly eases. In ten minutes, they're all smiling.

I continue to play, both for their benefit and my own. *Thank you, father...*

"Tell me there's something left to analyze." The Son of Samyaza glared into the monitor, the shaky image of the Son of Batraal and the smoldering ruin behind him.

"There's *always* something left to analyze, but we won't be finished for days. I admit, the outcome was... less than optimal."

"Less than *optimal*?" The leader of the Nephilim's teeth chirped, jaw muscles writhing, his fingernails digging into the armrests of his custom-made office chair. "Do we know anything at all about who lived there?"

"We know they were heavily armed, saw our men coming, and escaped in a steel-gray four-door sedan, which we found abandoned some blocks away. We found the remains of a gun safe in the ruins. They fired fully automatic weapons and used a white phosphorus grenade to destroy our agents' vehicle."

"Which tells us next to nothing. There's enough ordinance on the black market to outfit an army. Anyone with money can get it. What in all ten-thousand levels of Hell happened there?"

The Son of Batraal sighed. "It boils down to a breakdown in communications. Our agents encountered an old man in a bathrobe whose story didn't seem right. While they were investigating, the man shot the senior agent. The junior agent returned fire, and the man was killed. A car drove out of the garage, *through* the garage door, obviously intending to escape, and the agent exited the house intending to stop them. A woman in the car pinned him down with automatic weapons fire, at which point he called for air support. That's where the miscommunication happened. We had a drone on high overwatch, and the supervisor ordered a strike instead of simply following the vehicle."

"When the suspects had already escaped?" His teeth chirped as he ground them together. "I hope this supervisor is on a plane to the Yukon."

"He is being disciplined, as is the agent's superior, but all the drone supervisor saw was the house and the agents' vehicle exploding on the street. He had no information on the escaping vehicle, only that there was a firefight inside and outside the house with heavily armed suspects, and one agent was already down."

"And we end up with nothing," The Nephilim growled through gritted teeth.

"Not *exactly* nothing. We found their car, and suspect they stole a white Ford F-350, which we're looking for."

"If you find it, *try* not to blow it up before we can ask the driver a question or two."

The Son of Batraal glared at the sarcasm. "We've put out a bulletin, but there are about a thousand vehicles of that description in the greater Charlotte area. We have a plate number, but these are experienced fugitives; they'll have changed the tags already, if not the vehicle."

The Son of Samyaza's brow furrowed. "What makes you think they're experienced?"

"Weaponry, tactics, and skills. These weren't common criminals."

In this, at least, he trusted the Son of Batraal's judgment. "Find them. These agents were deployed on evidence linked to the Church of the Coming Dark. They may be linked to the surviving Ageless."

"We're searching, but their possible location is in a circle with a radius increasing at sixty miles an hour."

"I know that. I also know that the Ageless and this... hybrid, Canción, are responsible for destroying two of our kind and banishing several more. If you don't want a one-way ticket to Hell, or *oblivion*, find them and eliminate them."

The muscles in the other Nephilim's jaw bunched. "I *know* my job. You do yours."

"When you start doing your job *better*, I'll stop telling you how to do it!" The Son of Samyaza ended the call before the other could get in the last word. He had work to do if he was going to make anything useful out of this catastrofuck.

7

GETTING GONE

The sun was going down by the time they pulled into another crappy motel in the outskirts of another town Gippy had never been in. Greenville wasn't very green with the blistering heat of summer wilting the trees and grass. He parked the electric Subaru they'd bought in Spartanburg near the motel's office, making sure they weren't in view of any cameras. They'd changed cars twice before the legitimate purchase, abandoning the stolen ones after wiping them down with a solution of chemicals that destroyed DNA. Constant vigilance for fourteen hours on the road had him seeing double and yawning, but now, maybe, they could sleep and regroup.

"Get us a room for two nights, Jer. Two beds. Three people. We'll pick up takeout and eat in."

"Sure." Jeri had changed their appearance in transit. She dressed like a young professional, with glasses, sedate makeup, a wig to cover her hair, and only a tenth of her usual jewelry. He'd been transformed into an East Indian, with a wig of straight hair and makeup to sharpen his nose and cheekbones. "Back in a flash." She got out and did a corporate power walk to the office.

Gippy was proud of Jeri, seemingly as calm as a junkie on a trip so soon after her first firefight. He knew from experience that the aftermath of being shot at and returning fire often hit harder than the fight itself. Then he glanced at Chaki in the rearview mirror and sighed. She had regressed into a trauma-shocked silence, avoiding his eyes whenever he looked at her. Right now, he didn't have time to worry about her; they were on the run without any real plan at the moment other than to stay safe and anonymous. He had mixed feelings about Chaki; part of him felt sorry for what she'd been through, having experienced it himself on a much smaller scale, and the other part didn't trust her. Admittedly, a very small third part couldn't even think of her without remembering what the succubus Duvara had done to him, and hated her.

Jeri returned before the silence became oppressive and got in. "Number 107." She pointed. "She asked a bunch of questions, and there was a TV on in the office playing news. Terrorist attack in Charlotte."

"Of course, that's the news. Same old story." He cocked an eyebrow at her as he moved the car. "You didn't *answer* any of her questions, did you?"

"Sure, but I made shit up. We're up from Atlanta, house hunting. My brother and his girlfriend."

He pulled in backward to keep the tag hidden from the street and shut off the car. "I don't look much like your brother."

She shrugged. "Another mother. Come on, I'm sick of this car."

Her curt reply surprised him. Maybe the stress of the day was wearing on her after all. "Get used to it, we'll probably be moving on soon."

They moved Chaki and her things from the back seat into the room first. It smelled like disinfectant and stale cigarette smoke, but there were two beds and a bath with a window in the back big enough to escape through if they had to. While Jeri went back for their guitar cases and duffels, Gippy made sure the back window opened and slotted a tencoin in the metered shower to check the water, which came out the color of weak tea for a while before it cleared. He pissed, flushed, and came out of the bathroom to find Chaki sitting hunkered with her knees up on one bed, and Jeri on the other with her guitar case open, Empa's sword across her knees, wiping an oil cloth over the lustrous curve of steel.

"Badass bitch with a blade." He flashed a grin, flopped onto the bed, and pulled his phone. "Hungry?"

"Not really." She wiped the blade one more time, then sheathed it. "Too much junk food."

"Sorry, but there's not much around but fast food." He glanced to Chaki. "Any preferences?"

"Yes." Her eyes met his for the first time in twelve hours. "I'd like you to let me go."

"What?" The request caught him off guard.

"Let me go. I'm not a part of this, and I'm just slowing you down. I don't know anything, and I'll be fine on my own." Her lower lip trembled, but she seemed sincere.

Gippy opened his mouth, then bit off the argument he couldn't start. "Maybe when we're in the clear. I'll talk it over with Empa." He knew her answer would be a resounding 'No.' Despite her claim to ignorance, Chaki knew too much. She knew about Cora, Emil, and Canción, not to mention Jeri, who was still below the Nephilim radar. "Sorry."

Chaki responded by crossing her arms over her knees and looking away.

"I wish it was cooler out," Jeri said, taking Gippy off guard again, but the change of subject was welcome.

"Why?"

"Because I want to keep this close," She caressed the lustrous scabbard with her fingertips. "And wearing a long coat this time of year would be like a neon sign. Way out of place."

"Ah, right." He knew she loved that sword for two reasons: it was Empa's, and she was good with it. He thought for a bit, then suggested, "Maybe shift to your musician disguise and carry the case everywhere."

"Too fuckin' heavy with that beast in it." She nodded to the shotgun and two long bandoliers of shells strapped into the case. "The weight tells everyone it's not a guitar."

He frowned; Jeri had become a master of disguises, and not just makeup. She'd studied gait recognition algorithms, fashion, mannerisms, and even poker tells. "Never thought of that. What if you strap it over your shoulder?"

She shrugged. "Maybe, but I couldn't draw the blade quickly anyway." She sighed and put the sword back in the case. "Hard to disguise a three-foot piece of steel."

"True that." He remembered Empa's long duster, but Jeri was right; wearing something like that in summer heat would draw too much attention, besides being way too hot. "Should have worn an abaya, I guess. That'd cover it."

Shrugging, she closed the case. "And I'd sweat like a trick in church." She got up and put her sports jacket back on. "I'll get us some food. Any preferences?"

"Nothing too greasy. And be careful."

She grinned, drew her pistol—a slim-line Glock 42XC—and checked the breech. "Locked and loaded, baby." She reholstered the pistol at the small of her back and headed out the door.

He watched her go, suppressing the haze of worry that felt like a lead blanket. Jeri knew how to blend in and could handle anyone giving her shit. She'd learned that from living on the street, just as he had.

To pass the time, he checked his weapons. The Glock hadn't been fired, but he dumped the magazine, cleared the breech, then removed the slide to make sure it was clean. Reassembling the pistol took only seconds, his hands performing the familiar task without his exhausted brain's help. He opened his guitar case and checked the long rifle, booting up the LAWS targeting system to check the batteries. All well, he closed and locked the case and pulled out his phone.

He texted Empa, "Safe and sound in G-ville. Charlotte is all over the news."

Less than a minute later, Empa replied, "We're in Spartanburg.

Two officers killed by a terrorist bomb, such a tragedy. Neighbor interviews are interesting. Some wild misinformation."

He tapped, "Great. Did they find anything?"

"No way to know truth from fiction at this point. Someone seriously fucked up calling in a drone strike."

"Wouldn't have been a fuckup if we were still in the house when it hit." He glanced at Chaki and decided to pop the question. "Chak's freaked out. Wants us to let her go."

"No can do," came the reply. "She knows about Cora. Ns don't even know she's alive. Too risky."

"Agreed, but what to do with her. She's a PITA with PTSD, and the Ns might be looking for her, since she vanished from Carty."

"No choice. Try to keep her out of sight."

He gritted his teeth. "There's one choice, but you won't like it."

"We're not doing that," she replied, as he knew she would. "She doesn't deserve that, and there would be complications."

"Your call. You talk to Cora?"

"Tonight. We'll figure out our next step. Txt you in the AM."

"Ay-firmative. Sleep tight."

"How's Jeri?"

"Oh, good! Handled her baptism like a pro. Seems okay with it. Better than I was."

"Good. Hug her for me."

He smiled. "That all?"

"Don't get freaky on me, bro."

He chuckled and started surfing the news. Looking up, he found Chaki staring at him, a question in her eyes. "Sorry. For now, you're with us."

She just turned away, her shoulders hunched and neck stiff.

Gippy tried to ignore her; he had enough on his hands keeping them alive.

Knowing this will be a difficult conversation, I set up a three-way video call with Cora, Emil, and Canción and me on our end. Emil takes the news of Hank's death hard, as I knew he would. Emil's a man of peace; he finds the one simple truism of war impossible to accept.

"I'm sorry, but Hank was a soldier to the core. He volunteered to help us, knew what he was getting into, and saved Gippy and Jeri by putting himself in the line of fire." I can almost feel his rejection of that rationale over the phone. "He died a *hero*, Emil."

"Hero." Emil hates violence of any kind. "That doesn't make what happened right."

"No, it doesn't, but this is war, and people die. Thanks to Hank, we only lost one, not three." I don't know if he'll accept that, but I can't change facts, so I change the subject. "We seem to be out of danger, albeit homeless for now, thanks in large part to Gippy's street smarts and quick thinking. They've got Chaki with them, but I really don't see a valid reason to put off our family reunion. They're still going to act as overwatch for the rest of us. If you're okay with it, we can be in Nashville tomorrow."

"Don't get me wrong," Emil says, still obviously concerned. "I'd love to see you all together, but I don't want to put anyone at risk."

"You wouldn't be," Canción cuts in before Cora can respond. "And I want to see my mother. We have too much to catch up on that can't be said over the phone."

"And I'd love to see you, too, Canción, but Emil's right. It might be dangerous."

"I don't see how it could be," I assure them. "They might have tracked the burner phone from the number I left on the Coming Dark website, but that phone's gone, and so is the one the messages were forwarded to. There's no way I know of that they could have cracked our texts. Too many random virtual hosts, and they dump their data-banks hourly. Even so, we can change the venue."

"Well, *you* were always the cautious one," Cora admits with a smile. "And I'd like to sit down with my family. *All* of us."

Emil's blush is priceless. "If you all think it's safe, I'll be there."

"All right, then. We'll change the venue, maybe still on the Osage

Reservation, and plan for day after tomorrow. I'll find someplace in Ponka City." I can't help smiling at the prospect of the reunion. "We'll be in Nashville tomorrow, Cora. I still think it'd be safer if we traveled separately. Can you get a car?"

"Not a problem. I may *look* like a vagabond, but I've got money. Text me when you're close."

"Will do, and I'll text everyone the details on Ponca City."

"Thank you both for agreeing to this," Canción adds, clearly relieved. "I'll see you tomorrow, Mom."

Cora glows with pleasure. "Hasta manana, mi Canción."

I end the call and clap Canción on the shoulder. "Get some sleep. It's been a hell of a day."

"Right." He draws a deep breath and lets it out slowly. "Thank you for this, Empa. Really."

"My pleasure. I haven't seen Cora in centuries."

"*Centuries...*" He shakes his head with a wry chuckle. "I still have trouble wrapping my head around all this sometimes."

I laugh ruefully. "You'll get used to it... maybe."

Chaki opened her eyes. The only light in the room came from an ancient clock radio displaying 2:43, but that was enough. She'd kept herself awake by thrusting the needle under a fingernail every time her attention wandered. She'd been listening for hours: diminishing street sounds, air conditioning, the drip of water from the condenser onto the sidewalk outside, and the deep breathing of her two captors.

Now. It has to be now. Unlike the house, the motel didn't have motion-sensing security cameras linked to their phones. If she didn't wake them, she had a chance to escape.

She moved with agonizing slowness to keep the stiff sheets from rustling. When her bare feet touched the bristly carpet, the clock displayed 2:54. Easing her weight off the bed slowly to keep the springs from squeaking, listening for any change in their breathing, she stood. Gippy and Jeri were deep asleep, sprawled on the bed fully clothed. Chaki wore her jeans and t-shirt already, and her shoes were right beside her bed. She picked them up but didn't put them on, and took a step, just one, toward the pile of luggage, the droning AC masking her movements. All of their weapons were locked up in the guitar cases or in their holsters, but the ditch kit held money. She could make out the bag lying with the guitar cases, the neck of one case resting over half of the smaller bag. Another step, stop, listen, then one more. Squatting down, she reached for the bag's zipper. She couldn't lift the larger guitar case to take the bag without risking waking them up. She knew the zipper would make noise, but she needed cash. If she did it slowly enough, maybe they would sleep through it.

One click, another, another... slow, quiet.

Jeri snorted in her sleep and shifted.

Chaki froze, the bag's zipper barely an inch open. She waited, breathing slowly through her mouth, listening. Jeri's breathing settled down.

Don't be stupid. Get out. You can get money later.

She considered taking the whole bag again, but getting out of the motel room without noise would be hard enough without twenty pounds of luggage. She let go of the zipper and stood, cringing as her knees popped, but neither of her captors stirred. The door would be impossible—too many locks and latches to rattle, and the light from the parking lot would wake them up. It had to be the bathroom window. She took her time, one slow step after another, rough carpet transitioning to cold linoleum. Diffuse street light through the bath-room window gave her enough illumination to see. She eased the door closed, turning the knob to keep it from clicking, and locked it.

She put on her shoes, grabbed a towel from the rack, and did a quick search through Jeri's toilet bag for anything useful. She slipped a disposable razor, toenail trimmers, and nail file into her pocket, then turned to the window. The lock turned without a sound, and the lower pane slid up with only slight resistance, but scraped against the frame at the top. She cringed and waited, listening, but no one stirred.

Nice and slow... She inched the lower pane all the way up without any more noise. The screen would be the hard part, but she had tools and time.

The nail trimmers had a foldout pick with a little crook in the end. It was dull, but ten minutes of careful filing with the nail file sharpened the tip. She pushed the impromptu blade through the screen near the corner, holding the towel against it to dampen the noise. Slowly, meticulously, she used the trimmers to clip the screen, taking her time, click-click-click, pausing to listen every so often. In about an hour, she had three sides cut. She put her tools away, laid the towel over the edge of the opening, climbed up on the toilet seat, and worked her head and shoulders through the window.

The alley was empty save for some garbage and a stripped car. There was nothing for her to grab onto, but she squirmed forward until her hips rested on the edge. Wriggling forward, the edge of the window frame pressed painfully into her thighs, and the weight of her torso tilted her legs up like a seesaw. Embracing the pain, she pushed with her arms and feet to keep from bending her knees backward, and wiggled far enough for her hands to reach the ground. Tiny shards of broken glass pressed into her palms, sharpening her senses to razor acuity. She walked her hands forward, leaving blood behind, until her heels cleared the window, then pushed off. Rolling scraped her shoulders and back, but she came up with only minor abrasions.

Free, she started for the end of the alley, then stopped. She had to look tempting for what she had to do, and she needed a better weapon than a nail file. Clenching her hands, the tiny splinters of glass pressed into her flesh. *Glass... sharp... maybe...*

Searching through the trash, she found a large enough shard and took off her shirt. Brushing off the dirt and wiping the blood from her hands on the hem, careful not to get any on the rest. Then, she cut it off at mid torso, shortened the sleeves, and cut the collar out of the neck, deepening the V to show off her blood-red bra. She donned the shirt and checked herself over. No blood on her top, but her hands were still bleeding a little. She scrubbed them with the cut-off pieces of cloth, then carefully cut a few gashes in the thighs of her jeans, and undid the button at the top of the zipper, pulling them down on her hips to show her underwear. She tucked the razor-edged shard of glass in her back pocket and set out for downtown Greenville. She didn't know the town, but every city had a business district where the wealthy shopped and banked. With luck, she'd be on the road before sunup, on her way to recovering all that she'd lost.

All I need is money, a phone, and a ride. I can get all that from one horny businessman. Find him, and I'll be wearing my crown again in no time.

8

HOUSE OF CARDS

The pulsing vibrations of Gippy's phone jarred him awake to sliver-gray daylight invading the room around plywood-thick curtains. Jeri stirred beside him as he checked the phone, but rolled over. Knowing they would sleep like the dead, he'd set an alarm for 6 a.m. just to get the morning started. They'd packed a small hotpot and sachets of real coffee in their luggage, and he felt them calling to him.

Everything's brighter with coffee.

Swinging his legs off the bed, however, he found the other bed empty. A quick check confirmed that the door was still locked, but a cold shiver of dread tickled his spine. Fully awake with the surge of adrenaline, he stood up, checked his pistol, the guitar cases, and the bags. Everything looked secure. The bathroom door was locked, which calmed his pounding heart a little. He didn't hear water running, which meant she was probably on the toilet.

He rapped on the door quietly and said, "Chaki? You okay?"

No answer, but Jeri stirred at the noise. "Whasup?"

"Dunno. Chaki's in the bathroom, but..." He rapped again, harder. "Chaki! Answer me." Still nothing, and his heart rebounded to its previous racing cadence. "Shit!"

The bedside light snapped on. "Her bed's cold, Gip!" Jeri stood beside the second bed, her hand under the covers. "You don't think..."

"I think there's a window in the bathroom, and I'm a fucking idiot!" He backed up and readied a kick to the flimsy door, but Jeri stopped him.

"Wait! If you break it, there'll be questions." She hurried to her bag, unlocked the clasp, and recovered a multi-tool. "The locks on these things are just push trips anyway." One quick push with a leather punch and the door clicked open.

"Fuck!" A glance confirmed that Chaki was gone, the window open, screen cut, and a towel over the edge. "Fuck-fuck-fuck! Check the bags. See if she took anything."

"On it." Jeri hurried out.

Gippy checked the alley, spotting a few scraps of clean cloth among the trash. Following Jeri's lead that they didn't want to raise a stink about damage with the motel, he put the towel back on the rack, flipped the screen out, and closed and locked the glass. The cleaners might spot the cut screen, but probably not for days. On the counter beside the sink, he found Jeri's toilet kit open.

He took it to her. "Anything missing from this?"

"The ditch kit zipper was open a bit, but nothing seems to be missing. Our duffels and cases are still locked." She took the kit and examined the contents. "Nail clippers, file, and my razor are gone."

"Enough tools to cut the screen. There are some clean scraps of cloth in the alley. I should check them out, but we need to get on the road, too. If she went to the naffies, we could be in deep shit any minute!"

"And we need to switch cars again!" Jeri was already hefting bags and her guitar case. "And you have to text Empa!"

"Yeah, I do, but I need information first. Chaki didn't know where they were staying, so they're safe for now." They had everything in the Subaru in one haul, and the blessedly quiet electric motor hummed to life. Jeri got in the passenger's side after a final check of the room, and he asked her, "Key to the room?"

"Inside. We're booked for two days, so they won't even know we're gone until tomorrow."

"Good." He took them around the motel to the alley and wove his way through the trash. The last thing they needed right now was a flat tire. At the cut window screen, he got out and snatched up the scraps of clean material, showing them to Jeri. One of them was smeared with blood, and the others had a splotch here and there. "What do you think?"

After a quick examination of the pieces, she nodded. "They're hers. She cut her tee off at the waist, neck, and sleeves." She bit her lip and fixed him with a stare. "She's gonna trick, Gip. She cut her shirt to make herself look sexy. She tried the ditch bag but the zipper was too loud, so she'll trick for cash. Empa said she'd been a trick before."

He nodded. "That's better than going straight to the naffies, I guess. Come on. We need to move. You drive; I'll text E."

Jeri drove them north around Greenville using back roads while Gippy texted Empa.

"Chaki escaped. My fault. We think she's going to trick for $. So far, no sign of naffies."

"Shit! She knows too much! I'll warn Cora and Emil. Get out of G-ville."

"On our way north to Asheville. Gotta switch cars again."

"Good. Thinking she'll want a phone and money. More money than she can earn selling herself. Check the local news for crime. We need to know what she's planning."

Gippy thought furiously. "Think she'll contact her old thralls for help?"

"Or a Nephilim. She knows things that would be valuable to them. Payoff for her."

An idea snapped into his head. "Hey, I want to cruise downtown G-ville. Not many people up yet. Maybe we'll spot her trolling for tricks."

After a long pause came, "Dangerous."

He tapped, "We switch cars, new faces, and be careful. Might get lucky."

Her reply surprised him. "Your call, but eyes up. Don't blame your-self. Steady spirit."

Her confidence in his judgment buoyed his mood. He tapped, "We're focused. I'll be in touch," then turned to Jeri. "Get off the main road. We need to switch cars. I want to look around downtown Greenville for Chaki. We may find her trolling for tricks."

"Not many johns out this early." She made a turn off the highway onto a side road dotted with dilapidated single-family homes sporting chain-link fences and big dogs.

"Exactly, so maybe she hasn't scored yet. We might spot her." He pointed ahead toward a dodgy mobile home park. "Pull in there."

"You sure?" She turned into the gridded neighborhood, making a face at the trash-strewn yards, stripped cars, and mold-streaked trail-ers. "You boost a car here and yer likely to get shot."

"Damn right, but money and guns will get us what we need." He'd grown up in worse, but had to admit that this looked rough. Way in the back stood a brick ranch-style house, the yard crammed with cars and trucks, most of them stripped, but many might be drivable. The porch light and one window were lit. "There. That's a chop shop, or I'm a freakin' movie star."

"*Really* dodgy." Jeri sounded worried. "And it's early."

"Yeah, but they'll jump at the chance to take this one off our hands and give us a ride in trade. I'd bet on it." *That is if they don't shoot us first*, he thought.

"You'll be betting our lives, Gip. You gotta be a badass or they'll be jerks." She pulled in and shut the car off. "You talk; I'll back you up."

"I just hope they're awake and have had their coffee." Gippy got out and moved his pistol to the front of his belt, obvious beneath his long shirt. "Cover my ass."

"You know it." She recovered the Mach-10 from her bag and worked the strap over her head and left arm. Then she donned her business jacket over it. Without her wig, she epitomized a high-end gangster.

"Just don't shoot me if this goes sideways."

"Oh, man! You *never* let me shoot you!" She grinned, which shocked him, but he went with it.

"Been shot enough, thanks." Gippy walked slowly to the door and knocked, rattling the rusty screen door.

A big dog barked inside, and a woman said something he didn't catch. The dog yelped and fell silent, then the door rattled and opened, with the screen door still closed. A black man in jeans and a greasy t-shirt filled the space without much left over, though Gippy spotted a skinny woman in the hall behind him in a nightgown.

"Whachu want?"

"Need a new ride and I got a trade." He hooked a thumb over his shoulder at the Subaru. Jeri leaned against the front fender, her arms crossed, her right hand undoubtedly resting on the grip of the machine pistol.

The man looked him up and down, then at the car. "Hot?"

"Nope. Bought it in Spartanburg."

"You on the run, then?"

"I *might* be, but the car's not in my name. You can have it in pieces in a day and be money ahead."

The man frowned. "Lotta work."

"Take it, ya lazy shit," the woman behind him growled, stepping forward. "2040 Subie Cross electric, and the tires look good. Don't even need to break it up. New VIN and we eat for a *month*." She was obviously the brains behind the operation, while he was the muscle and mechanical know-how.

The big man cringed at her tone and nodded. "Yeah, okay. Take yer pick?"

Gippy glanced at the collection of vehicles. "What runs?"

"The Hyundai rice-burner's the best I got. It's a mash-up, but it'll get ya there. Burns that eco-ethanol shit, but it'll take gas too." He glanced back at the woman. "Straight up trade?"

She nodded once.

"Tags match the car?" Gippy asked.

"Close enough," she said. "I'll get the fob and you can start it up."

"If it runs, we got a deal." He turned back to Jeri and nodded. "We good!"

"Excellent." She started unpacking their gear.

In five minutes, they were on the road headed south back into Greenville, though their gear barely fit in the smaller car. Gippy had doffed his wig and wore a baseball cap and a t-shirt two sizes too big. While Jeri drove, he slouched down low, watching the streets.

Pickings were slim so early in this po-dunk little town, but Chaki knew where to watch for what rated as "high rollers," even here. The cleanest streets with the best-maintained buildings and the highest level of security were her hunting ground. She found a spot to wait and leaned back against the corner of a building at the end of an alley. She could duck out of sight if a Naffie cruiser rolled by, but that was less of a concern than some balls-in-one-hand bible-in-the-other redneck. Hooking wasn't illegal, though she was out of place here, but some smaller towns had "Morality Police" that would as soon run her out of their community tied to the hood of a pickup truck as report her to the authorities.

The sky lightened, and the foot and vehicle traffic picked up slightly. The town wasn't exactly prosperous, but there were shops, and people ran those shops. One building in particular held her interest; a three-story structure with pillars in the front, and a sign that read "Community Bank." She didn't know if this was a franchise or an honest-to-goodness home-grown financial institution, and didn't honestly care. Banks meant money, and people who specialized in that money were her favored prey.

Finally, a blue Caddy pulled up to the curb next to a sign that read "Bank Manager Only," and a middle-aged white guy in a suit with a severe haircut and a stiff back got out, briefcase in hand.

"Perfect," Chaki murmured, pushing off her corner to swagger toward him before he could vanish into the building.

Men like this one were as predictable as snow in winter and heat in summer; their souls ruled by greed, money, and status, but longing for a dip into the wild side. She caught his eye without even trying, and his steps slowed. She smiled as his gaze roved over her from neck to toes, then back up as she kept swaggering toward him. His tongue touched his lips, and his fingers fidgeted at the handle of his briefcase, and she knew the hook was set.

"Lookin' to start the mornin' right, mister bank manager?" she asked from three steps away.

His steps faltered. "What are you... um..."

"What *am* I?" she chuckled and licked her lips for him. "I'm just an independent business woman out trying to make a livin', *jefe*, and I haven't even had my breakfast yet." She dropped her eyes to his belt. "And you look like my very *favorite* dish."

He swallowed hard enough for her to hear it and glanced around, obviously to see if anyone was watching them. No one was, and his gaze returned to her. "Maybe I could buy you breakfast."

"Oh, you can *buy* me, jefe, and I'll be happy to..." her eyes dropped again, "eat your breakfast."

His head jerked up and down. "Where would we...?"

"Just step inna my office, jefe, and we'll transact a little business." She turned and strutted back to her corner and the alley cast in shadow by the low morning sun. His polished shoes clicked along the sidewalk behind her, following her like a dog after a bitch in heat.

She turned into the alley and progressed far enough that nobody from the street would see them in passing, then turned and eyed her prey. He was nervous, shaking in fact, and she couldn't help but smile.

"Don't worry, jefe. Nobody's watching us." She backed him up against the wall of his bank and groped him, feeling his urgency. "You're just ready to bust out already, aren-cha?"

He shivered as she ran her fingernails up the bulge in his trousers. "Um... how much do you..."

"Oh, let's not worry about that until later, jefe." She pressed herself against him, expertly loosening his belt. "I'm just *dyin'* for the taste of your cock."

He drew a sharp breath as she lowered his fly and slid down him.

His briefcase hit the ground, and his fists knotted in her hair as she freed him from his stylish plaid boxers. She let him control her for about five seconds, then wormed her hand into his pants and grabbed him by the balls. Her other hand fished the shard of glass from her back pocket.

She bit him hard, squeezed, and jammed the glass into his stomach.

He tried to scream but couldn't. His hands wrenched her head back, then let her go as she squeezed even harder and twisted the glass in his gut.

"*Now*, jefe, we're going to conduct a little *business*."

They cruised the few blocks north and south of Main Street. The area of downtown had once been the historic and business district, but, as everywhere else, had fallen on hard times. Many of the historic buildings had been repurposed as residential, the storefronts converted to bar-windowed shops and groceries with roll-front security doors. Still, the streets were clean and there was some foot, bicycle, and even vehicular traffic. This early, many of the shops were still closed, but when they rounded a corner into a side street, Gippy stiffened. Four black and gold NAFAS cruisers were parked at the mouth of an alley beside a bank, and a small crowd had gathered across the street.

"The fuck?" Gippy slouched lower and pulled his hat down, feigning sleep.

"Looks like one's a stiff wagon," Jeri offered, slowing to pass the lone cop waving them through. "Someone got dead."

"Someone *important*." Poor people died every day in every city, and nobody gave two fucks. This one warranted four cop cars and a stiff wagon. Gippy met Jeri's meaningful gaze, and said, "Or rich. Think she'd murder someone for cash?"

"Maybe, if her trick went bad." She considered for a moment, then added. "Or she needed something more than money."

"We need to find out what happened. Ask one of the gawkers."

"Sure." Jeri toggled down her window as they neared the cop and waved at a nearby onlooker, "What happened?"

"Rich banker got jacked," an old woman replied with a shrug. "Someone cut him up like a pig fo' chitlins."

Gippy had no idea what chitlins were, but it didn't sound good.

Jeri looked duly horrified. "Daym! Robbery?"

The woman snorted a laugh. "Whachu think? Got his pants down and started cuttin'. Wallet, phone, and car all gone, and left him cut open from izzard to gizzard."

"Double daym!" Jeri drove on and glanced at Gippy. "*Gotta* be her."

Gippy recalled his time with the succubus, Duvara, and shuddered. "I think you're right, but man... Murder's a serious rap, especially when it's someone important. She's gonna end up shot dead if the naffies catch up with her."

"If she's got a car, she's on the road."

"Yep, and the naffies know what she's drivin'." He shook his head. "She's not stupid, but I just don't get it. She could'a just walked into the local cop shop and reported herself kidnapped, and we would'a been up to our asses in alligators."

"Unless she wanted something besides just turning *us* in." Jeri shook her head, then suddenly stopped. "Not cops, but *Nephilim*! I'd bet my virginity she's headed for home."

"Albuquerque?" It made sense, kind of; especially since she hadn't gone straight for the cops. "She'll use the stiff's phone to contact her network. We need to find out what she's drivin' and find her fast!" He pulled out his phone and tapped the app that monitored police frequencies and bulletins. The murder was all over the feed, an APB for an unknown female assailant, and some very grim details about the crime. Chaki had clearly gone—or always had been—completely bat-shit crazy. "I'm thinkin' she played us, Jer."

"Like a pro; no doubt. Where to?" Jeri asked.

"Dunno yet. I'm working on the details. Find someplace out of the way to park. Once I get the scoop, we'll touch base with Empa."

"*That's* gonna be a fun conversation," she muttered, pulling the Hyundai into a closed down gas station.

"Fun like one of her sparring sessions," he agreed, frowning at the phone as he read the reports. "Naffies are stirred up like a kicked hornet's nest about this. The guy was a bank manager. Car, money, and phone taken, but not his ID or credit cards. And... *Jesus*, she took a *finger*, probably to access his phone."

Jeri winced. "And maybe the car. She could already be calling in the Nephilim."

"Bet on it." Gippy scrolled through the police logs. "Dude's car was a blue Caddy Nebula; they've got an APB out on it."

"And if they find her, she'll sing like a diva," Jeri said.

"If they don't gun her down first, which would probably be good for us." Gippy cringed at his own cold logic. Deep down, he felt sorry for Chaki, but if she'd murdered some poor dude just for his car and phone, she was beyond redemption. He secretly lamented not putting a bullet through her brain months ago. "I gotta fill E in. Drive north. She'll be headin' for a big city, and Asheville's closest." He started texting, and Jeri started driving.

Chaki wiped the blood from her fingers onto her torn jeans as she drove the flash car toward Atlanta. She hadn't intended to make such a mess, but the moron wouldn't give her the access code to his phone. Only at the end had he finally caved, telling her everything was print locked. Then it had been easy. But while the car was nice, it didn't have any paper towels or even napkins in the glovebox. Consequently, the blood from their encounter was a problem. The cops would be looking for the car, and being pulled over covered in blood would end up with her either in cuffs or dead.

Arrested would be bad, but dead would be worse. She had no doubt that Hell was a real place, and that her soul would be going there once her heart stopped beating. That was why she needed to hook up with another succubus, and she now had the information to buy that deal. Two Ageless and Canción for one free ride to Hell on the back of a demon. She just had to make contact with the right Nephilim.

To that end, she tapped the 'call' button on the wheel and said, "Call 'Skin-Tone Productions' in Los Angeles, California."

"Calling Skin-Tone Productions," the car responded, and a ringtone sounded over the car's speakers.

"Skin-Tone, how can I help you?" a female voice answered.

Wow, a real person on the first ring? Labor must be cheap in LA. "I need to speak to Walker Trenton. Tell him Chavela Almonte's calling. He'll take my call." Unfortunately, she couldn't remember her incubus contact's direct number. All her contacts were on speed dial, and Empa had destroyed her phone. Of course, if she hadn't, they probably would have been hit with a cruise missile in Mexico.

"One moment please," the voice said, and Chaki wondered if the voice was real or some AI sim.

She drove and waited. At least traffic was light, even on the notorious I-85. Barely enough to use all five lanes, most of it smoke-belching tractor trailers, AI-piloted, but manned with armed guards hauling food into the megacity. At least the shitty condition of the pavement kept them at a reasonable speed. Even if she could drive faster, cops had stopped pulling cars over for speeding before she was born, so no worries there. Finally, the line clicked, and a familiar voice came on the line.

"Chaki? Thought you were *dead*, bitch!"

"Duvara is, but I'm alive and kickin'." She tried to fill her voice with Duvara's old confidence, something she no longer possessed, but she had to pull it off. Being a scared human would only get her an eternity of agony. "Look, I got a serious issue, and I need to talk to the head Nephilim honcho. I got a line on two Ageless, and the... *thing* that can destroy demons and Nephilim. I want to make a deal."

"A *deal*?" He sounded incredulous, which was unusual for an incubus. "Whachu mean, bitch? We don't *make* deals with Nephilim. We give and they take, end of story."

"They will this time, but I'll only talk to the Son of Samyaza." She knew Trenton served as the senior Nephilim's primary contact to

Hell. That was her in; start at the top and make her pitch. "Get him on the line and tell him if he wants the bitch who's been sending Nephilim to Hell, call this number."

"I'll send it up the food chain, but you askin' for trouble, puta."

"I already *got* trouble, pendejo. That bitch Ageless took me prisoner, and I had to *kill* a guy in Greenville to get away. I'm *literally* driving a stolen car with blood on my hands. Maybe you could tell the jefe to call the dogs off of me."

Trenton snorted. "I ain't tellin' him shit, puta. *You* tell him."

"Look, if I get shot by some dick-in-hand cop, he gets nothin'. He deals with me, and we can end the fucking war in a *week!*"

"End the *war?*" Trenton sounded genuinely shaken. "Fuck me on a bike, puta. You serious?"

"*Dead* serious. I need you to move on this *now.* I'm up to my eyeballs in scorpions, you know?"

"All right, all right, don't start pissin' blood. I'll make the call."

"Do that." She ended the call and took a deep breath, letting it out slowly.

The car's nav app told her to take the next exit, and she moved over, earning a horn and a finger from a trucker. "Just get me on I-20 and get the fuck out of my way, bitches."

HIGHWAY TO HELL

The Son of Samyaza stared at the text in disbelief. The human host of Duvara was alive and had escaped the Ageless. She wanted to make a deal, but only with him.

Finally, a fucking break!

"Are you *listening*, Miaka?"

The accusative question snapped his attention back to his desk's monitors and the angry faces of several telecom CEOs all around the globe. "Something's come up. I'll rejoin the meeting in ten minutes."

"Something more important than—"

"Not more important, but more *urgent!*" He hated placating humans worse than he hated the prospect of being banished to Hell, but there was more at stake here than his own future. The whole War of Souls hung in the balance. "Ten minutes." He cut the conversation off with a single keystroke and tapped the highlighted number on his phone. It barely rang once before a woman answered.

"Yes?"

"I was told by Walker Trenton to call this number."

"Son of Samyaza?"

"Who is this?" He knew it was her, but there was no point being careless.

"Chavela Almonte. I hosted Duvara, who you should know by now was destroyed. If you want the ones responsible, you'll cut the bullshit and listen to me."

The Son of Samyaza gritted his teeth at being dictated to by a human, but he needed what she knew. "I'm listening."

"I've got a line on *both* living Ageless and the son of Terpsichore and Azkeel. His name's Canción, and he can destroy demons *and* Nephilim."

"*Both* living Ageless? There's only one. Empa's the last."

"No, there are two. Terpsichore's alive. If you want them *all*, you'll make a deal with me."

"A deal?" Nephilim didn't make deals with humans, but the prospect of destroying the last surviving Ageless and the anomaly who could destroy his kind was something he couldn't turn down. "What *kind* of a deal?"

"I want back in Hell's network. I want to be possessed again, and not just by some low-level scumbag succubus. I want Lilitu."

He snorted a derisive laugh. "The Queen of all Succubi? A princess of Hell? What *else* do you want, a throne beside the Father of Lies himself?"

"Since that's where Lilitu's sitting right now, yes! That's *exactly* what I want."

"That's not going to happen. Humans don't make demands from Hell!"

"Then you're going to *lose* the War of Souls, you arrogant fuck!" she howled. "Canción can rip you right out of your human body and shred your soul like fucking hamburger! I know! I was there when he tore Duvara away from me and crushed her like an empty eggshell! I can give you all three of them, Empa, Terpsichore, and Canción, but I'll only do it *after* Lilitu possesses me! Now stick your ego up your ass and tell the Father of Lies to take his *dick* out of Lilitu's mouth and put her to work!"

Rage smoldered within the Nephilim like a percolating volcano, but he had to admit that the woman was right; for the chance to win the War of Souls in one stroke, he would make a deal with a human.

Whether the Father of Lies would agree to this bargain was something else entirely.

"I'll put forth your proposal, but the decision's not mine. It's *His*."

"Fine, but call off your hounds. I had to kill a banker in Greenville to get away. I'm driving a stolen Caddy with his blood on my hands. If I get pulled over by some dick-in-hand Naffie goon, you lose everything I know."

Or I could tell them to apprehend her and torture the facts out of her, he considered. Then again, the human who had hosted Duvara was no stranger to torment. She'd probably laugh in his face. He bit back his pride and said, "That I can do."

"Good! I'm driving east on I-20 through Atlanta on my way to Albuquerque, then to you. We do this deal in person, you and me. Tell NAFAS I'm untouchable, a government operative, diplomatic immunity, whatever."

"Very well, consider it done. We'll put eyes on you and make sure you get here safely."

"Fuckin' A." She severed the connection, leaving the Son of Samyaza to smolder in impotent rage.

He called the Son of Batraal, who picked up on the first ring. "News?"

"Yes, from a most curious source. The former hostess of Duvara wants to make a deal." He filled the other in on the details, including the shocker that Terpsichore, the mother of the creature that could destroy Nephilim, was alive. "Flag that car and make her untouchable."

"Will do, but that won't stop some jackass small-town cop from putting a bullet in her head."

"If that happens, I'll see you burn in Hell. I'm contacting our Lord as soon as I'm off the phone with you. It's *His* decision whether to deal with this human or make some other arrangement, but if she dies, we have nothing."

"Can't we just arrest her ass and put her on a plane to LA?"

He'd already considered that but knew it would get them nowhere. "No; not yet, at least. She just escaped from the Ageless Empa. If we're lucky, Empa will go after Chaki. Get eyes on that Caddy and never let it out of your sight. Put radio chatter out on police bands, which I'm sure Empa will be monitoring. If she picks up a tail, we may bag an Ageless *without* the human's help."

"I'll have high-altitude drones on her in five minutes."

"Excellent. I'm sending her data to you now." The Son of Samyaza severed the connection and forwarded Chaki's file to his subordinate with a few taps on his phone. Then, he ruminated for a moment, considering all the potential double-crosses from both ends. Could Chaki be working for Empa? Was this a ploy to get to him, to destroy him as they had other Nephilim? And this creature, Canción, the spawn of Nephilim and Ageless, the angels of music and destruction. What other powers might he wield? And with two Ageless still alive, could they beget more? The possibilities were infinite.

"Not my call," he mumbled, dialing the number for his demonic minion.

"Yes, master?" the incubus answered.

"Contact your creator. We need to consult with Him on an opportunity." *Opportunity*, he realized. *That's what this is, now. An opportunity to win the War of Souls in one decisive stroke.*

I end the call with Cora and Emil, feeling the bridled anger and disappointment from Canción like icy flames. "I'm sorry, but with Chaki in the winds, we can't—"

"I understand," he interrupts. "That doesn't mean I have to *like* it. Disrupting their lives like this every time something happens to us... I don't know how you live like this."

"That's the only way we stay alive, Canción." I examine him, gauging his level of calm. His knuckles are white on the steering wheel as he pilots us toward Asheville. "The only way we've survived so long is to constantly move, run, hide, evade. We've been doing it for *millennia*. Cora understands this as well as I do."

"Okay, but that's not living, that's just surviving."

I keep forgetting how young he is, how inexperienced, impulsive, and stubborn. The last two he gets from Cora, but she's somehow honed those traits into survival skills. Canción's not that sharp yet. "You can't *live* if you don't survive, Canción."

"No! *Really?*" He snaps a glare at me. "But what's the point if all you do is stay alive?"

"The *point?*"

"The *point!* Why survive if there's no *joy* in your life? Why go on?"

Father, please give me patience, I mutter beneath my breath. "Because it's bigger than us. It's about all of mankind, not just us."

"What?" Confusion flickers through his anger.

I'm stunned for a moment, another of my assumptions about this volatile young man shattered. "I'm sorry, Canción. Maybe Cora never told you this, or intended to but didn't have the time." I consider how to break the news to him, and decide the direct approach is best. "You must know that we're not entirely human, Cora and I."

"Well, sort of, I guess, but—"

"No *but*, Canción. We were *put* on Earth for a reason. We were supposed to balance the war. That balance has been shattered over the millennia, especially with the information age. If we, the last two Ageless, die, the spawn of Hell will corrupt every remaining human on earth. When that's done, the Four Horsemen will be released, and they will wipe the planet clean. There'll be *nothing* left."

"I..." He clears his throat and lapses into Spanish. "Why would God do that? What's the purpose?"

"Purpose?" I shake my head. "It's *war*; the purpose is to win or die trying. Ageless have been dying for five thousand years, and God's love takes them home. You kill a Nephilim, and they just respawn."

"But that's... *cheating.*"

I snort a laugh. "Yeah, Hell cheats. Who would have thought *that?*"

"But, it's a losing strategy. God must *know* that!"

"Maybe she does. I'll ask her one day. In the meantime, we survive and bring love and hope to the few people we can. That's our only weapon." I fix him with a steady stare. "Or was, until now, at least. Now, we have a chance."

"But... there are too many of them and they have too much power! We'll *never* destroy them all."

"Never say never." I smile thinly at his incredulous stare. "That's another thing that Gippy taught me, something I'd forgotten; after over a century with no hope, he reminded me. I gave him something to fight, and he showed me that I still could. I'd virtually given up, and he and your mother gave me a chance to win. It's a small chance, but that's more than I've—"

My phone vibrates and chimes with a voice call.

"It's Gippy." I take the call. "Sup?"

"Weird shit, E. Every Naffie frequency east of the Rockies is lit up like a brothel on Saturday night lookin' for Chaki. I guess murdering a banker gets some attention. But there's some weird code going around now. Not at first, but it just hit the airwaves."

"What code."

"Just a bunch of letters in that 'Alpha, Bravo, Charlie' shit you do."

"Phonetic. What letters?"

"Um, let's see... 'Subject is Delta-November-Alpha under any circumstances, by order of DHS.' Then it gives an authorization code. You know what that means?"

"DNA? Not in that context, no." I wrack my brain but come up empty. "I don't get why she stole a car instead of just going to the police and reporting herself kidnapped. That would get her a phone call, and she could contact her network."

"Right? So, Jeri thought she might be headed for Albuquerque, tryin' to hook up with her people there."

Not a bad theory, but... "Why not *call* them?"

"We trashed her phone. When was the last time you actually *memorized* a phone number?"

"Well, I do it out of habit, but I suppose most people don't."

"*Nobody* does, E. That's old school. Computers do our thinkin' for us these days, right?"

"Right." I forget sometimes how much technology has changed humankind. "So, she killed someone to get a phone, money, and a car, and she's driving to Albuquerque to hook up with her old network, but she's not possessed anymore. She won't have any power over her thralls."

"Maybe, but will *they* know that?"

"Probably not. Once a succubus seduces someone, there's nothing supernatural keeping them in line. Just..."

"Yeah, I know. But her contact list is probably backed up on the cloud somewhere. All she'd need to get that is an account number and password. Why not do that?"

"No idea. Maybe she needs something. Keep monitoring police frequencies. If they stop her, we should hear it. If we can get to her before they do, we have a chance to stop this."

"I'm on it."

I end the call and glance at Canción, whose smoldering mood warms me like a cast-iron wood stove. "What are you thinking?"

"I'm thinking that going after her will be dangerous. She may have already contacted a Nephilim. I don't want my mother in on it. We should just vanish and regroup."

"You're not wrong about the danger, but if Chaki hooks up with the Nephilim network, they'll have one thing they didn't have before: Your description."

"But no actual photos. Not like you and mother." He fixes me with a cold stare. "Maybe I should just strike out on my own."

"No way. She also knows where we've been, so she could find your picture on the cloud; cameras are everywhere, and you can bet your image is out there somewhere. You don't want that." He doesn't understand what he's up against. "You're not trained for this, Canción. I've been evading Nephilim for centuries."

"I thought you said millennia."

"We tried to fight them for the first few thousand years before we realized that they just respawned, that Hell was cheating, as you so aptly stated." I sigh and try to focus, but the memories of so many cousins murdered by the Nephilim grips me like a bear trap. "We paid for our folly in blood."

1 0

UNTOUCHABLE

Chaki put off stopping for fuel as long as she could. The Caddy's hybrid engine got excellent mileage, so it was getting dark when she finally pulled off outside of Memphis. This, she knew, was where things could get dicey. Police didn't surveil freeways, but gas stations were another story. She also only had cash, which meant pre-paying at the register. There would certainly be cameras inside, and probably also at the pumps. If the Nephilim hadn't called off his hounds yet, the AIs looking for her would flag her plate, and she'd be in trouble. She'd picked an out-of-the-way station, but cameras were everywhere.

Time to put up or shut up. She pulled up to the pumps, locked the car, tucked the dead banker's finger in her pocket, and headed for the station. The door was locked but with a wave to the guy at the register, he buzzed her in.

She flashed a smile and strutted her stuff up to the counter. "Two K on pump three." She dumped the T-notes into the slot. "I gotta pee."

"Sure." He raised his eyes from her tits to her face, took the bills, and scanned them. "Restroom code's two-one-three-four."

"Thanks." She bounced away, absolutely positive that his eyes were on her ass, not the dried blood on her hands and clothes. She punched

86

in the code, locked the door, and washed in the sink, scraping the blood from beneath her nails with the shard of glass she'd used on the banker. Clean except for a few flecks of blood on her shirt and smears on her pants where she'd tried to wipe it off, she headed for the car, flashing the attendant another smile as she passed.

So far, so good. She popped the gas fill door with the dead banker's fingerprint and started pumping. Before the pump stopped, however, a NAFAS cruiser pulled into the station, blue and yellow lights flashing as it stopped right behind her car.

"Well, fuck."

Two men got out and leveled guns at her over the car doors. She raised her hands and faced them, eyes wide in feigned shock. She opened her mouth to speak, but one of them cut her off.

"Step away from the car! Keep your hands where we can see them!"

Chaki complied, taking two steps sideways. The pump was still running, and a stray bullet might be very bad. She would rather die by gunshot than burn to death, but the end would be the same: an eternity of torment in Hell. They stepped out from behind the doors and approached, guns still leveled. One was young, the other older and fat. They didn't wear the bulky vests under their shirts like usual NAFAS cops, and she decided they must be from a small-town department.

"Problem officers?"

"Just shut up and don't move," Fatty ordered, sighting at her chest as he gestured the other one forward.

"You're making a mistake," she said as the younger one did a quick and cursory frisk for weapons.

"Blood on her shirt and pants, sarge," he said, taking a step back. "No weapons, no ID."

"Move to the back of the car and put your hands on the trunk, feet back and spread wide."

It was time for some attitude. "You need to check with your boss on this, pendejo. You should have gotten the news. I'm untouchable." At least she hoped that was the case. If the Son of Samyaza hadn't called off the hounds, she was screwed.

"Shut the fuck up and *move!*" Fatty's finger moved from alongside the pistol to the trigger.

"I'm *moving*, all right? Just don't fucking shoot me!" She stepped slowly over to the car and put her hands on the trunk, feet back, legs spread wide. "If you pull that trigger, your ass won't be worth the bullet!"

"Shut up!" The younger one slammed a hand between her shoulder blades, forcing her down on the hood. "One twitch and I'll end you, whore."

Chaki gritted her teeth at his much more thorough search. He found the shard of glass in her back pocket, then the banker's finger.

"Jesus, Sarge, there's a fucking *finger* in her pocket!"

"A *what?*"

"A human finger!" A gun barrel pressed to the back of her head hard enough to hurt. "What the fuck?"

"Guy gave me the finger, so I *took* it!" she snapped. "My name's Chavela Almonte. Now run that through your computer before you make a life-fucking mistake! Check it!"

"Secure her!" Fatty ordered.

As the younger cop zip-cuffed her hands behind her back, she heard the other calling in the Caddy's plate, the APB, and her name. She couldn't hear the reply, but his expletive-laden response almost made her smile.

"You're fucking *kidding* me! She's covered in blood and has a severed *finger* in her pocket!"

The younger cop hauled her upright and turned her toward the squad car. Fatty was red-faced, glaring at her, his gun still in hand but pointed at the ground.

"I don't care who gave the goddamn order! She's got no ID, blood all over, a stolen car, and a human finger in her pocket. Nobody walks away from that!"

More silence, and the man's face only got redder. The Son of Samyaza had followed through; NAFAS had put the word out on her, and these backwards-ass dumb fucks were just getting the news.

"I can't *believe* this bullshit!" Fatty growled.

"What the fuck, sarge?" the cop holding her asked.

Chaki smiled. "Told you. I'm untouchable."

"Shut up!" the cop snapped.

The fat cop just stood there, his flabby jowls trembling, eyes staring at her in disbelief. They stood like that for over a minute, Chaki smiling, the fat cop glaring, and the young cop holding her by her bound wrists. The pump clicked off and she glanced at the display: 58.3 liters, 1240 NADs.

"You mind hurrying this up? I need to get my change and move on. I'm on a schedule."

The cop holding her wrenched her wrists. "I said shut up! Sarge, what's up?"

"She's some kind of government spook. Do Not Apprehend under *any* circumstances. Cut her loose."

"The fuck, Sarge? She's got a—"

"I know what she's got! She's also got a pass from NAFAS Secret Service Command! Now cut her loose!"

The cop muttered obscenities as he pulled a multi-tool from his belt and snipped the cuffs.

Chaki rubbed her wrists. "Thanks. Now, can I have my finger back?" she held out a hand.

The younger cop's lip curled, but he withdrew a small plastic bag from his shirt pocket and dropped it into her palm. "I suggest you hit the road before I make a mistake and shoot your ass."

"Aw, that's not very nice." She brushed past him and pulled the gas nozzle from the car. "I might just have to file a scathing report, officer... 214839. Now get the *fuck* out of my way." She slammed the nozzle back into the pump and stalked off for the office to get her change. She didn't even look back. She was untouchable, immune, and things would only get better from here on out.

Once I'm wearing Lilitu's crown, nobody in Hell or on Earth can touch me.

"Got her!" I lurch up from the rock-hard motel room bed, eyes bleary from staring at my phone.

"Wha?" Canción blinks away sleep and sits up. "Chaki?"

"Suspect of Greenville SC murder approached, questioned, and released under NAFAS Secret Service DNA orders..." I tap for details. "Looks like a gas station just off I-22 south of Memphis."

"Memphis?" Canción rubs his face. "She's headed west."

"She is. Maybe Jeri was right and she's headed for Albuquerque." I tap a quick message to Gippy, pocket my phone, and start grabbing gear. "Come on. We're on the road and you're driving."

"You think going after her is smart? They'll be following her."

"Yes, they will, and we'll be following them following her." I flash him a grin; this is the first break we've had since she escaped, and I'm not about to waste it. "Now grab your shit, soldier. We're on the road in five."

"I'm not a soldier," he grumbles.

"Might want to reconsider that." I pause at the door and fix him with a hard look. "When there's a war and you've got a gun at your hip, you're a soldier whether you want to be one or not."

He makes a face, but picks up his duffle and golf club bag. "More wisdom from the ages?"

The ages... How many wars, how many deaths, how many souls... I force the plague of memories down. *Steady spirit.* "I could tell you stories all night, Canción. Come on."

We're in the car, on the road, and headed for I-40 in less than my predicted five minutes. I'm checking the weather when my phone vibrates in my hand.

Gippy's text reads, "You see this? Looks like DNA stands for Do Not Apprehend." with a link.

I tap the link, which pulls up a NAFAS law enforcement bulletin posted on an interdepartmental shared server. The APB on the dead banker's car has been called off. The next line, however, takes me aback. "Suspect is NAFAS Secret Service operative under Federal immunity. Destination Los Angeles, CA. Do not approach, restrain, or apprehend."

I relay the news to Canción as I text to Gippy, "Chaki has friends in high places. What's going on?"

He texts back, "Probably called some Nephilim to call off the hunt. But why LA?"

"No idea," I reply, then add. "Whatever she's planning can't be good for us. Think we can take her before she gets there?"

After a long pause, he sends, "Maybe, but that would be *really* dangerous. Bet your ass naffies got eyes on her."

He's not wrong, but letting Chaki go would also be dangerous, especially for Canción, our secret weapon. Then my phone pings with a weather alert; severe thunderstorms are forecast overnight east of Knoxville with possible tornadoes. I grit my teeth at the possible delay.

Delay... The idea blossoms in my mind like a starburst, and I text, "They'll have eyes on high. Sat or drone, maybe both, but the weather will blind them. The southwest is getting hammered this time of year. We time it right, and we're invisible. In and out before they can respond."

After an even longer pause, during which I'm sure Gippy and Jeri are discussing options, he sends, "Chaki's already murdered one guy. We need to take her out for good."

My heart skips a beat. Again, he's not wrong, but the thought of killing Chaki feels wrong. Yes, she killed an innocent man, but I've seen inside her mind. Abuse and desperation made her fall for the trap Hell sets for so many. Possession pushed her over the edge. Now she's wielding the only power she can grasp, selling us out to her former masters, but to what end? One thing is clear: if we don't stop her, she'll out Canción, and put the Hounds of Hell on Cora's trail, not to mention Emil's.

There's too much at stake. I tap, "Okay," and feel as if I've committed a horrible sin.

"Sorry, but it's the only way," he responds.

"I know. No other option. Hell to pay if we don't."

"Literally. Now, where do we do this?"

Details click into my head like dominoes falling one by one. "LA's too big. We can find out where she lives in Alb. Think we can get there before she does?"

"Maybe. We drive in shifts. She'll probably stop for sleep. I'll get her address from the chop shop where she works."

I smile at his train of thought. "Good. I'll tell Cora and Emil. Stay in touch."

"You know it!"

"We're trying to set up an ambush in Albuquerque if we can get there first," I tell Canción. "We'll have weather tonight, but I'll keep an eye on it."

"I grew up in the hurricane zone," he reminds me.

"All right, then. Just don't wreck us." I text Cora the details and switch back to my weather app. So far, the tornado warning is north of I-40. We might slip through before the heavens open up.

I pause my playing as my phone vibrates in my pocket. The girls' smiles fade, but their eyes are still bright and full of joy they haven't known in over a year. Their mother, Niki, soothes them and hands them two packaged snack bars. I smile my thanks—the last thing I want is tears—and pull my phone.

Empa's text is long and worrisome. A cross-country chase after a psychotic murderer under surveillance doesn't sound wise or particularly safe, but letting her go will put Canción in danger. The problem is, Chaki's got an eight-hour lead.

I text, "See you in Alb. Got a plane to catch."

"Plane?" she replies. "You crazy? They may know you're alive. Airports have security."

"Not born yesterday, Cuz. Trust me." I turn off my phone and clamber to my feet. Three pairs of eyes watch me as I shoulder my bag. "Sorry, but I've got to go. The room's paid through the month, and you've got money for food." As I start to slip my penny whistle into my bag, the horror in the girls' eyes stops me. "Hey, now, don't be sad." I kneel and hold out the flute to them. "Take this. Learn to play. Music is our friend, remember?"

"Thank you," Niki says as the girls take the flute in awe. "For everything."

"No problem. I'm glad I could help." I've given her enough money to keep them fed and housed for a while, but a woman alone with two young kids and no support doesn't have much of a chance. "Try to get back on your feet, and be safe. There's always hope."

She nods and tries to smile, but I see the future in her eyes. It's been a long time since she's had hope.

I leave them, trying to ignore my breaking heart. At least this time I'm not leaving the place in flames.

I ping an auto-cab before I step out into the rainy night, tapping in John C. Tune airport via the bus station where I left my stash. I know I can convince a private pilot to fly me to Albuquerque for cash without any questions, and small airstrips don't have much for security. I just hope the weather isn't too crazy. Tornadoes and small airplanes don't play well together.

11

ON THE SCENT

Gippy pushed the piece of shit rice-rocket as hard as he dared. Weather and the winding freeway through the mountains slowed him down, but the car had newish tires, which kept them on the road. The sun had just gone down, but he couldn't decide if that made visibility better or worse with the spray from other vehicles lit up by his headlights. But he was no stranger to long road trips and ran through rhymes, songs, and riddles in his head to keep himself awake.

"Spotty cell service," Jeri complained, her face lit by her phone.

"Maybe wait 'til we're through Knoxville. The weather should clear up." He squinted as they passed a tractor-trailer throwing blinding spray, two wheels touching the rumble strip for a moment.

"Try to keep us on the road, please."

"Sorry. Fuckin' automated trucks drive like there's no human beings on the road." They cleared the spray, and he took a breath. "Any luck?" While he drove, Jeri worked on finding Chaki's personal information.

"The chop shop where she works doesn't have a website, but I found some info on a foreign car service listing with what you gave me. Got her full name, Chavela Almonte. Looking for her home address. Hope she pays her taxes."

Gippy concentrated on driving and let her work. They'd both been trained by Empa in people finding—a necessary skill in the hunting of Nephilim—and the Ultranet had everything if you just knew where to look. Employment records, tax records, drivers' licenses, and criminal records were all there for the snooping. He and Jeri were Oh-Gees, off-gridders, with no official identities; one of the very few advantages of being street people who had never held real jobs in their lives. If you believed the census data, about a quarter of the people in NAFAS were Oh-Gees.

"Man, E wasn't lying; Chaki's got a long rap sheet. Prostitution, drugs, assault, most of it as a kid."

"Yeah, and she just cut some innocent guy up for his car. Don't start feeling sorry for her." He understood that they were supposed to be the good guys, but putting a bullet in her brain back in Cartagena would have saved a lot of trouble. Maybe that was just his brain screaming for vengeance for what she'd done to him when she was possessed by Duvara.

"I'm not, but..." Jeri sighed and shook her head. "I just wonder if that couldn't've been me, ya know?"

Gippy knew Jeri had tricked for a while, but she'd never been into hard drugs, not like him. Her addiction was sex, so doing it for money or even a place to sleep for the night was a win-win for her. He had never tricked, had never trusted strangers enough to go there. But there was one more thing he knew for certain about Jeri.

"Not possible, Jer. You've got a good soul. Chaki dug her own hole all the way to Hell, then let that... monster in. It's a wonder she's sane at all after that."

"Ever think that maybe she's not?" Jeri glanced at him, and he could tell by her tone that she was serious. "Maybe she thinks she's still possessed."

"Could be, but Empa's been in her head and never mentioned it. That's not our problem anyway. Finding her and stopping her before she sells us all out to the Nephilim is our problem."

"Which makes me wonder again why she hasn't already, ya know?"

"I know." He shrugged and changed lanes to pass another truck. "I think she's makin' a deal, but with who and for what? Money maybe; enough to set her up for life."

"No way to..." She paused, scrolling furiously. "Yes! Got her home address. A place called Casa Roja. One of those communal housing things, not too far from the chop shop. I'm sending the address to Empa and Cora."

"Good. Maybe we can beat her there and end this before things go to shit."

"Sending the address to the car's nav system," she said.

The map screen bleeped, and a route appeared. "Twenty-one hours, if we don't stop to eat, sleep, buy gas, or take a piss."

"And coffee," she added. "No way I'm spending twenty hours in this car with you if you haven't had your coffee."

"True that! Get some sleep. We still got three hundred miles on this tank. I'll wake you when I'm tired."

"Deal!" Jeri reclined her seat, flung an old sweatshirt over her eyes, and sighed.

Gippy glanced at her, then fixed his eyes on the road. *Just keep the rubber on the pavement, Gip.*

***

Chaki woke to the chime of the banker's phone and lurched up to slap the noisy thing silent. She'd driven as far as she could without sleep but had almost run off the freeway at two in the morning. A cheap motel outside Amarillo had supplied a bed, and she'd set an alarm for seven a.m. Now she felt more exhausted than ever.

Her eyes started to close, but she jerked awake with a curse. "Fucking weak piece of shit! Get up!"

She lurched out of bed and staggered for the bathroom, cursing beneath her breath with every step. Exhaustion had never been a problem with Duvara riding her soul. The succubus had pushed her beyond human limits without a care, and Chaki had borne it. The demon gave her power over these weak humans, and Canción had ripped it away, but she'd have that power again.

She tore her clothes down from where she'd hung them over the shower rod to dry, slotted a ten-coin, turned the shower on cold, and stepped under the chill spray. The water wasn't exactly icy, but it took her breath away. She scrubbed without soap—there wasn't any—dried with a towel the texture of a gravel road, and glared at the weak human in the mirror. Her ink stood out starkly against her skin, obscenities in Spanish, violent pornographic images woven into the script. She still had a scar where Gippy had bitten her and ran her fingers over it, remembering the delicious pain. Grabbing a nipple, she pinched hard, savoring the memory of tormenting him.

"Not much longer..." she finger-combed her hair, pulled on her slightly damp clothes, and stalked out of the bathroom. She thought about stopping to buy some better clothes but discarded the idea. She'd have everything she needed once she reached Albuquerque. She did, however, need to eat and refuel.

A gas station, two energy bars, and a canned double espresso later, she was on the freeway. Checking the time—8:15—she knew Ernesto would be in the shop. She tapped the call button on the wheel and said, "Call Tuercas y Tornillos Motors, Albuquerque, New Mexico."

"Calling," the car replied, followed by a ringtone.

"Ernesto," he answered, sounding irritated with the single word.

"Hey, pendejo. It's Chaki."

"Jesucristo! Where you been, bee-ach! Two months and not a word, I thought you be *dead*!"

"Not quite, but it was close. Some serious shit went down and I'm on my way back. Hey, I'm drivin' a hot Caddy Nebula. I need to make it vanish and score a new set of wheels; an SUV, somethin' with some miles that won't attract attention."

"What kind of trouble you in, puta?"

"Nothin' I can't fix, but I'm in a rush. I'll be there by noon. You got somethin' for me?"

"No problema, chica. Just swing by when you get in. Oh, and your friends been houndin' my ass like a pack of pit-bulls. You should call them."

"Can't. I lost my phone."

"I'll text you the number. Just get 'em off my back. I got a business to run and without you behind the desk, I'm goin' loco!"

"Best hire somebody new, ese. I'm in the wind. Don't know where I'll end up." Wherever she landed, she knew it wouldn't be behind the desk of a chop shop.

"Bitch, you *killin'* me," he whined.

"Get over it, homey. See you in a few hours." Chaki ended the call and started running through all the things she needed. If she could get in touch with her thralls, they could line everything up for her, and she'd be in and out of Albuquerque in a flash.

Less than a minute later, the phone chimed with an incoming text. A phone number with an Albuquerque prefix. *Perfect!* She tapped the touchscreen to call the number.

It rang once, then, "Hola?"

She didn't recognize the voice. "It's Chaki. Who's this?"

"Chaki! It's Bernado. Whassup, chica! Thought you'd fallen off the planet! We was all worried."

"I was in some deep shit, but I'll be back in town about one this afternoon. Look, I need to get out west. Pack up my shit and get ready for a road trip. Oh, and I need a new phone, cash, and a weapon."

"A *weapon*? Seriously?"

"Seriously. And get your homies together. We goin' to LA, ese, and I need some muscle." She really didn't, but once the deal was made, it'd be nice to have a crew. The queen of succubi would undoubtedly want to set up a serious network of thralls.

"All right, then. We on it like white on a stockbroker. You steppin' up in the world?"

"Big time, and I'm takin' you all with me! Get ready to roll."

"Balls to the wall, chica! We'll be ready."

I wake at the nudge from the pilot and a squawk over the headset, "Comin' into Double Eagle in ten minutes."

"Thanks, Victor." I straighten up from my slouch and twist my neck to get the kinks out.

We're clearing the Sandia ridge, the valley opening up before us and the sky threatening to the north, towering thunderheads piling up on the mountains. No lightning yet, at least. I've had enough lightning for a lifetime during our flight from Nashville. Not my first time flying through storms in the dark in a small plane, but I'll never get used to it. Victor, my pilot, assured me he avoided the worst of it, and we survived, so I can't fault him for the tumultuous ride.

Albuquerque is clear below us, heat wavering in the air, even this early in the morning. It's not the city I remember from two hundred years ago. The Rio Grande has grown with the changing climate, gouging a canyon through the urban landscape and flooding some of the lower-lying areas, but the sprawl has tripled the city. The little commuter airport we'll be landing at is now surrounded by trailer parks and dirt roads instead of raw desert. There's a vast crater south of the airport near the highway where terrorists bombed a massive distribution center, the poor, misguided fools. I remember the news story, the lies that the company was using children for slave labor, rallying vigilantes with access to munitions. Over a hundred distribution centers were bombed on the same day amid anti-capitalist war cries.

I wonder now if the Nephilim were behind it, rallying support for tyranny under the guise of security. The misinformation age seems to be the death knell of the human race, and I have no way to stop it. Money and propaganda have altered the souls of humankind in a most horrific way. Ironically, the poor have less access to the deluge and aren't as deluded. Perhaps Matthew will turn out to be correct in his prophecy, and the meek will inherit the earth.

I stir from my musing as the groan of deploying landing gear reaches me over Victor's conversation with the tower. He puts us down as smooth as silk sheets, and the ancient twin-engine Navaho taxies to the tiny buildings that house the airport. Victor is an old hand, but rules are rules, and there will be an inspection, albeit a cursory one. There's not enough air traffic these days to support the massive bureaucracy of NTSB/TSA that once ruled the skies, but bureaucracies, like dinosaurs, leave fossils behind.

We come to a stop, and I wait for Victor to give me the all clear before stepping out. I grab my shoulder bag and two guitar cases from the back—one case significantly heavier than the other—and I thank Victor and head for the building. He doesn't even wave. For what I've paid him for anonymity, he's already forgotten I exist.

I've cleaned up, of course, adding a red wig and old cowboy hat to block the ubiquitous cameras, and enough makeup and jewelry to fool a cursory inspection. A low-cut shirt will draw eyes away from my face, and shit-kicker boots change my gait. I'm sweating with the heat by the time I'm indoors. The terminal—if you can call it that—is only slightly cooler than the blistering tarmac outside, but it feels like an icebox. I put my cases down, hand the tired-looking official my ID—at least the one that matches my current appearance—and a smile as he glances up at me from my photo.

"Carla Winston, welcome to Albuquerque." He hands my ID back without a twitch, clearly bored stiff.

"Thanks, darlin'." I pocket the card, pick up my cases, and do the cowgirl stroll back out into the blazing desert heat.

There are no taxis, and I can count the vehicles in the parking lot on one hand. A grinning man in a dirty t-shirt and jeans accosts me immediately.

"Need a ride, pretty lady?" Two gold teeth glint in the sun beneath a drooping mustache.

"No thanks, pardner." He's too eager, and I get a slimy vibe that is warning enough. I scan the vehicles in the lot, and spot an old woman sitting in a pickup truck with a rifle in the gun rack only a hundred feet from where I'm standing. Her dark eyes are on me like a bird dog's on a pheasant. I stride toward her as if I know her, and she opens the driver's door to step out. Two long salt-and-pepper braids flop down the back of her denim shirt, her wrinkled face a teak-hued blank, dark eyes in a permanent squint.

"Just put your guitars in the back." She's read me accurately.

"Thanks." I comply and ask, "How much to the South Valley, Five Points?"

"Depends on the 'hood." She shrugs and gets back in the truck.

I walk around and get in the passenger side. The door creaks, the seat is cracked, and the rifle looks barely operational. I realize it's a decoy as I spot the pistol-grip shotgun in a rack between the driver and passenger. The woman is obviously not to be fucked with. I think I like her. I give her the address I received from Empa's people and get in.

"Dodgy, but not so bad in daylight. Three cees." She starts the truck, which sounds well cared for.

"Fine." I slam the door and pull a wad of crumpled bills from my jeans. To the woman's credit, she doesn't even watch as I peel three off the roll. "I'm looking for a friend, but I don't know if she's there yet. Mind if we do a drive-by? I don't want to get stuck in that neighborhood alone with my luggage."

"Damn straight, you don't, gringa." She pulls onto the access road, eyes still on the road instead of me. "One more cee for the trouble."

"Sure." I peel off another note and drop them on the seat between us.

"You ain't a musician, I'm guessin'." She scoops up the bills and stuffs them in her hip pocket.

"Oh, I am, but that ain't *all* I am." I grin at her, and she snorts a laugh.

"And those cases don't carry guitars?"

"One does—a twelve-string dreadnought—but I only use it in emergencies."

Another snort, and she drives on in silence. She isn't using a nav system and is staying off the main thoroughfares. She's careful; I like her even more.

After the better part of an hour, we arrive in the neighborhood, high walls with jagged tops of razor wire or broken bottles, and a lot of big dogs. Some of the walls are pocked with bullet hits, but there aren't many people out this early.

She drives as if she knows where she's going until we round a corner, and she nods ahead. "You picked a busy place."

There's no lie; three pickups and a few bikes crowd the street around the roll-back gate of a two-story casa. We drive by slowly without drawing any attention, but I don't spot a blue Caddy inside the fence, just a few more vehicles and several busy people loading things into a big pickup and a smaller SUV. I spot more than one firearm before we're past.

"Your friend there?" my chauffeur asks.

"I don't think so." I grit my teeth; Chaki has obviously called ahead, marshaling her forces. This is more than I can handle alone, but I can't just let her drive off into the sunset, either. I need transportation. "Know somewhere I can buy a vehicle that won't raise eyebrows?"

"I do. A cousin of mine runs a shop not too far from here." I reach for money, but she waves me off. "Forget it. On my way. Dunno what you're up to, but you need the help."

"I never turn down help. Thanks." I know when to keep my mouth shut.

A dozen blocks later, on a corner with a main thoroughfare, she pulls into a fenced lot full of vehicles in various states of disrepair and disassembly. We get out, the air filled with dust and the scream of power tools. I take a moment to slip the holstered revolver from my shoulder bag, clipping it to my belt before I slam the door.

"Mateo!" my guide yells, and a swarthy middle-aged man in a baseball cap looks up from an engine sitting on blocks.

He flashes a gap-toothed grin, his face lined with deep grime. "Shasha! Cómo estás?" He drops a power tool and wipes his hands on his grimy overalls.

"Bien." She waves at me as we approach. "My friend here needs a ride. Got anything that runs?"

He eyes me up and down with a lop-sided smile. "Sí, but nothin' up to *her* standards."

"My standards are lower than you think," I respond, which earns a grin. "And I need to blend in."

"You blend in like a hawk among crows, lady, but I got somethin' you can work with." He gestures to several parked heaps, none of which would raise eyebrows. "Those all run. Take your pick."

I give them a cursory examination, all of them rusty and several with cracked windows. I don't know what I might need, so four-wheel drive seems wise. "The Bronco?"

"Sure!" His brows furrow, thoughtful. "Ten kay?"

I flash him a skeptical scowl. "How about *seven*."

"Nine. She's better than she looks, and the rubber's good. Runs on emulsion or diesel."

"Eight-five, then." I have plenty of money, but it's the principal of the thing.

"Done." He flashes another gap-toothed grin. "I'll fuel her up."

I turn to the old woman and hold out a hand. "Thank you."

She takes my hand without a smile, her grip warm and strong. "De nada. Keeping money in the family's all good." She helps me move my bags. I stow the heavier guitar case in the front passenger seat, reclining it all the way so I can lay it flat. To my surprise, the Bronco starts with a single stab of the button.

Mateo hands me the fob, and I hand him the money. Done deal.

I do a drive-by of the house again, but nothing has changed. There are more people out front than I'm comfortable with, and most of them look like gangers of one stripe or another. There's still no blue Caddy in sight. I park around a corner half a block away to watch, engine running for the AC as the desert heat intensifies. After half an hour, I text Empa, "Watching Chaki's address. Bunch of rough types packing a couple of cars, but no sign of her."

In moments, I receive. "We're about three hours away. Keep in touch."

I text, "Count on it," and sit back to wait.

12

THRALLS

I'm less than an hour east of Albuquerque when my phone chimes. The display on the dash tells me it's a video call from Cora. I wonder why she's not texting as I stab a button on the wheel to answer. Her face pops up on the dash screen—*A red wig and a cowboy hat? Really?*—the oblique view from a phone in a cradle as she's driving. I feel Canción tense in the passenger seat.

"Whassup, Cuz?"

"I'm on the move. Three vehicles packed full of people, luggage, and weapons pulled out of the house without any sign of your girl or a blue Caddy. I don't know where they're going, but I'm following. Where are you?"

"Less than an hour from the city, and Gippy and Jeri are half an hour behind me. Keep your distance. They're probably going to pick her up." A realization comes to me in a flash: Cora's all alone, no backup, and outnumbered. "Look, Cora, this isn't a good idea. Those must be Duvara's thralls. Chaki's going to be surrounded by her own private gang of thugs. We should pull out and vanish."

"Not yet." She glances at me and grins. "No way they've spotted me yet. You'll be here before they leave town to even the odds. Weather's turning to shit, too, which will keep aerial surveillance down."

I shake my head, forcing calm. "But it'll still turn into a gunfight. Too dangerous."

"Not if we play it right," Cora argues. "I'm forward obs, you're the shooter. I *know* you carry a long gun. Don't tell me you can't take out a target from half a mile. One bullet and we're done."

I think for a moment, and she's right, but we need a field of fire to do this right, and Gippy's got a longer gun than I do. "Okay, but we have to wait until she's in the open, east of the city, and I need Gippy. He's got a sniper rifle. A mile will work if we can get her to stop, half a mile if she's moving. We'll set up ahead of her if we can. You're our eyes, I'll play spotter, and Gippy's the shooter. One bullet." Her face transforms into a scowl as I speak. "What?"

"I don't want Canción in the middle of this. Drop him off in Albuquerque." A mother's concern hones her words into razors.

I open my mouth to reply, but Canción snatches my phone from the cradle.

"Mom, stop it. This is all *about* me. I'm not a kid anymore, and I'm not going to sit in a motel room while you risk your life to protect me. Not again. I watched you die for me once. I can't *do* that again."

There's pleading in his voice, but something more, too. I see it in Cora's face as he speaks; her worry melts away, the wrinkles between her eyes smoothing. This is between mother and son, not my argument, so I keep my mouth shut, but I watch her take a deep, calming breath, nod once, then smile.

"All right, but be *careful*, my son. Listen to Empa and do as she says. She's good at this, better than me."

"I will, and please don't worry about me. Be safe. Don't get too close to them."

She nods. "I'm fine, my love. Just be careful."

"We will be." Canción hands the phone back. "Sorry."

"Don't be." I pop it back in the cradle. "We'll get ahead of you and set up. I'll call you when we're ready. Let us know if anything changes."

"I will." She grins. "Brings back memories, doesn't it?"

I realize it does. "Constantinople, but we had only flags instead of cell phones."

"Same tune, different instruments, cousin." She nods again. "I'll be in touch."

The call ends, and I look at Canción, feeling his tension. "Are you okay?"

"Yes." He points to an old, burnt-out car a quarter mile ahead. "Pull over up there, please."

A twinge of concern writhes like a ball in my gut as I comply. I wonder if he's going to be sick. Before the car stops fully, he gets out, faces the wrecked car, and shouts a pure note of sheer energy. The wreck moves a foot forward, the trunk lid caving in.

I stare in shock as he gets back in. "How..."

"I took her fear."

My mouth gapes. "Over the *phone?*"

"Yes. All I had to do was make eye contact. I was doing that for years before the Nephilim found us, and she never knew." He stares quizzically at me, as if he hasn't just opened up a world of possibilities. "You going to drive, or what?"

"Sweet mother of God." I pull out and put my foot down. We have an ambush to set up, and a hundred details to work out. I push 'Call' and say, "Call Gippy."

He answers on the first ring. "Sup?"

"Lock and load, brother. We're setting up an ambush east of town."

"Fuckin'-A! About damn time!"

"One bullet. One mile. Cora's bird-dogging for us. Get on maps and look for high ground where we can have some cover, a mesa or something, as close to the city as possible. Give me coordinates when you have them.

"On it." The call ends.

After only a minute or so of silence, Canción asks, "What's 'Constantinople'?"

I blink at him, then realize once again that his upbringing probably didn't include courses in ancient history. "A city in Eurasia—originally

Byzantium. It was besieged dozens of times through history. One of the most contested pieces of real estate in the world. It controlled the sea route from the Mediterranean into the Black Sea. It's Istanbul now, and the rising sea has claimed a lot of it, but it's still a bottleneck between Europe and Asia. Your mom and I fought there a number of times."

"Why?"

I examine his eyes to see if he's serious. "Because, back then, we thought we could win. We were wrong." I turn back to the road, then add, "Until now."

I feel my feral self reemerging, ready, even eager, as I follow the cars into the Barillas district. There's some traffic now, which gives me cover, but I keep my distance. We don't go far—over the old railway yards and down into the chaotic mix of shops, dilapidated buildings, homeless shelters, and fenced lots littered with shipping containers converted into family housing. I'm three cars back as my quarry turns onto a wider boulevard, even busier. Before I make the turn, the lead SUV pulls into the central turning lane in front of an auto repair shop with a fenced lot full of half-stripped foreign vehicles. I make the turn and spot a shiny blue Caddy in front of the shop.

"Gotcha!" I drive past, turn right into a dodgy electronics repair shop, and adjust my passenger side mirror to view the auto shop.

I don't spot Chaki right away, but as the ten rough people get out of the pickup and two SUVs, a dark-haired woman in a ripped t-shirt and jeans emerges from the office. She greets the tall man in the fore by leaping up to wrap arms and legs around his torso. Another man and woman join in, creating a messy Chaki sandwich. When the clinch breaks up, she greets the others, pointing to the shop and another SUV parked in one of the bays as she talks. They begin moving things from the pickup truck to that one, and I now realize what she's doing; trading the stolen car for another for the trip to LA. From the sheer volume of all they've packed, she's not planning on coming back, but what hold a dispossessed minion of Hell has over the succubus' former thralls, I can't imagine.

"Unless they don't know," I hypothesize.

I snap a pic with my phone and send it to Empa with the message. "Found her. Looks like she and her crew are all going. Maybe ten and Chaki."

"20 minutes out," I get back. "We're going to set up east of the city near I-40. 34.979 -107.128. Keep us updated."

I punch in the location and smile. A low mesa near a bend in the freeway, perfect for a sniper. "Will do. They may be on the road in 30. Put your foot down."

"We'll be through the city before they get on the freeway."

"Probably three SUVs," I add. "One white, one green, one gray. Maybe a faded red pickup, too. They're moving stuff from the pickup into the green SUV, so maybe leaving that one behind. I'll keep tabs and let you know when they're OTR."

"Good. Be careful."

"You know it, Cuz." I put the phone down and slouch in my seat, hat low. Chaki and her crew aren't in a hurry, which is good, but the longer I have to sit here, the more likely I'll have to move or attract trouble. I unclasp the latches on my guitar case and check the contents. I hope I don't need the arsenal, but firepower is never a bad idea. Forty minutes later, they've finished and are ready to leave. The green SUV takes the lead, followed by the white, then the gray. The pickup turns the other direction back the way we came. The trio heads north, so I pull out and cross the median to follow.

When I'm sure they're headed for the freeway, I text Empa, "OTR. Freeway in five. Three SUVs, green, white, and gray in that order. Two in each. C is in the passenger seat of the green one. I'm a block back."

"We're in position and setting up. We'll be ready."

"Good." I squint up at the burgeoning clouds rolling down from the north, streaks of virga obscuring the mountains, but no lightning yet. Hopefully, the storm won't be bad enough to foil us, but bad enough to keep high-altitude drones out of play. It's a safe bet there are Nephilim eyes on Chaki. I trust Empa to have an escape route planned; I just pray that Canción is as far away from the conflict as possible.

"Talk to me." The Son of Samyaza paced before his desk of multi-screen displays, half of them dark, the other half showing multiple views of Albuquerque from air and ground. One showed the suited Nephilim who was the Son of Batraal and chief investigator in the NAFAS Secret Service.

"Our assets are flying just below cloud cover. We're running data from them and every ground camera in the area through the FAIT system, and the AI has found something." The Son of Batraal motioned offscreen, and several of the displays merged into one, showing a confusing tracery of lines across a low-altitude 3D image of the city. "A late model Ford Bronco followed Chaki's thralls from her home to Tuercas y Tornillos Motors, where she exchanged the dead banker's Cadillac for an SUV. The tailing vehicle parked in view of the shop and is now following them toward the freeway."

The view shifted again, an evolving linear progression of high-resolution images through the windshield of the beat-up Ford Bronco. "This is real time," the Son of Batraal confirmed.

The Son of Samyaza squinted at the parade of images, a woman with red hair wearing a bedraggled cowboy hat, denim shirt, and sunglasses. "ID?"

"Working on it, but there's not much to see. She's obviously avoiding exposing her face to cameras."

"Not Empa," the Nephilim said between clenched teeth.

"No, but you said Chaki mentioned another Ageless, Terpsichore. I'm running the best images we have from her in parallel and letting the AI compare." A parade of images streamed beneath the real-time ones, most of them old, blurry, some even in black and white. "We should—"

Red line drawings flared around mouths, jaws, lips, and noses of the two streams of photos, and the text, "ID Confirmed to 98% probable certainty. Real-time subject is the fugitive, Terpsichore."

"Got it! She's the Ageless!" the Son of Batraal crowed in triumph. "We can take out the vehicle with laser-sighted munitions right now. Just give the word."

The Son of Samyaza opened his mouth, instinctively jumping at the chance to destroy one of his long-time enemies, but his recent conversation with the Father of Lies stayed his tongue. This was exactly the opportunity Hell had been waiting for, but not what he or the Son of Batraal had expected.

"No. Follow that vehicle and ready your strike team."

"What?" His subordinate's face recentered on a screen, his dark eyes wide, clearly puzzled and angry. "We have the shot! We should take it!"

"No. The Father of Lies has other plans for Terpsichore." The Nephilim's lips twitched into a sardonic smile. "You have my orders. Carry them out."

"Fine, but if this turns to shit, you can't blame me!"

"If this turns to shit, you need to be ready to clean it up! Ready your strike force! Now!"

"They're ready; six LASSO drones on site and two Defiants orbiting at 3000 meters, just above the cloud deck, loaded and ready to deploy. Just give the word and the objective."

"When the time comes," he said, his smile intact. "As soon as they're in the clear."

13

THE JAWS OF HELL

Chaki leaned back in the seat as they accelerated onto I-40 and sighed. "Next stop, LA." Her plan was coming together beautifully.

"So, what's in the city of fallen angels?" Bernado asked.

She chuckled at the irony. "We're gonna meet the biggest fallen angel of them all, ese, and he's gonna be my bitch."

He barked a laugh, not knowing that she was telling the absolute truth. "And, seriously, where you been for two months?"

"You don't wanna know. Thought it would be an easy gig, but it turned into Armo-fuckin-geddon. But I'm back, and I'm gonna be badder than ever once we—" Her new phone buzzed in her pocket. She pulled it and blinked at the screen. "Ernesto? What the fuck?" Why the mechanic would want to talk baffled her. They just said their goodbyes minutes before, but she punched answer and said, "What, did I forget my vibrator or somethin'?"

"Na, chika, I'm havin' that bronzed and mounted on a plaque." He barked a laugh. "Just thought you might want to know you got a tail. Chan from across the street buzzed me and said a beat-up Bronco pulled into his place right as your homies arrived. Chick in the driver's seat just sat there until you left, then pulled out right behind you. Maybe some NAFAS spook."

Chaki grinned a rabid dog smile. "Did Chan say what she looked like?"

"White chick, red hair, cowboy hat."

That didn't sound like Empa, but... "And she was alone?"

"Yep, just her."

Not Empa, then. "Thanks, bro. I'll deal with it. I owe you a solid."

"And I'll collect, chica." He ended the call.

Chaki looked at Bernado. "We got an opportunity, homey."

"*Opportunity?*" He cocked an eyebrow at her. "What kind?"

"The kind that'll put another jewel in my fucking crown. Get your homies on the line. We got a tail, and it's time to snip it."

I hang back as we leave the city, keeping the three SUVs barely in sight. There's not much traffic, and I can't afford to be spotted. I have my phone locked in on Empa's position, and she's tagged me to keep track of mine. Twenty-six miles to the strike point. All I've got to do now is watch.

Lightning flashes to the north. The storm is coming, and a deluge would ruin visibility for a sniper, but we should be finished before it hits. I bite my lip, watching the sky and the distance to the strike point on my phone's split screen ticking down. We're less than two miles away when the two trailing SUVs pull off the freeway onto an exit.

"The hell?" I thumb the call button on the steering wheel and say, "Call Empa."

She answers before it even rings. "Problem?"

"Maybe. Two of three vehicles just took an exit. Chaki's still in the lead coming your way."

"How far... Never mind. Our spotter sees them. You should consider bailing."

"Keep your eyes on the prize, cuz. Take the shot if Chaki comes in range."

"Gippy's got crosshairs on her car. Our spotter's watching you."

"Fine. I'm coming to an underpass where they turned off. Tell me what the two SUVs are doing."

"They're taking the on ramp! Coming up behind you! Bail now!"

"Shit!" I swerve into the central median before the merge, throwing up a pall of dust. I'm headed the other direction before it settles. "I'm out! Take the shot!"

"Not in range, and the two are crossing to follow you! Gaining fast!"

I hammer the accelerator, but the Bronco accelerates sluggishly. "Fucking piece of shit!" I flip the catch on my guitar case, drag the M4 from its bracket, and chamber a round as the two SUVs close in. I'm not going to outrun them, and I'm outnumbered. There's no cover, either. I am well and truly screwed. My only hope is to turn around and get close enough to Empa for some fire support.

"Time for rock n' roll." I wait until they're close, then slam on the brakes. They swerve and brake hard, tires smoking. The M4 roars in the confined space of the cab, blowing out my passenger side window as they scream past. I don't wait to see if I hit anything, but swerve hard across the median again and stomp the gas pedal to the floor. "I'm coming back toward you! Take Chaki out if you can, then cover me. I might get there before they catch me."

"Gotcha. Chaki's pulled off out of our optimum range, and the other two are coming around behind you. About one klick and you'll be in our range."

"Half a mile..." *Less than thirty seconds...* I press my foot harder on the accelerator, but it's bottomed out.

The two SUVs, one bullet-riddled but still functional, are closing fast again. Far ahead, I can see an SUV on the shoulder. I'm between Hell and high water with nowhere to go and no place to hide.

Desperate, I replace the empty magazine, lower my driver's side window, and pull a frag grenade from my case. I gauge the distance to my pursuers, counting the seconds as I pass a mile marker. When they're three seconds behind, I pull the grenade's pin, release the lever, and drop it out the window. The first SUV swerves, evidently seeing me drop something and wanting no part of it. The second doesn't, and the detonation riddles the grille and windshield with shrapnel. The vehicle swerves out of control, hitting the median sideways and rolling at high speed.

"Nice shot!" I can barely hear Empa over the roar of wind and tinnitus, but before I can reply, she adds, "Chaki's coming your way now, wrong way. The other's still closing."

"Thanks for the update!" I spot the oncoming vehicle easily. Every other car on the freeway has pulled off into the desert; explosions and gunfire will do that. I wonder if I should do the same, relying on the Bronco's four-wheel drive, but there's nowhere to hide out here. I also don't have time to think of another option.

Propping the M4 out my window, resting the forward grip over the rearview mirror, I gauge the vehicle rushing at me at almost two hundred mph, and pull the trigger. They swerve, though I doubt I hit anything, and blast past me with only feet between us. I glimpse a spider-webbed windshield, so maybe I did hit something.

Then my rear window disintegrates, and something hits me hard enough to slam me into the steering wheel. I drop the rifle out the window and grab the wheel with my left hand—my right's not working too well for some reason—fighting to keep the Bronco straight. I make it to the median and skid to a stop without rolling, which astounds me, before the pain arrives.

"I'm hit!" I yell over the growl of the dying engine.

"You're two klicks out. Extreme range. We may be able to cover you."

"Thank Christ!" I reach across with my left hand to grab the Baretta M9A4 from my case, and manage to open the door and get out without faceplanting. My shoulder is blown to shit, but there's no exit wound. Trying to move my right arm sends lightning lancing through me. I stagger around the open door, which gives me some cover, and try to assess my enemies.

Both SUVs have passed me and turned around, one approaching down the median, the other on the pavement. They'll pass me by on both sides and riddle my ride with bullets. I brace my pistol over the hood, wishing I was a southpaw, and unload on the eastbound foe. My aim is shit, but I manage to hit the windshield with a couple rounds. Then, half the windshield is painted red from a high-velocity bullet from behind.

Thank you Empa!

Unfortunately, the SUV careens out of control right at my car, and I have nowhere to go.

The impact sends me flying, but the Bronco takes most of the damage. I find myself lying in the dirt; my chest hurts, and my right arm hasn't gotten any better. My pistol is missing, but it was empty anyway. My ears are ringing like cymbals, but I hear a vehicle roar past, braking hard on pavement.

Move, Terpsichore. You can still get out of this, but you've got to move!

I roll over onto my left side. The Bronco's close, steam rising from the point of impact with the other SUV. I crawl back, using the door to clamber to my unsteady feet. My chest hurts when I breathe, reviving the memory of being kicked by a mule, undoubtedly broken ribs. I can't tell if my ears are playing tricks, or if there's thunder, or music. *Maybe O' Fortuna?* That would be so appropriate...

I reach across to drag my guitar case toward me and retrieve another grenade. I also have the revolver still in my belt holster.

The last SUV, Chaki in the passenger seat, leaning out with a pistol in her hand, scribes a circle around me. The woman's grinning like a fiend as she levels the weapon in my general direction and opens fire. Her aim is even worse than mine left-handed. I can't pull the pin from the grenade with my right hand, so I use my teeth. Her eyes widen as she sees what I'm doing, and she screams something. The vehicle swerves madly in a power slide, all four wheels spitting dust and gravel. I'm staring at the grille as the pin comes free.

As I raise my arm to throw the grenade, the grill slams into the door, crushing my legs against the frame and sending the bomb flying back through the cab and out my missing passenger side window. The explosion is even more mind-numbing than being hit by a car, the vibration of shrapnel ripping through the Bronco telegraphing up my broken legs.

"Got you, bitch!" Chaki lunges out of the SUV, still grinning like a maniac as she reloads her pistol. The tall hombre gets out of the driver's side, a pump shotgun in hand, mirroring her feral glee.

I'm in no condition to fight either of them, pinned as I am, but I can reach my pistol. I might get a shot at one of them, but not both. I glance at my phone, wondering if I might be delivered by another miraculous shot from Empa, but a jagged piece of my passenger door is sticking through the screen. Thunder rumbles overhead, a strange, high-pitched howl. I fumble the revolver from my belt, but even through the tinnitus I realize that it doesn't sound quite right.

Puzzled looks fix both of my enemies' faces, and they shift their gazes skyward. I take the opportunity to raise my pistol.

Chaki, the SUV, and the driver are suddenly torn to shreds of blood, metal, meat, and bone. The hornet's nest howl of rotors and a heavy gun blast me back as the helicopter passes only a few yards overhead. I stare in blind shock as the heavy helicopter banks, the dual coaxial rotors and tail propeller screaming as landing gear extends. Another hilo banks in from the other direction, landing to my right, and a dozen soldiers debark from each.

"Well, shit."

I have been delivered from the frying pan and dumped directly into the fires of Hell. There's no way out of this, and I have no doubt that Nephilim are behind it. Chaki was nothing but a lure. I took the bait, and they now have their hooks in me. But I don't intend to end up like so many of my cousins have in the past, tormented interminably by the minions of Hell. I raise my pistol, but not toward the soldiers.

A single gunshot, and my left arm jerks before the pistol's muzzle reaches my chin. My deliverance clatters to the Bronco's floor, my arm a shattered ruin. I've failed once again. The soldiers close in, a few more rounds making sure there are no witnesses from the other vehicles. Three soldiers approach me, two flanking one in the lead, black uniforms and gear with no insignias. A syringe rises in the hand of the leader.

Canción... I know my son is watching me from a distance and shudder to think what this will do to him. *Please, Mother of my father, give him peace.*

The soldier wrenches my head to one side and slips the needle into the bulging vein in my neck. In seconds, the drug takes me down the dark hole of oblivion.

Canción sat underneath the camo netting as if chiseled from stone, eyes fixed through the binoculars at the scene unfolding below. He wanted to grab a weapon and charge down to save Cora, but he knew he couldn't. They could do nothing, and the inability to help his mother tortured him, so he sat there and stared… just like he had once before. Visions of fire, a green jungle, explosions, and the rattle of gunfire raged through his mind, but he felt no anger, no frustration, no pain. He was frozen.

"They're taking her alive, E," Gippy said from beside them, prone on the rocky ground, viewing the proceedings through the scope of his rifle.

"It was a trap from the beginning." Empa lowered the spotting scope and glanced up at the threatening sky. The low-altitude drones were still there, of course, their engines masked by the storm, but their electronic eyes were trained on Cora, not the four hunkered on the top of the nearby mesa. If they'd seen them, they would all be dead by now.

Jeri sniffed behind them, probably crying. "What can we do?"

"Nothing." Empa had already told Gippy not to fire. A mercy shot came to Canción's mind, but it might have gotten them all killed. It was a wonder they weren't painted by targeting lasers after his first shot, before they heard the howl of the heavy helicopters above the thunder.

Then, one other option comes to Canción's mind. "If they're taking her alive, we may be able to find her." He put down the binoculars and strode toward the camo-shrouded cars.

"Don't move!" Empa barked, stopping him in his tracks. "We're invisible under the camo netting, but if we move, we're all dead, and Cora has no hope at all."

He realized she was right. The drones overhead couldn't see through the RF-blocking camouflage above their heads, but if he stepped out, they would. White fire flared from the wrecked vehicles as the soldiers use phosphorus grenades to destroy all trace of evidence.

"Hope?" Canción's usually melodious voice sounded like cold stone dragged over pavement. "They're going to *torture* her. It's what they do!"

"Yes, they are, but..." Her eyes fix with his, and he can feel her impotent rage bubbling beneath the placid surface of stillness. Then her brows knitted, and her emotions roiled. "Maybe not."

"What?" Canción watched the two helicopters take off, bank, and climb to altitude under the coming rain, heading east.

"Why take her alive when they could have killed her at any time?" Jeri asked. "Hell, they probably spotted her in Albuquerque. One missile and they're done. They didn't even have to sacrifice Chaki."

Gippy looked up from his scope as the hilos roared past, barely three hundred yards away. "And she was the one person who could have painted every wanted website in NAFAS with your picture, Canción. They wanted her alive, so they had to have a *reason*."

"Correct; a *very* good reason." Empa's unnerving gaze remained fixed with Canción's, and he felt the wheels moving behind her eyes. "You're the first of your kind, Canción, but that doesn't mean you'll be the *last*."

"What?" Canción's thoughts spun like bald tires on a gravel road, gaining no traction. The only thing he could think of was his mother in the hands of monsters, and what they'd do to her.

"When Gippy was possessed, the demon learned everything he knew. He told the Nephilim about you, your origin, but we didn't know what you could do at that point. When they assaulted your home in Las Brisas, they planned to kill you and *abduct* me... to make offspring of Ageless and Nephilim of their own, whom they could corrupt from birth."

The bottom dropped out of his raging emotions, his knees thudding to the rocky ground. "They want to make more like *me?*"

Jeri drew in a startled breath. "But that'll take months! Then *years* before they're grown up. Seems foolish."

"Does it?" Empa looked from face to face. "The Nephilim play a *very* long game, Jeri. Entire wars were staged for no other reason than to seed despair, hate, and misery. If others could do what Canción does, but for Hell, it might be worth the wait. They could make dozens like him and turn them into weapons that would poison the minds of the whole world."

"Fuckin' hell," Gippy growled.

Canción felt like he might throw up with the ramifications; his mother confined and restrained, forced to give birth. Rain began to patter the desiccated ground around them, fat drops splatting on stone and dusty soil, a gift from the heavens or the tears of angels. His numb mind latched on to something Jeri had said.

"Time…" His single word was nearly drowned by the oncoming hiss of the deluge. "If that's their goal, it'll take time, and that's to our advantage." He started to move again, but Empa's hand closed on his arm.

"Not yet. The drones are still up there, undoubtedly scanning with IR. This camo netting reflects the same as the surroundings, but if we try for the cars, they might spot us. As you said, we've got *time*, and we know they're going to LA."

"Do we?" Canción looked puzzled. "Why not some secret military base?"

She shook her head. "Because what they're planning will require privacy and seclusion, and while the Nephilim control much of NAFAS, humans still hold many positions of power in the military. Those helicopters *weren't* military, or if they were, they were black ops of some kind. No, they'll take her to someplace completely controlled by them, someplace invulnerable to outside scrutiny or supervision. They flew west, not north, not Denver, so I'm guessing LA. And Chaki was headed there, not Phoenix. She undoubtedly spoke to a Nephilim there."

What she said made sense, but even narrowing the search down to LA, finding her would be like picking a single diamond out of a mountain of salt. "And how do we find her?"

"I don't know, but we've got time." Water dripping through the camo netting started plastering Empa's hair flat before she pulled up the hood of her poncho. "We wait thirty minutes, then pack up and head west. We'll figure this out once we're in LA."

14

CROSSROADS

The Son of Batraal led four Secret Service covert ops soldiers through the double doors of the private facility's laboratory, which looked like an ER triage center. Between the soldiers rolled a stretcher, and upon that stretcher lay the wreck of a woman, both legs distorted, her left arm a tattered mess of blood and fractured bone, while blood pooled under her right shoulder.

"Alive?" the Son of Samyaza asked.

"Of course, and not as bad as she looks. Bleeding's under control, and her wounds are already closing. Sedated and stable."

"Excellent!" He nodded to the room's other occupant, another Nephilim, the Daughter of Yomyael, Angel of Insanity. "Dr. Feriday, see that she's processed."

"Yes, yes!" She grinned—yellowed teeth beneath a hooked nose and thick wrap-around glasses, the right lens fitted with an electronic magnifying and recording loupe—and waved toward a treatment bay. "Here, here. We're all set up for her."

"She looks like she's been through a meat grinder," the Son of Samyaza observed as the soldiers wheeled her past.

"She was." The Son of Batraal looked at him with knitted brows. "Weren't you watching the feed?"

"No, I had a *meeting*." His lip curled, and he shot his immaculate cuffs. While he was, deservedly, in his own mind, one of the most powerful information brokers in the world, he despised dealing with so many arrogant, self-serving humans every day. "Sometimes I regret taking on this position, despite its advantages. The misinformation age is *exhausting*."

His subordinate snorted in derision. "You want to trade jobs?"

The son of the angel of pride gritted his teeth. "Not for all the souls in Hell. Now tell me what happened."

"Someone must have tipped Almonte that she was being followed. Her..." He glanced at the soldiers moving Terpsichore and lowered his voice. "Her *people* exited the freeway and moved in to attack Terpsichore. She probably thought taking out an Ageless would earn her points. We couldn't risk a missile strike without endangering the prize, so the hilos moved in to take out the threats. Terpsichore killed or injured four of them but was injured, then pinned between two vehicles. Our strike pilot killed Almonte and her accomplice before they could kill Terpsichore, then the ground team intervened when she tried to take her own life." He gestured to the table where the Daughter of Yomyael was fitting restraints and placing an IV. "There she is, damaged but alive."

The Son of Samyaza nodded once without looking at him. "Well done."

"Do you mind if I ask why we didn't take her out with a missile?" the Son of Batraal asked.

"Because our Lord wishes us to use her to produce others like this... anomaly who is responsible for destroying two of our kind." The Son of Samyaza turned slowly to scrutinize his subordinate. "Since you've been unable to *find* the anomaly, and just killed the one person on Earth who could give us a lead in doing so, we'll be taking the long game in this new arms race."

The Son of Batraal's face flushed darker at the admonishment. "You told me to use Almonte as bait. You *didn't* tell me to keep the bait alive. Bait, by definition, is expendable."

His lip curled. "No, I *didn't*. I also didn't tell you to defecate this morning, but sometimes I assume my subordinates can think on their own. *Evidently*, they cannot."

Rage and frustration flushed the Nephilim's features; rage at being denigrated by his superior in front of soldiers under his command, and frustration at his inability to respond. The Son of Batraal could call in a drone strike that would bring this entire building down, but Hell would respond, and the Son of Samyaza would respawn. He couldn't even argue the facts, which were undeniably in his favor. All he could do was whirl on his heel and stalk out, his escort in tow.

The son of the fallen angel of pride turned to his prize without another thought for his subordinate. He approached the table and the Daughter of Yomyael who hovered over the Ageless like a vulture awaiting death.

"How is she?" he asked.

"Healing with remarkable speed, as they do. I should remove the bullet from her shoulder before that progresses too far. The bones of her legs are out of alignment also, so I should probably reset them before they heal awry." She looked up from her patient/victim with a mien of utter indifference. "Unless you don't care if she's crippled."

"I don't, as a matter of fact." He turned and started for the door. "Intervene only to keep her alive, which will probably be unnecessary. When she's healed, we'll begin the procedure and preparations for the interrogation. If anyone can give us information about this... *Canción*, she can. Make her compliant. Do whatever you need to do, but don't damage her so badly that you risk miscarriage."

The Daughter of Yomyael grinned sickeningly. "Of course."

With utter confidence in her abilities—if not her mental state—he departed the treatment room, passed the security station, and boarded the elevator to the floor of his private residence and office. He had another meeting in less than ten minutes. He would rather have had his teeth pulled than attend, but didn't have that option.

I haven't been to the City of Angels in decades, and the changes catch me off guard. Of all the post-climate crisis coastal cities in the northern hemisphere, it has fared the best. Of course, we came in from the north, turning off of I-40 at Barstow, then south on I-15, so we didn't see the worst of the flooding.

The Gulf of California has advanced north across the former US/Mexico border to swallow Mexicali and the Salton Sea. The coastal canyons north of San Diego have become protected harbors, and shipping terminals have cropped up. The megacity of LA/San Diego has become the shipping capital of North America, although nothing compared to the days of yore. Trans-Pacific shipping is a rarity with cyclones curving up from the tropics as far north as British Columbia and rolling across the big pond to ravage Asia. But there is still some intercontinental commerce, and fleets of smaller, faster ships race across in spring and fall along the equatorial zone, where the weather is less violent.

The coastal highways are gone, of course, and the lower, southern quarter of LA county south of downtown is underwater, their once proud buildings nothing but hazards to navigation these days. Anaheim is beachfront property, though there is no beach, only a hundred-foot seawall. The downtown area, and north and east, however, have exploded with the displaced population. Huge apartment buildings cropped up in the once sprawling suburbs, and massive desalination plants transform the sea into potable water. Agriculture has changed as well, becoming more climate resilient. The cyclones dump billions of acre-feet of water every year. Cisterns and reservoirs capture a lot of that, the liquid gold pumped into miles and miles of greenhouse factory farms girded by chain-link and barbed wire fences and guarded by small armies. Food has become the new gold rush of California.

We regroup in yet another crappy motel room in Pasadena, just off the 210, paying a fortune for a double room. I end one of the most difficult phone calls I've ever made, informing Emil what happened in New Mexico, and begin the long and arduous search for clues where in this vast megalopolis we might find my lost cousin.

Gippy sits on the floor cleaning his rifle, Jeri is cross-legged on one bed with my naked sword balanced upon her knees, and Canción paces. Of the three, I worry most about Canción. Gippy radiates cold determination like an open freezer, and Jeri bridles her nervousness and fear like a team of unruly horses. Canción, on the other hand, is on the verge of a full-blown panic attack. He's been silent during the drive from Albuquerque, but the pot of his temper is starting to boil. I'm on my phone, trying to ignore all three of them without much success.

"How do we find her?" Canción's question is as predictable as it is frustrating.

"Working on it," I say without meeting his gaze.

"Question is, should we even try?" Gippy looks up from his dismantled rifle, eyes flicking from face to face.

"You're not being funny," Canción growls.

"Not tryin' to be. Serious as a heart attack, in fact." He raises the barrel of his rifle and peers down the bore. "Think it through. Even if we can find her, she's being held by Nephilim, and probably not just one. These fuckers have more power at their fingertips than the president of NAFAS. You can bet your sweet white ass that Cora's being kept under high security. Even if we *can* find her, getting her out will be impossible."

Canción stops his pacing and glares at Gippy. "We're finding her and getting her out. End of discussion."

"No, it's not," Gippy counters, locking the barrel back into the frame of his rifle. "And I don't take orders from you, I take them from Empa. She says we walk away, we walk away."

Canción steps to loom over Gippy, fists balled at his sides. "*I'm going to find my mother and—*"

"And calm the *fuck* down!" Jeri snaps, her hand settling on the hilt of the katana.

"Everyone, *please* calm down. We have time, and Gippy's not wrong; even if we can locate Cora, getting her out will be *more* than difficult." I fix Canción with a pleading gaze. "Losing our tempers with each other isn't going to help." I let my gaze slide to Gippy. "Nothing, however, is impossible. The *first* step is to find her, then we work out a plan to get her out. If extraction looks like suicide, we find a way to... end this."

"*End* this?" Twin chips of glacial ice—Emil's eyes—narrow. "What's *that* supposed to mean?"

"I mean end Terpsichore's life, Canción. I know how you feel, but—"

"You have no *idea* how I feel!" His anger resurges, a nova in a night sky. He's a loose cannon in every sense of the word, and I don't know what to do with him. He needs to learn patience and caution, but now isn't the time to tell him so.

"Dude, you're wrong." Gippy fits the lower receiver of his rifle into the upper and taps in the two takedown pins. "She *knows*. She's been through this before, more than once. The Nephilim have captured other Ageless, and unlike your mom, they weren't interested in using them for anything but *entertainment*. Empa found them and ended their lives as an act of mercy. Sometimes mercy's the only thing you *can* do for someone you love."

As Canción stares in utter shock first at Gippy, then at me, I remember Gippy sighting down the barrel of his Glock at my forehead, offering me mercy when I thought I was unable to continue. If he'd pulled that trigger, it would have been an act of love, saving me from capture and endless torment.

"He's not lying, Canción. I've taken the lives of people I loved to end their torment at the hands of the Nephilim. If you remember, I *tried* to take Gippy's life when he was possessed by an incubus. Think of what they're planning for your mother and ask yourself if eternity in Heaven isn't better than *decades* of torture."

The color washes from Canción's features, and I wonder if he's going to pass out. "Fine." He swallows hard, color flushing back to his cheeks, and resumes pacing. "So, finding her is the first step. How?"

"And as I said, I'm working on it." I show him my phone. "FAA has a record of two Secret Service helicopters entering Los Angeles airspace, but not their destination or flight paths, which were classified. So, we know she's here somewhere."

Gippy looks up from his rifle. "Secret Service? Not the Federal Security Force?"

"Yes, which means we may have thrown a wrench into their network by eliminating the Daughter of Ariquiel."

"Who?" Canción asks, temper still simmering under his poorly maintained control.

"The Nephilim who nearly murdered your father. She was a commander in the FSF." I glance at Jeri and smile at the memory. "She's put that sword through Jeri, pinning her to a wall, and would have killed me, but Jeri saved me."

"Badass bitch with a blade," Gippy says with a wry smile.

"But, you said..." Canción stares at Jeri in shock. "How?"

"I pulled it out." She sheathes the blade in one smooth motion, her girlish features as unresponsive as stone. "Then cut that bitch's arms off with it."

"And we later exorcised the Nephilim, but they obviously still have someone high in the covert law-enforcement branch. Secret Service used to be *strictly* law enforcement and protection, but they've... metastasized into something closer to the Nazi SS in the last two decades."

"And they flew my mother... where?" Canción asks.

I shake my head and return to my phone. "That information is classified, and the FAA is serious about its secrets. We don't have the IT skills to crack their network. If we want to go there, we'll have to hire someone willing to put their neck on the chopping block."

"One more thing to consider," Jeri offers, still utterly calm despite her inner turmoil. I'm proud of her composure. "They used Chaki for bait to land an Ageless. They know about Canción. Could they be using Cora for bait to eliminate him *and* you?"

I consider that for a long moment, then shrug. "Maybe, but it seems too convoluted." Truthfully, I hadn't thought of that possibility before, and I'm proud again for her out-of-the-box thinking. The problem with such a plot is Occam's razor. "If we can't find her, it's a lousy trap, and if we can, it's too obviously a trap. Too many assumptions on their part. They would have to know *we* know Cora was taken, in the first place."

Jeri nods. "I get it."

"And why kill Chaki at all?" Gippy snaps the bulky LAWS scope onto his rifle and boots up the telemetry, running the rig through sighting diagnostics as he speaks. "She knew where we'd been, and all they had to do was analyze security camera footage. She could have pasted Canción's picture all over the Ultranet."

"To save Cora for themselves," I point out. "She was their bird in the hand; more important than the former host of a succubus. Also, the hilo gunner might have had orders of priority, and Cora trumped Chaki by a lot. Chaki was going to kill her, so they eliminated the threat."

"That's… cold," Canción comments.

"Yes, it is." He's learning our enemy, but slowly. After Boquete and Cartagena, I'd have thought he'd be farther along in this, but he evidently isn't. I wonder if deleting his own negative emotions, specifically fear, has sheltered him in a harmful way, at least when it comes to dealing with threats. "We have to think like they do to find her."

"They'll interrogate her," Jeri adds, way ahead of Canción in understanding our enemy. "She doesn't know where and when we met up with Emil, or anyplace else we'd been, but they won't buy that."

"True." I see Canción's dread rising again and put a stopper in it. "Which adds a time imperative, but doesn't change our plan. We find out where she's being held, analyze the situation, and work out our next step."

"So, LA's a big place, like twenty-five *million* people." Gippy puts on the headset and stares into space, calibrating the sighting system. "What's that thing you say? Needle in a…"

"Haystack, and that's putting it mildly."

"So, I'm thinkin' Chaki's still our best lead to follow." Jeri wipes the sword's scabbard with a clean cloth and lays it aside. "Where was she going? Who was she coming here to meet up with, and *why?*"

I nod. "You're right, but Chaki was borderline psychotic. Her motivations for coming here could have been anything."

"I still think she made a deal," Gippy offers. "Canción's face isn't on every network in North America, so that was her bargaining chip. She wanted something, and she had to come here to get it." He shrugs and shuts down his rifle's targeting system. "Money, power, whatever, but something she knew the Nephilim could give to her."

"Power..." That tweaks something in my mind. "Chaki's contact in the Nephilim network was the Daughter of Ariquiel, who we sent to Hell. With her gone, she needed a new contact."

"How do you know that?" Canción asks, slightly calmer now that we're working on his goal.

"I sifted through her mind." He blinks at me as if he thinks I'm joking. "I'm a healer, Canción, and Chaki had a lot of mental trauma. I did what I could for her, but that evidently wasn't enough."

He looks shocked. "And you call what *I* do invasive?"

"It is invasive, but what I did for Chaki was like... first aid or trauma surgery. If I hadn't, she would have stayed in a catatonic state." I nod to Gippy. "I helped Gip, too, but he wasn't as far gone, and he gave me consent." I sigh and shrug.

"So, who would she contact in LA to get in touch with the Nephilim network?" he asks, shifting gears like a bloodhound on the scent, unwilling to deviate.

His question is pertinent, for Chaki contacted the Nephilim somehow. "Let me think for a minute." I put my phone down and close my eyes, trying to sort through all the details of Chaki's damaged psyche; her years on the street, her seduction by Hell's minions, her possession. Prostitution, drugs, abusive pimps, being sold like a commodity, descending into utter depravity... Then the man who offered her the one thing she'd never had before: power. He'd opened the door to Hell for her, and she'd invited Duvara in, but who...

"Walker Trenton." The name pops into my mind like the visitation of a fallen angel. "He's the producer of an adult film studio and hosts an incubus. After we exorcised her Nephilim superior, Chaki contacted him to be put back in touch with the network. He's the conduit for a major player in the Nephilim network."

"Conduit?" Jeri asks. "What's that?"

"Nephilim can't commune with Hell directly, so they have to do it through demons. Every Nephilim has at least one conduit, a possessed human, through which they can send intelligence and receive orders."

"From Hell?" Gippy blinks at me. "Like, from the *actual* devil?"

"The Father of Lies, Lucifer, yes." His name tastes like brimstone on my lips, but I know that the old myth of Him knowing when His name was spoken aloud is only that, a myth.

"So, we find this Trenton and locate his Nephilim contact. Then we find *them*, you do your mind probe thing, and we find my mother." Canción's already working on the next steps, his eagerness throwing caution to the winds.

"It won't be that easy, but yes, that sounds like a plan." I'm already searching for Walker Trenton, and I don't like what I'm finding. "Trenton's been up on charges for human trafficking more than a dozen times, but nothing has stuck. He clearly has friends in high places. He's not going to be easy to get close to."

15

THE SIN OF PRIDE

I awaken, which is a surprise within itself, memories of gunfire, explosions, blood, and agony rising like broken glass on a sandy beach. My legs ache, but when I try to shift, I find that I'm completely immobilized. *Not good.* The light through my eyelids is bright and blinding white but I refrain from opening them, the surface beneath me yielding, the temperature cool enough to prickle my skin. The air smells processed, sterile, and I hear only a background hum of HVAC and electronics. I take a more thorough inventory of myself, moving minutely to test my environment and wellbeing: left arm, legs, and right shoulder hurt; I have straps across my thighs and chest; restraints on my wrists; and something on my head, as well, tight enough to ache. *Really not good.*

"She's awake," a voice says nearby, so I open my eyes.

The light is momentarily blinding, but a man in a lab coat and scrubs stands at a medical monitor nearby, his eyes on the screen, not me. I wonder how he knows I'm awake but suppose it's one of the squiggly lines on his monitor. I try to turn my head and can't. I look up and see a circular framework with wires. As well as restraining my movements, it probably has some type of EEG telemetry. Looking down reveals a hospital gown, and that I'm in a large medical suite.

Then a prickling wave of discomfort that I'm far too well-acquainted with sweeps through me.

"Good morning, Terpsichore. Welcome to our little facility." I can't turn to face the Nephilim, but she leans over close enough for me to see her face. She's an older woman, thin, with hair pulled back from a skeletal face of high cheekbones, thin lips stretched over horsy teeth, and cold gray eyes. "I hope you're comfortable. We've gone to great lengths to prepare this place especially for you. You're going to be here a *very* long time, so... make yourself at home." Her low smirk of amusement turns my stomach.

I say mute, knowing that pissing off my captors will only make things worse. They're far too experienced to be fooled into killing me if I anger them. There will be no escape that way. Instead, I analyze my surroundings as much as I can. Besides the male at the bank of monitors, there's one more attendant besides the Nephilim, a woman working over another hospital bed. I can't see what she's doing, but there's a thick black cushion atop the bed, and another on a hinge that will close over that one. There's a disconcertingly Terpsichore-shaped depression in the upper cushion. A surprising amount of laboratory equipment crowds the tables and counters around the room, including fume hoods, centrifuges, glassware, and a plexiglass box fitted with a microscope and some kind of manipulation apparatus. I spot only one "Exit" sign over a pair of double doors with hazed glass panels. I could be a thousand feet underground, for all I know, or in a private hospital for that matter, but as far as I can tell, I'm the only patient in the room.

All for me... I suppress a shiver that has nothing to do with the temperature.

"I'm the Daughter of Yomyael, and I'll be asking you a number of questions before we begin our procedure. Right now, we're running tests to make sure everything's in order."

Yomyael... the angel of madness. That doesn't bode well, but she doesn't seem like a raving lunatic. I wonder what procedure she's referring to, but refuse to give her the satisfaction of asking. I'll know soon enough.

Instead, I close my eyes and compose music in my mind. I've been a captive before, though never of a Nephilim—Ageless generally don't survive that—and I know that patience is currently my only weapon. Planning escape is pointless; when the opportunity arrives, if it arrives, I'll take it. I don't dwell on the dismal probability of that opportunity arising. There's no point in depressing myself.

"My first question is where we might find information on your son, Canción."

The music in my mind dies, and my heart begins to pound in my chest. *Canción...* What is he going through after watching me being taken? What will he do? *Please, Empa, don't let him come after me.*

"That hit a nerve," the man at the monitors says. "ECG spike, heart rate and BP elevated."

"Of course, it did," the Nephilim coons. "She knows that we discovered what her little boy can do. Now, *tell* me, Terpsichore, where is he? How do we find him? And where is the sad old priest who harbored Azkeel, Emil Farrel? Where is *Empa?*"

I struggle for calm, but it's a dim light from the bottom of the well I'm in, and that well's only going to get deeper. *Please, mother of my father, take my soul...* I know that won't happen—it would be too easy, and I was put on Earth for a reason—but I can't help asking.

"No, huh?" The Nephilim sighs theatrically. "Oh, well, no matter, really. We'll find them all eventually... with your help."

I open my eyes and stare up at her, unable to keep myself from responding. "What in *Hell* makes you think I'll help you?"

Her smile is sickening. "Well, not *willingly*, but eventually you'll crack. Everyone does."

I close my eyes again, but now I only see visions of the atrocities committed by Nephilim over the ages.

The Nephilim cackles a discordant laugh. "Oh, don't be so *dramatic!* We're not going to *torture* you. Those old methods never worked very well anyway. We have better ways these days, less *invasive* ways to encourage you to help us. Besides, we have to be careful not to... damage our investment." A hand pats my forehead, motherly in an unnervingly creepy way. "You're going to produce an entire generation of weapons for us, Terpsichore. Only when we have them fully conditioned and trained, maybe in thirty years or so, will we allow you to die."

Weapons... Now I know why they captured me alive, why they used Chaki as bait to lure me into the open. They'll make more like Canción and corrupt them with the hatred of Hell, and there's nothing I can do to stop them.

I would weep, but I don't want to give her the satisfaction.

"We've taken the Ageless, Terpsichore, alive, and our Lord's plan is proceeding." Brushing the lapels of his jacket, the Son of Samyaza preened with pride. The amassed Nephilim, present only virtually, of course, exchanged murmurs of excitement, surprise, and satisfaction, even those who had disagreed with the plan to capture the Ageless rather than simply destroy her. "We're performing a non-damaging interrogation, but should be able to harvest ova, fertilize them, and implant within a few weeks."

"Why question her at all?" a Nephilim from Argentina asked. "You risk our prize and the displeasure of the Father of Lies."

"Because there's still a creature out there who can destroy our kind, Daughter of Akibeel." He considered the get of the angel of pestilence for a moment, lamenting that she wasn't male and, therefore, a potential contributor to the first generation of weapons. Perhaps they would try parthenogenic fertilization in the future, for a being that could wield a plague through music would be valuable indeed. "Which brings me to the next consideration we must face; who will sire the first generation of Terpsichore's offspring?"

"I'm surprised you didn't insist upon using your *own* seed," another Nephilim grumbled.

The others didn't always appreciate his position as their sovereign on Earth, and discord had historically run rampant through their ranks. The age of instantaneous global communications had changed all that, but there were still disagreements, if not outright war, between the sons and daughters of the Gregori.

"I considered it, but we need something we can weaponize." He smiled smugly. "Perhaps in the future, if we need a leader for our new army."

"If it's a leader you need, use Kokabiel's seed," another suggested.

The Son of Samyaza nodded once, for the grandchild of the fallen angel of stars, commander of Hell's legions, would be formidable indeed. "Again, a good suggestion for the future, but weapons first, then commanders."

"And I'm too busy to leave my current project," the Son of Kokabiel stated. "We're near a unification agreement, and a combined Russo/Chinese influence would play well for an all-Asia conquest."

"Agreed," he said with a nod. "So, other nominations?"

There were several, and the sniping and posturing ran rampant for long minutes. Finally, the candidates were whittled down to five: Ramuel, Angel of Decay; Zavebe, Angel of Disease; Armoros, Angel of Unmaking; Mamu, the Australian Aboriginal Angel of Destruction; and Sathariel, Angel of Deception.

Hell had never been a democracy, so the Son of Samyaza made the decision. "Son of Armaros, make arrangements to come here as quickly as possible." The Nephilim, Glen Renquist, COO of a strip-mining operation in the Appalachians of West Virginia, was close by, with nothing he couldn't leave to subordinates. "The other nominees will donate seed to be frozen and shipped here. I'll be in touch to update you all on our progress."

He ended the conference with the flick of a key on the arm of his chair and leaned back, toggling the control to swivel around to gaze out upon his empire, glowing with his victory. *Yes, a weapon that can merge unmaking with music will be formidable indeed...*

16

CITY OF FALLEN ANGELS

As Empa had predicted, finding Walker Trenton hadn't been difficult. Tax records gave them his home address, office address, income, and contact information. The Ultranet was full of information and misinformation on the guy, and weeding through it all, sorting fact from fiction, took time. They crawled into every noisome detail of the man's existence, and the results nauseated Gippy on a visceral level.

He was rich, influential, and always in the company of beautiful young women and men, as well as armed private security. The San Fernando studio he ran was nothing short of a fortress; walled, monitored with electronic security, and manned with a private army. Empa had called it a concentration camp, which Gippy had to look up. The comparison was apt. People went in and never came out. What did come out was about two thousand adult films per year, most of them legal, though about a third of them weren't. The connections between the last third—the truly horrific ones, many involving children—and the studio were impossible to legally verify, but the rumors and scuttlebutt were hard to deny. Walker Trenton bought, sold, and used up young, beautiful human beings in the vilest ways imaginable.

If they didn't need information from Trenton's head, Gippy would have been pleased to put a bullet through it on general principle. The thought of getting close enough to the man to spring their plan made his skin crawl, and it certainly wasn't going to be easy. Getting into the studio wouldn't have been hard, but getting out alive with what they needed would have been impossible. The man's house—a thirty-thousand-square-foot, walled and gated mansion halfway up Kagel Canyon—would be harder to access, but only half a dozen guards were on duty at any given time instead of a hundred. Getting out would be possible, if not easy, so that had become their target. The grunt work of planning, preparing identities, and acquiring everything they needed to get in, secure Trenton, and get out alive without ending up on every news broadcast on the Ultranet, had taken weeks and a small fortune of Empa's money.

Their way in would be simple: talent scouts for the industry often showcased their "product" for Trenton by appointment only. Getting such an appointment had taken another week, and some imaginative fabrication of identities and reputations. Unfortunately, since Empa's face was all over every wanted site on the Ultranet, Gippy would be their front man. He would be posing as a talent scout, Central American by birth, living in Las Vegas, and specializing in finding people for all manner of specialties. Canción and Jeri would be taking on the roles of that talent. Empa would stay out of the view of cameras and handle the linchpin to their plan.

Their limo pulled up to the security gate at precisely ten a.m., and Empa lowered the tinted window just far enough to speak. "Antony Narvaez here to see Mr. Trenton." She wore a chauffeur's suit, complete with a hat and sunglasses that hid most of her face from the cameras covering the entry. Her mouth, nose, chin, and cheekbones were augmented with silicone prosthetics.

Gippy wore a bit of that as well, but just enough to sharpen his features. They were betting their lives that Trenton's security system didn't include AI facial recognition software connected to the NAFAS database.

"One moment, please," the voice of a guard answered.

Their appointment was legitimate, of course. Nobody walked into

Walker Trenton's home without one. More of Empa's money well spent.

"Please enter. Mr. Trenton is expecting you."

The gate rolled aside and, Gippy noted as they drove through the substantial barrier, rode in a recessed steel track. The gate itself was beautiful—a bas relief of sensual shapes, both male and female, without achieving actual pornography—but not simply ornamental. Double-walled steel behind the sculpture and reinforcing cables kept anything short of an assault vehicle from driving through it. They'd downloaded the specs for it and how its lock could be overridden—thanks to the Los Angeles Fire Code Enforcement and their shitty network security. If everything went as planned, that wouldn't be necessary, which didn't make him feel much better as the barrier rolled closed behind them. In his experience, things rarely went as planned.

"Party time," he whispered as Empa pulled around the circular drive and parked in front of the grandiose entry. Two security guards approached, both eyeing the car professionally. Gippy knew their names, addresses, and professional histories. All six currently on the premises were former military and knew who they were working for, which made Gippy feel a little easier about what was going to happen to them—if shit didn't go sideways and they all died, of course.

Steady spirit, Gip. Just play the part.

Neither of the guards approached close enough to open the passenger door. Gippy waited for Empa to get out, step around, and open the door for him. He got out, shot the lapels of his five thousand NAD brushed-silk suit, and grinned at the guard. "Buen día. A lovely hacienda, and the view... asombrosa." He made a point not to look at Canción or Jeri as they exited the limo behind him and ignored Empa utterly.

"Good morning, Señor. Follow me, please." One guard turned without another glance and strode for the impressive front doors, while the other motioned them to proceed, then followed behind.

Gippy made a casual gesture for the others to fall in behind him and strutted behind the first guard, his neck itching with the other behind him. Empa, of course, stayed with the car, which was the part of their plan that he hated most. Canción might be able to suck a demon from their host like an oyster from its shell, but Empa could feel a Nephilim from twenty feet. They were walking into an incubus's lair, and he'd rather have angelic radar than a demon-killing magic wand. For all they knew, they could be walking into a room full of Nephilim and not know it.

The entry was under surveillance, of course, but Gippy ignored the hidden cameras and nodded as the first guard opened one of the double doors and gestured them through. Inside stood a woman taller than Gippy wearing a black business suit and white collarless shirt fixed with a diamond pin. This was Trenton's butler/head of security, Maria Vaca, a former special forces covert operative, which really meant assassin. She looked to be about fifty, but Gippy didn't doubt for a second that she could take him apart like a puzzle if he gave her the slightest provocation.

He smiled his most winning smile and swallowed his nerves. "Buen dia, Señora."

She didn't return the smile, but her eyes roved over him from head to toe, and then Canción and Jeri behind him. They lingered on Canción longer than they had Gippy, which didn't surprise him. Sometimes, he couldn't help it either. "Mister Narvaez. Follow me, please."

They knew the layout of the house from construction schematics, but the décor was a shock. Blinding white with garish gold accents everywhere, from moldings to furnishings to the frames of pornographic artwork throughout the ages. Asian, Greek, Indian, and European paintings and sculptures cluttered the entry hall, dining room, and vast living room with no discernible sense of arrangement or organization. The theme, however, ranged from simply erotic to graphic brutality.

Gippy tried not to stare, maintaining a façade of casual amusement as he followed Vaca through the museum of torrid insanity. The sunken living room was dominated by a gold and crystal chandelier depicting daisy-chaining gold-winged alabaster cherubs engaging in all manner of imaginative sex. Beneath it stood an equally imaginative sculpture of gold-accented demons of every imaginable type in an orgy of violent copulation with damned humans.

Gippy ignored all of it, focusing on the silver-haired man reclining on the far side of a circular white leather couch, a steaming cup in one hand, a tablet in the other, seemingly oblivious to the young man and woman performing fellatio upon him.

"Mr. Trenton, Mr. Narvaez," their escort announced emotionlessly, stepping aside.

The man's attention snapped up from the tablet to his butler as if surprised by the introduction. His eyes shifted from Gippy to Canción and then Jeri, and recognition registered. "Ah, right. Sorry, I got carried away." He nudged the two aside from their attention to his phallus and stood, pulling his white and gold silk robe closed. "Work, work, work, you know. You two scamper off and keep yourselves occupied for a while."

The couple, also robe-clad, rose and hurried off without a word or a glance at anyone else, eyes down, gaits listless. Gippy wondered if they were on drugs.

"So, Mr. Narvaez, what have you got for me?"

"Something a little *different*, I hope." Gippy stepped aside and motioned his charges forward. Canción wore jeans and a snug white t-shirt, his hair in a casual tousle, exuding his mother's angelic beauty. Jeri wore a hijab with a translucent veil and a full abaya. Through the veil, you could see gold chains linking her nose, lips, eyebrows, and trailing off under the fabric. The robe hid her shape completely, and her hands were tucked out of sight. "Cory here is... well... gifted in many ways, and Magda is a submissive with a predilection for pain and piercings."

"Hardly unique, but I'll admit he *is* a pretty one." Trenton stepped forward, his eyes roving over Canción from head to toe. "Well, let's see if you can—" The demon-possessed man's steps faltered as their eyes met, still a few steps away. Trenton's mouth gaped, and his entire body convulsed.

Adios, pendejo, Gippy thought.

"Sir?" The bodyguard, Vaca, stepped forward. "Are you—"

Trenton's eyes rolled up, and his knees folded, but Vaca was quick and reached him before he hit the floor. Even as she lowered him, one hand touched her collar.

"Medical emergency. T has collapsed in the living room. Dr. Dillon to the living room. Security to me. Comms, call EMS." She spoke in a calm but loud voice, and missed Gippy speaking in a much softer tone into the cuff of his suit.

"Package down. Drop the hammer." He then switched off the radio in his pocket and stepped away from Canción.

Jeri backed away in the other direction, her hands still under her robe.

The front doors burst open, three guards hurrying in. Another joined them from the dining room. Then a deafening crack sounded from the parking circle, drawing the attention of the four guards and bringing Vaca to her feet. The sound, an EMP bomb in the trunk of the limo, killed all electronics on the estate that weren't hardened, including the security cameras, cell phones, and radios. Their own gear was shielded, but only if it was turned off.

"What the fuck?" Vaca reached beneath her coat and drew a pistol, striding toward the door.

"What the hell was *that*?" Gippy bellowed, drawing the security chief's attention long enough for Jeri to jam a Taser into the back of her neck.

As Vaca collapsed in convulsions, Canción turned to face the entry hall and unleashed the energy from the incubus that he'd ripped from Trenton. The four guards were still facing the front door, weapons in hand, when the pulse of force hit them hard enough to send them sprawling. From almost fifty feet, the impact probably wasn't enough to kill them, but it certainly knocked them momentarily senseless. Empa stepped into the doorway with a pistol in one hand and a Taser in the other.

"Still one more, Jeri. Second floor stairs." Gippy stepped on Vaca's pistol and drew a syringe full of ketamine from his pocket. The 16-

gauge needle plunged into her butt cheek, and he depressed the plunger. By the time the Taser wore off, she'd be gorked.

"Got it." Jeri dropped the discharged Taser and drew her pistol and Empa's sword from under her robe, hurrying to take up a position beside the wall where the stairs emptied into the room.

"Here." Gippy discarded the empty syringe, handed Vaca's pistol to Canción, and pulled his own, keeping his knee between the woman's shoulder blades until she stopped twitching. "Check Trenton."

Canción complied without comment, kneeling beside the comatose man. "Alive but out of it."

"Good." A glance confirmed that Empa had secured the other four guards, whether they needed it or not. "Watch for the doctor. He should be here any—"

As if on cue, a balding man entered the room from a hallway carrying a large first aid kit. His eyes widened at the sight of armed strangers, and his mouth gaped. "Wha..."

"Shut up and get on the floor!" Canción advanced on the man, Vaca's pistol leveled at his face.

The doctor dropped the kit and hit the floor like a sack of dirty laundry. Before Canción reached him, however, a shot rang out from the stairwell. Canción fell, then a man screamed.

Gippy lurched up, but by the time he could train his pistol on the stairs, the last guard was on his knees, clutching his bleeding wrist. His severed hand lay several feet away still clutching the pistol he'd fired. Jeri held the bloodied sword under his chin.

"On the floor, asshole!" Jeri ordered.

"You cut off my fucking hand!" the guard screamed.

"And your head's next if you don't lay flat!" She kicked him between the shoulders, and he faceplanted hard, still clutching his bleeding wrist.

Gippy turned to find Empa already at Canción's side, a hand pressed to his bloody shirt. "Alive?"

"Yes. Superficial, just a lot of bleeding. Secure the shooter."

"On it." Gippy joined Jeri, who stood with one foot on the bleeding man's back, the edge of Empa's sword at his neck. Her other hand held her pistol close, aimed at the back of the shooter's head. "Nice job."

"Not nice enough," she growled.

"Don't worry about it. He'll be fine." Gippy knelt and cinched a cable tie around the man's bleeding wrist, then another around both forearms. Two more secured his legs, then he emptied another syringe into the man's backside. "Done. Help me with Trenton."

"Sure."

Empa already had Canción on his feet, though his shirt was bloody, and both of them looked a little shaky, which told him she'd taken some of his injury. She'd cable-tied the doctor's hands and feet as well. Gippy hurried to Trenton, who lay in a fetal ball, breathing fast, eyes closed tight.

"Can you two get him to the car?" Empa asked.

"Drag his ass if nothin' else. Come on, Jer."

He and Jeri tried to hoist the man to his feet, but his legs wouldn't hold him. Empa and Canción were in no condition to help, so they made good on Gippy's claim and dragged the older man up the steps of the sunken living room, past his bound and unconscious security guards, and out the front door. He began to mutter in a language Gippy remembered from his time possessed as they levered him into the back of the limo. It was a language no human used, the tongue of demons.

"Tape his mouth, Jer. I gotta get the gate."

"Sure." She helped Canción in, then piled in after.

"You good to drive, E?"

"As soon as I get the computer rebooted. Two minutes." Empa opened the driver's door and unsealed the electromagnetically shielded compartment under the dash that protected the car's computer, which had also been shut down before the detonation to keep the electronics from being fried.

High rollers valued their security, which included armored windows, flat-proof tires, and anti-electronic warfare systems. Proof that money could buy you virtually anything. The hardened system had been designed to protect the electronics from an EMP at the request of some uber-rich prepper, or at least that's what the dodgy fellow they'd leased the car from had said. Unfortunately, there was no way to test it other than to fire the EMP, which, if it damaged the car, would have put their operation back weeks. If it didn't reboot, they couldn't start the car and would have to find another ride.

Gippy muttered a prayer to the God of Computers as he hurried to the box that controlled the gate motor and put a bullet through the lock. Inside, he threw the emergency release lever that disengaged the motor from the drive chain, then grabbed the gate and pulled. It was heavy but rolled open slowly. By the time he got back to the car, Empa had it running.

"I can drive if you need me to, E," he offered.

She shook her head. "No, I'm good. Make sure Trenton's okay."

He piled in the back with the others where Jeri was affixing a bandage around Canción's waist. The bullet looked to have entered and exited without piercing anything vital, a bloody mess, but nothing more than a deep wound across his abdominal muscles.

"Lucky as fuck, dude," Gippy said with a grin as Empa gunned the engine.

"Not just luck." Canción nodded to Jeri. "Probably would have killed me if she hadn't cut his hand off. The gun went off as the sword went through his wrist."

"Badass bitch with a blade," Gippy nudged her and grinned even wider as she blushed. "Package secured, and we'll be invisible in ten minutes! Well done!"

"Yes, well done," Empa seconded as they rolled out of the open gate and down the hill toward LA. "Now all we have to do is pray that this asshole knows where they took Cora."

The hiss of deafening white noise fades, and blinding white light stabs through my eyelids. Something inarticulate comes from my mouth, not quite a cry, the most discordant sound I remember ever uttering.

"Good morning, Terpsichore." A hand grasps my chin, the vile touch of a Nephilim turning my stomach. "Are you well rested?"

"Nughhh," I manage through chapped lips, my tongue thick in my mouth.

"No? Well, that's to be expected." Fingertips pry open my eyelids and an even brighter light stabs into my skull. I try to pull away, but the device that holds my head immobile is like a vice. "Amphetamines and sensory deprivation don't lend to restful sleep."

"Bugger yourself, demon." My voice is hoarse, and for some reason, I'm speaking ancient Greek. Sometimes my brain reverts to my mother tongue; especially when I'm being tortured.

"Delightful." The grip on my chin relents, and the voice is softer as he speaks to another. "Anything useful?"

"Not yet. She's... resilient. Keeps singing nonsense tunes, even with the audio blanking."

I recognize that voice; the woman's been asking me questions for... days? Weeks? Years? I can't remember how long, or even where I am anymore, but I remember the questions, all about Canción. So far, I don't think I've given them anything useful, but my short-term memories are slippery.

"She'll crack eventually, but I don't want to stress her too much now that the implantation's finished. We don't want a miscarriage."

"No, we most certainly do not," the first voice agrees.

Implantation? Miscarriage? I try to remember all they've put me through, and can't. They've been feeding me with a tube and giving me drugs through an IV. My body is currently swathed in a yielding but tough material, but I recall blood tests and having my legs propped up in obstetric clamps. I shiver with the hazy memory of a cold speculum. I blink my eyes open. A medical facility, tubes and monitors, wires, and a soft pressure holding me immobile, like sandbags, but warm. I strain against it, but can barely feel my own skin.

"We have time, but I want that... thing neutralized." The male Nephilim adjusts the cuffs of his expensive suit, smiling down at me as if I'm a prize butterfly pinned in his collection. "There's no telling what damage he could do."

"Understood. I'll proceed carefully." The woman leans close, flashes that damned light in my eyes again, and nods. "Back to oblivion for now, Ageless." She lowers a headset over my eyes and noise-canceling earphones over my ears. I try to struggle and feel the pinpoint braces pressing into my skull. All sound and light vanish, drowned in white noise and blindness.

Oblivion... I struggle to concentrate, to think, to remember music. *A song... any song... My song... My Canción...* The music, my memories, my entire long life all slip away like water through my fingers.

I've delved into the minds of the formerly possessed on more than a few occasions, but I wouldn't want to make a career of it. Exploring Trenton's psyche feels like diving into a cesspool on fire. I've witnessed atrocities that modern humans would think of as utter barbarity, and they wouldn't be wrong, but the things that this man has done shock even me. I tell myself that it was the demon that did these things, not the near-catatonic human being cowering fetal on our motel bed, but it doesn't change the fact that this cruelty happened. Witnessing it through his memories leaves me sickened and angry, ready to lash out at anything within reach. But I can't blame Walker Trenton; in fact, I pity him. Unlike Chaki, he didn't ask to be possessed; he was tricked into it, similarly to Gippy's ordeal. I doubt he will ever recover from almost forty years with that filth polluting his every thought, and there's very little I can do to help him.

After what seems like hours wading through Hell, I find what we need and pull away from the man's mind. Because I am what I am, I can't help but heal some of his trauma, but it's like putting a Band-Aid on a full-body burn. I can't delete his memories, and those will torture him for the rest of his life.

"Well?" Canción is pacing again, which I find irritating.

"I know who Trenton's Nephilim contact is, and we've just poked the dragon." I move from the bed to one of the rock-hard armchairs, staring at the shivering wreck of a man, wondering if he'll ever be fully sane. "It's the Son of Samyaza, the fallen angel of pride, leader of the Gregori. He's likely the head of Hell's entire network on Earth."

"Son of a…" Gippy stares at me, and I feel the wheels of his mind racing.

Canción is not impressed. "So, who is he, and how does that help us find my mother?"

Impatience… I take a breath and let it out slowly, steadying my tortured spirit. "He's Joseph Miaka, Chairman and CEO of NAFAS Transmedia. And it doesn't help us in the slightest."

"Fuuuuuck," Gippy groans, shaking his head.

Canción stops pacing. "What? Why is that bad?"

"Because the dude's untouchable. Transmedia's *literally* the information hub of the whole freakin' empire. They decide what news is news, and what bullshit is truth. Propaganda central."

"Why does that make him untouchable? We find out where he lives and—"

"Because it's not so simple," I interrupt, rubbing my temples as if I can score away the memories of Trenton's mind. "Pull up Grand Hope Tower on your phone. That's the nerve center of Transmedia, and that's where Joseph Miaka lives. The top three floors are his private residence. He's quite likely the most influential man in the world, worth over three *trillion* NADs. He *controls* the narrative that NAFAS uses to control the populace."

"And he's a fuckin' Nephilim." Jeri bites a nail, beginning to understand what we're facing.

"Not just a Nephilim, their Hell-appointed commander-in-chief." I nod to Trenton. "He was Miaka's connection to Hell, and we just cut the line. And the most recent conversation he was privy to was about Cora. They've got her for certain, but we still have no idea where they're holding her. They'd need a medical facility to… do what they're planning."

Canción snaps a glare at me. "Don't sugarcoat it."

"I'm not, I just…" I rub my temples. "I feel like I might puke."

"But you said we poked a dragon. What do you mean? So, Miaka's a bigshot. He can't know we're onto him, can he?"

"I don't know how often they speak, but the disappearance of Trenton *won't* go unnoticed. Even if it doesn't make the news, which it will, Miaka will eventually try to contact him, fail, and find out he's been abducted. He'll then go through another Nephilim's demon to contact Hell. One question to the Father of Lies, and they'll know Trenton's incubus is gone. Miaka will know it was us, or more specifically, *you*, Canción."

"Shit." Canción resumes pacing, realization dawning.

"And he'll assume you're with me." I try to think if any Nephilim or demon knows my capabilities, but five thousand years is a long time, and with Trenton's horrible life fresh in my mind, I'm having trouble remembering what I had for breakfast. "He may or may not come to the conclusion that I know what Trenton knows."

"And there were witnesses to Trenton's abduction," Gippy adds, as if we need icing on the shit cake. "Even if we fragged the electronic records of us being there, they'll have our descriptions. They'll be hunting for us."

"Everyone's descriptions but mine," Jeri says, drawing our attention. "I wore a hijab. I'm still invisible, and I'm the only one the motel manager saw face to face. We're probably safe for now."

"Probably," I agree, "but that doesn't help us in the long run."

"And Miaka lives in a fuckin' *fortress*, so we're no closer to finding Cora," Gippy adds.

"Aren't we?" Jeri wags a finger. "I mean, think it through. Since we exorcised the Nephilim who ran me through in Cincinnati, Mr. Porn Hub here was Chaki's go to. She kills the banker to get a phone, and calls him, then she's on her way here with her whole crew. Was she coming here to hook up with Trenton, or someone else?"

I don't know what good this does us, but I can find out. "Give me a minute." I lever myself out of the chair and sit beside the bed again, peering into the shattered mind of Walker Trenton. In minutes, I have it. "Chaki called him at the studio. She wanted to make a deal with the Son of Samyaza. Trenton called him and gave him her number. He didn't know what the deal was, but she told him she had information that would end the war." I sit back and stare at Canción. "She was going to out us, specifically you."

Gippy nods. "Then they spotted Cora following Chaki and murdered her to get their hands on an Ageless."

"Because one Ageless was all they needed to create more like me." The muscles along Canción's jaws writhe and knot.

"Exactly," I agree, thinking there might be a light at the end of this rabbit hole after all. "And this is something that the Son of Samyaza would see to himself. He's the son of the Angel of *Pride*, after all. He wouldn't delegate it. And there's no more secure place to conduct this project than his very own fortress."

"Cora's in Grand Hope Tower?" Jeri asks. "I thought you said they'd need a hospital."

"A medical facility, and money can buy anything. Doctors, equipment, you name it."

Gippy blinks at me and shakes his head. "Jesus! She may as well be on the fuckin' *moon*!"

Canción's temper flares so hard I feel it across the room. "So, what? You want to just *leave* her there?"

I struggle for my steady spirit, but his raging anger is like a forest fire. "It's not a question of what we want. It's a question of what we can and can't do, Canción. Grand Hope Tower is unassailable. They have the highest tech security in the world, and an army of soldiers. We're also on their radar now or will be soon."

"I'm not," Jeri reminds me. "I could walk in there in a business suit and nobody'd know."

"And we have an EMP bomb," Gippy adds, nudging Jeri with a grin. "I mean, you paid a friggin' *fortune* for the thing. Seems like we ought to get more than one use out of it."

They both have valid points, and the EMP only needs rearming. But there's one thing they haven't thought through. "And getting out?"

They all stare at me like I'd just pissed on their birthday cakes, but none of them have a reply, much less a solution. The silence is deafening until a voice breaks it from a most unexpected quarter.

"E...vac."

Four pairs of eyes snap to Walker Trenton as if a dead man has just spoken.

"What?" I didn't even think he *could* speak or understand what we were talking about. "Evac? Evacuation?"

His eyes swivel toward mine, and he nods once very slowly. "S... O... P. Bomb threat."

I blink at him. "Well fuck me on a donkey."

Gippy snorts a laugh. "Daym, E! You been hangin' 'round *me* too much!"

"Well, yes, or not really, but he's right. Ever since nine-eleven, there have been strict evacuation protocols for big buildings. A verifiable bomb threat or explosion will force them to evacuate the building. If we time it right, we can escape with Cora using the *thousands* of people who work there as cover."

"Still, getting in's gonna be a *bitch*," Gippy adds. "Jeri might be able to walk in the front door, but we can't."

"No, we can't, but big buildings also have a lot of things delivered." Jeri has Grand Hope Tower pulled up on her phone. "Four *thousand* people work there. Ten restaurants, two gyms, bars, clubs, even a damn *theater*."

"But you can bet your ass they have cameras linked directly to the NAFAS facial recognition network at every door, including the delivery entrances." Gippy frowns over his own phone. "This damn thing takes up an entire city block! It's *huge*!"

"Tallest building in North America," Canción adds.

They're all on their phones, but I'm thinking of our other source of information. "Walker. Have you ever been to Grand Hope Tower?"

He nods, barely a tremor, but an affirmation.

I don't trust him to help us, but the information we need is there for the taking. I kneel down beside the bed and stare into his eyes again. "I need to know what you know, Walker. Will you let me in?"

Again, that quiver of a nod.

"Thank you. Just relax and think of your last visit there. I'll do the rest."

He nods, and I delve once again into the horrors of his life. This time is slightly easier, for he's compliant and his surface thoughts are on our goal. The reason for his visit, however, is appalling and predictable. He brought the entertainment for a party being thrown for telecom executives, a stretch SUV limo full of beautiful men and women from his studio. I see the entry ramp, the security checkpoints with cameras, and the roll-up steel gate that leads into the vast parking garage beneath the building. Banks of elevators take them up, but there are more security guards accompanying them, because access to the top floors is restricted.

I back out of his mind before I see what happens at the party. "We have a way in, but security's tight. Four guards at the delivery entrance, security gates, cameras, facial recognition at the front door, and more guards for the elevators to the upper floors. This is going to take some work."

"A diversion," Gippy suggests. "We create a shitstorm of a diversion at the main entrance to the building. It'll pull in every security guard not nailed to their seat. We paintball the cameras, take down the guards, use their IDs to get in, then park a van in the basement with the EMP."

"And the elevator guards should have access keys or codes for the upper floors." Canción shows me his phone, a scrolling article on the lifestyles of the uber-rich. "Miaka's residence takes up three floors, all of it restricted. That's *got* to be where they're holding my mother."

"A safe bet, but not a certainty. We need to know for certain." He glares at me as if I'm killing his buzz.

"And facial recognition at the front door is a problem," Jeri adds. "I found a promo video. Everyone swipes their ID and smiles for the cameras at the entrance turnstiles. We either need to forge a fake or steal a real ID and somehow get my face in their system."

"Or find someone who works there that you can impersonate," I suggest.

"That's a thought." She returns to her phone. "Three thousand eight hundred and twelve employees go in every day. We should be able to find *someone* who looks like me."

"Personnel files?" Canción suggests.

"We need a hacker," Gippy points out. "Not only for that, but for floor plans, security systems, delivery companies that service the place..."

I start making notes. "What else? The devil's *literally* in the details. We have to think of everything."

"So, we get Jeri in, she preps the loading dock, taking out cameras and security; we pose as delivery or service workers. Pop the diversion to draw security guards. Meet up at the loading dock. You look into the memories of a security guard for passwords, security, and where they're holding Cora. We get her, blow the EMP, and get the fuck out with everyone else being evacuated." Gippy cocks an eyebrow at me. "Plan?"

"A *rough* plan." I add to my notes. "Maybe blow the EMP when we reach the restricted floors. We'll have to go through their security to get Cora, and they'll set off alarms at some point. This will be complicated, and good plans are simple." I glance again at Trenton. "And we need to figure out what to do with our friend here."

He just closes his eyes and shakes his head.

"We can pay someone to watch over him, then release him when this is all over." Gippy shrugs. "He can't do anything to us but give them descriptions once we're in the wind, and I'm sure they'll have those anyway. And I got an idea for the distraction, but it's gonna cost some bucks."

I shrug. "For Cora, money's not an object."

"Thank you," Canción says, and I see in his eyes that he's sincere. "Really, all of you. You're risking your lives for my mother, and... I don't know what to say."

"Say you won't do something impetuous once we're inside," I suggest. "We work out this plan down to the second, execute it, and get out with Cora. That's our only goal."

He nods. "Deal. You're in charge."

"Fan-fucking-tastic!" Gippy claps his hands and rubs them together. "Let's get to work!"

"All we need now is a donkey," Jeri adds with a lascivious grin.

THE WRATH OF HEAVEN

Jeri swiped Loretta Watkins's stolen security badge at the main entrance to Grand Hope Tower and smiled for the cameras, just another of thousands of worker bees reporting for the day. She held her breath while cameras compared her face to the ID. Loretta was sleeping in her apartment, courtesy of an anesthetic IV drip monitored by a paid attendant. Of the thousands of employees that came and went every day, she had been the one similar enough to Jeri—along with some imaginative makeup that made her look twenty years older and about fifty pounds heavier—for her to pass the facial recognition system. Or at least the disguise worked on their test runs. If she didn't pass now, alarms would go off, the entire mission would fail, and she'd be arrested.

Lucky, lucky, lucky, she muttered to herself as the cameras examined her, thanking God they had no magnetometers. She had enough gear under her padded outfit to set one off from fifty feet.

They'd discovered through a paid hacker that Transmedia had separate security stations at every working floor, each one proprietary to the work being done in that department. Some were just another ID scan and facial match like the front door, while others included print scanners, retinal scans, and even voice recognition, as well as magnetometers. Luckily, Jeri wouldn't have to worry about those... yet.

The turnstile beeped, and the light flashed green. She exhaled and walked into the building, praying that she didn't bump into anyone who knew Loretta Watkins. She pulled her phone from her pocket and texted as she walked, along with hundreds of others doing the same. She typed, "I'm in." The time was 8:07 a.m.; she had twenty-three minutes.

"OK. We're on station," Empa replied a moment later, which meant the others were ready to bring the mocked-up van through the security checkpoint into the delivery garage under the building.

Jeri's job was to clear the way for them.

They'd spent two weeks getting ready for the operation, securing the services of a dependable hacker, analyzing the massive building's layout, and researching every business that supplied Grand Hope Tower with everything from food to clothing to equipment. For the preparations, Empa had rented a shipping-container-sized storage unit. They stored their vehicles and gear and set up a workshop. Jeri had been their driver for the week, since her face was the only one not on the wanted feeds. They honed their plan into fine detail, with contingencies and bail-out options at every interval, but the other three would never get past the security cameras in the loading dock without some help from Jeri. To get up to the first security checkpoint, they'd pose as a food service that specialized in vegan fare, because it was delivered daily in small shipments. They bought a van the same model as the company used and mocked it up to pass a cursory check. That wouldn't get them through the checkpoint, but it would get them close enough.

Jeri followed the flow of workers to the bank of elevators that would put her closest to the freight elevator on the loading dock, pressed the down button, and waited. Since most people were going up, ten minutes passed before a down-bound lift arrived. She texted as she waited, "On lift," and hit send when the doors opened. She'd be out of cell service in the elevator and the sub levels, so the clock was now unstoppable, at least for her. In about fifteen minutes, the distraction they'd arranged would take place whether they were ready or not.

The elevator's single security guard barely glanced at Jeri and the two maintenance workers who boarded with her, even though she wore a business suit and they wore jeans and blue button-downs. There were seven floors below street level: S1-3 parking levels, S4 delivery and trash removal, and S5-7 physical plant. She got out on the delivery level without a word from any of them and walked toward the express lift they'd chosen.

The loading dock was cavernous, built to accommodate full-sized tractor-trailers, and cameras covered all doors and elevators. When she was out of sight of any cameras, thankful for the crappy lighting typical of parking garages, she pulled the disassembled paintball pistol from under her padded disguise and carefully put it together. Lastly, she attached the CO2 line to the port, pulled the spring-loaded firing mechanism back, which also jacked a ball into the chamber, and checked the laser sight. It was calibrated for thirty feet, which would put only her legs in view of the video cameras when she fired. Ready, she checked the time—three minutes to spare—drew in a deep breath, *Steady spirit,* and let it out slowly.

There was nothing left to do but wait until all hell broke loose.

At precisely 8:30, the Los Anarquistas Motorcycle Club sent a hacked driverless taxi careening into the front of the building. It hopped the curb, took out a bike rack, and hit the towering Armorglass windows at thirty mph without hitting a single pedestrian. The vehicle wasn't heavy, so it didn't quite smash through into the main lobby, which prevented any innocent bystanders from being injured, exactly as Empa had asked them to do. The impact sent guards and workers outside and inside scattering and set off multiple alarms.

The two armed security guards outside the main entrance reacted predictably, approaching the empty vehicle with their hands on their weapons, but the crash was only the beginning of the diversion. A high-speed parade of motorcycles howled down the avenue, gangers spraying the building with gunfire and screaming slogans for free speech, equal rights, and burning down Corporate NAFAS. Not a single bullet hit anyone, but the barrage sent the two guards to their bellies, and set off even more alarms, pulling every non-essential security guard from their posts to defend the frontal assault.

The distraction had cost Empa a hundred thousand NADs, half up front, and half to be deposited in the club's account at noon once the job was done. She hadn't even flinched at the expense, calling it money well spent.

As yellow lights flashed and alarms began sounding, Jeri leaned out, centered the laser light on the nearest security camera, and fired the paintball gun. The ball splashed black paint over the dome of the camera, obliterating the feed without damaging the device—which would have set off yet another alarm—and blinded the security feed that covered the express freight elevator.

"Easy peasy." She strode to the edge of the next camera's field, took aim and fired, blinding one of the cameras covering the loading dock.

"Hey, what are you doin'?" Two guys unloading a cargo van stared at her blankly, but she'd prepared for this.

She aimed her paintball at them and advanced. "Get in your van. Now!"

"That's not a real—"

Jeri shot him in the forehead with the paintball gun, pulled the taser from under her jacket, and shot the other in the chest. The first reeled, his eyes full of paint, and the second fell twitching to the concrete.

She changed the Taser cartridge, shot the first guy before he could recover, and had them on their stomachs, hands and legs zip-tied and mouths taped in a matter of seconds, but they were too heavy for her to lift into their van.

"Later. Finish the job, Jeri!" She reloaded her Taser, calmed her hammering heart with another deep breath, and moved.

Ten steps took her around a corner and put her on the edge of the field of view of the camera covering the loading dock office. One shot blinded that camera as well, then she tucked the paintball gun through her waistband and advanced. The man and woman inside weren't security, just logistical staff, but they had phones in the office. They stared at her dumbfounded as she approached the door. She smiled, pulled a fake badge from her pocket, and waved it at them.

"Security! There's an emergency!" That distracted them long enough for her to reach the door.

"Who the fuck are—" The man started to reach for something on his desk, but the door wasn't locked, so Jeri just opened it and shot him with her Taser.

The woman stared at her open-mouthed, eyes wide in terror as her coworker fell to a twitching heap.

Jeri leaned in, blinded the interior camera, and pointed the paintball gun at the woman's face. "On the floor!"

She didn't argue, dropped, and lay flat. The fact that Jeri had only tazed her partner, not killed him, might have expedited her compliance, or she didn't know what a paintball gun was, but Jeri didn't care. More cable ties and duct tape secured them in moments. She checked her watch and blinked in surprise; 8:33 a.m. Only three minutes had passed.

Time does weird things in your head in combat, Empa had warned her. *Don't get freaked out if you find half an hour has passed in the blink of an eye, or what seemed like an hour only lasted five minutes. It's your brain in survival mode. Just go with it and do the job.*

"Do the job, Jeri." She left the office, locking the door behind her, and cleared out the rest of the cameras until the entire loading area and freight elevators were blind.

She checked the time, 8:37, and looked toward the loading dock entrance. "Now all I need is the cavalry."

I watch through binoculars as a delivery truck passes through the security checkpoint. We've been on station for half an hour, and deliveries have slowed. Most food deliveries are finished by eight a.m., but there are always a few late arrivals, so we shouldn't raise any eyebrows.

"One minute," Gippy says from the driver's seat.

"What if your biker friends don't show?" Canción is anxious and overeager, a stallion chomping at the bit.

"Relax." I've told him not to play devil's advocate, but he can't resist. "If they don't show, we regroup and try again."

"They'll show," Gippy assures us. "Gangers got a rep to uphold, and this kinda gig is right up the LA's alley. They live for this shit. Oh, and they're not friends, they're business associates."

"Besides, they only get the second half of the cash after the job's done," I point out.

"But what if—" Canción shuts up as yellow lights begin flashing from the security checkpoint and three of the four guards dash for the building.

Sporadic gunfire echoes through the canyons of glass and steel, sounding like popcorn through my open window. I check my watch. The Los Anarquistas are right on time.

"The fertilizer has just hit the air conditioning," Gippy quips, shifting the van into gear. "Put on your party hats."

I hunker down with my baseball cap low and my weapon out of sight. Canción takes his position at the van's back doors. We each have our jobs to do, and Gippy's is the hardest, but his disguise is better than mine and my face is higher on their recognition list. They only have CG sketches of his and Canción's from our assault on Trenton's mansion, and while they're good, they're not perfect. If they get my picture before we can blind their cameras, the entire NAFAS security network will light up like a Christmas tree on Black Friday, and we're fucked.

We roll up to the gate and Gippy toggles down his window. The guard steps out of the shed waving us off, but Gippy plays his part to a tee.

"Whassup, bro?"

"No entry. There's an emergency." The guard takes a step closer, his hand on the grip of an M4 slung at his chest. "You'll have to come back later."

"Bro, I got twenty cases of shit in here that's gonna go bad by 'later.' We got two other deliveries to do this mornin' and we're already late!"

"Not my problem." He waves us back, glancing behind us. "Just pull back and—"

Gippy's Taser cracks, the prongs lodging in the guard's neck. It's not an optimal hit, but Grand Hope security all wear body armor, so a chest shot won't work. He spasms, and Gippy smacks the van's door into him, dropping the taser and pulling his paintball gun.

The moment he fires his Taser, I fire my paintball out my window at the high-angle camera and score a hit. Canción opens the back and fires at the rearview camera twice. Gippy steps on the twitching guard's weapon and paints the camera in the security shed with one shot.

The paintball guns were Jeri's idea, and I approved wholeheartedly. There are hundreds of cameras throughout the building, and most are monitored by computer algorithms, not people. Computers aren't as good as people at interpreting null-data, so we should have minutes before the outages are reported. We have to get inside before those minutes run dry.

Gippy and Canción grab the guard and haul him into the back of our van, while I override the gate and raise the rollup door into the loading dock garage. We're back in the van in less than twenty seconds. Gippy races down the ramp and through the gate, screeching to a stop inside the rollup. I paint another camera black, and Canción gets out to close the gate behind us.

I key my walkie-talkie. "We good, J?"

"Clear," she replies, and I can breathe again.

Sending her in alone had felt like putting my hand in a garbage disposal with someone else's finger on the switch, but we needed someone on the inside, and she was the logical choice. She also flatly refused to be left behind.

"Fuckin' A." Gippy guns the van as the back door slams closed, squealing tires through the loading area, and backs into the loading dock like a pro.

"'Bout time you got here," Jeri says as she hops down from the landing. "I need a hand putting these two heavy assholes in their truck."

I get out, kiss her, and survey her handiwork. "Nicely done!"

"Thanks." She blushes, which warms my cynical heart. "I feel like I'm getting good at this 'beating up men' thing. Thinking of a career as a dominatrix. Now help me with these two fat asses."

We load the two delivery men into the back of their truck, add the twitching security guard, and close the doors. We then change into security guard uniforms I bought from a local vendor. They even have the same patches as the Grand Hope security, and matching body armor and helmets. Buy three, get one free! What a deal! What we *don't* have is the RFID badges that the guards use to pass through security checkpoints. They're all keyed to individuals, so while using the gate guard's badge might open a door, it won't get through an ID checkpoint. Consequently, this is where things get dicey.

In less than a minute, we're changed and armed with the same standard M4 carbines and Colt sidearms the guards use. The weapons aren't my favorites, but they're serviceable, and since all the guards carry the same, we can resupply ammunition. Gippy's carbine is outfitted with his LAWS VR laser sight, which isn't standard issue and might draw some stares, but in the convoluted labyrinth of the building, shooting around corners will be invaluable. He also wears the guard's helmet with its integral radio set to their working frequencies, so we can hear their chatter. Jeri carries a long satchel over her back that holds door breeching charges, a few specialty explosives, and, of course, my katana. She refused to leave it behind, and in the close quarters of an office building, it might be better for her than a pistol. She's even rigged the bag with a zipper that will allow her to pull the blade without taking it off. At her hip, she wears a yellow-painted single-shot paintball gun that looks like a Taser, as well as the standard Colt. My Taser is real.

Ready, we call the secure express freight elevator using the guard's ID and wait. Canción fidgets, and I feel his emotions raging. Of the four of us, he has the least training, though more live fire experience than Jeri. Frankly, I feel more comfortable with her in a firefight than

I did with him in Cartagena, but I know he won't freeze when the shooting starts.

The doors finally open, and there's only one guard instead of the usual two, but his hand is on his weapon. His face visibly relaxes as he sees four people wearing uniforms and weapons identical to his own. His hand leaves the grip of his carbine to hover over the panel of buttons covering the top 70 of 150 floors.

"Where to?" he asks.

"One forty-eight," Gippy says as we get in, fumbling the security guard's RFID long enough for us to get into position. When he swipes it past the pad, however, the buttons of the top three floors flash red.

The guard blinks at him. "What's wrong with your—"

Jeri and I are behind him, and as she fires a paintball at the elevator camera pickup, I jam my Taser into the back of his neck. He goes down like a bridegroom's trousers on his wedding night, and Gippy has his ID before we can even tape his mouth and zip his hands and feet. When he swipes the guard's ID, however, the three top floors still blink red.

"Fuck." He looks at me askance.

"Plan-B." Evidently, not all security personnel have access to the restricted floors. We're prepared with contingencies for everything we could think of, and this is one we're ready for. "One forty-seven. We take the hard way up."

Canción and I grab the guard, pull him out of the elevator, and stash him in the loading dock office with the others. He's coming out of the effects of the Taser, so I take a moment to delve into his mind.

"Well?" Canción asks, trembling with expectation.

"Nothing. He's just a guard, not cleared for the secure levels. Doesn't know what goes on up there and doesn't care."

"Then how do we—"

"Not here!" I cut him off with a significant glance at the other two fully conscious workers staring at us. "We'll talk on the way up."

He glowers but follows me out.

When we get back, Jeri has already liberated a door charge from her pack and clipped it to her belt. Gippy pushes the button for 147, and we're on our way up. It only takes four minutes, our ears popping repeatedly, but it seems like an hour. Canción fidgets, and I tell him to relax, but he only glares.

"We'll find her. All we need is someone to interrogate. Stick to the plan."

"Be a duck," Jeri says. "Smooth on the surface but paddling like hell where nobody can see it."

He glares at her too.

"And remember, if you fuck this up by doing something stupid, I'll shoot you in the ass," Gippy adds.

Canción's face flushes, and he opens his mouth, but I intervene.

"Easy, now. Everyone just chill. We're right on schedule and have had *zero* serious problems so far." I pull out the radio transmitter that will detonate the EMP bomb in the back of our van. "Once we kill the power, we won't have to worry about alarms, comms, or cameras."

"Or elevators," Gippy adds. "It's a long way down."

"A long way to carry mom if she's..." Canción swallows hard enough for the rest of us to hear.

"We *find* her first," Gippy reminds him. "Three floors, and more than 100,000 square feet to search."

"We cross that bridge when we get there, Canción. Deep breaths. Steady spirit." I take my own advice, counting the floors as we soar into the heavens.

⁂

Joseph Miaka's phone vibrated in his pocket, and a yellow light began to strobe through his cavernous office. "Hold on," he told the members of his conference call, "There's some kind of emergency in the building." The Son of Samyaza pulled his phone and glared at the screen, but there were few details. His desk monitors were all occupied by the faces of sat-comm specialists from all over the globe, so he used his phone to call his personal assistant, Dema Sikal.

The woman's face appeared before the first ring tone even chimed.

"Sir?" Her large, dark eyes were wide, darting like fireflies as she scanned her own multi-screen displays.

"What's going on?"

"Emergency on the ground floor, sir."

"I know that, Dema. Give me details." The woman had a PhD in communications but sometimes seemed unable to communicate effectively. She was also one of the few humans on the planet who knew exactly what he did on a global scale, using information and misinformation to grind the hope of mankind into the dust. She did not, however, know what he truly was.

"Violent extremists have driven a vehicle into the front of the building and are firing weapons from the street, effectively pinning everyone inside. They're shouting the usual anti-NAFAS rhetoric, free speech, human rights, anti-fascist nonsense." Her nose wrinkled as if she'd just smelled flatulence. "We've called the authorities."

Free speech? Miaka tried to keep the smirk off his face. *Like that's even a thing anymore.* Violence in LA wasn't uncommon, but with his project on the cusp of success, he didn't like the timing of this seemingly random attack. "See that this nonsense is cleared up."

"Of *course*, sir," she replied with a 'Well duh!' tone, which meant she was already doing it and didn't need his help.

He ended the call, but his phone vibrated again before he could return it to his pocket. A glance and he gritted his teeth. "I should have sent that ass back to West Virginia!" He answered the call. "There's an emergency at street level, Renquist. It's being taken care of."

"What kind of emergency?" The Son of Armaros, Angel of Unmaking, wasn't the type to be put off. He had done as ordered, donating the seed to inseminate Terpsichore, but then refused to leave, insisting on staying long enough to see his progeny.

The senior Nephilim on Earth gritted his teeth again. *If I have to deal with this dimwit for eight more months, I'll kill his host myself!* "A mob of extremists with no means to do anyone inside any real harm, so forget it. Local authorities will clean up the mess." He twisted his neck and adjusted his collar, forcing calm. "We're quite invulnerable up here. There's nothing to fear."

The Son of Armaros shot him a sour look at the insult. Nephilim didn't fear anything. "You've always been such an arrogant fuck, Miaka."

Refusing to rise to the bait, he severed the call and returned to the pedantic nonsense of his business. He longed for the day when he could wipe this whole planet clean and receive his just reward for millennia of faithful service. A seat beside his father at the right hand of the Father of Lies; a billion years of glory and just reward... *And perhaps some payback for all those who doubted my greatness.* That day was coming soon.

He returned to the video conference call. "Now, ladies and gentlemen, where were—"

Then the lights went out.

18

BASTION OF HATE

Empa was avoiding cameras, so Canción took the lead as they stepped out of the elevator onto the 147th floor. At first impression, they'd emerged into a shipping and receiving office, complete with a reception desk. Two receptionists sat behind it wearing company blues with the logo for Transmedia emblazoned on their chests. A single tired-looking security guard stood behind them with his thumbs in his belt. A spare pallet jack and several delivery carts were lined up to their left, and a pair of wide double doors stood closed beyond the desk. The receptionists glanced up, clearly bored, and went back to work. The guard cocked a questioning eyebrow.

"Checking stairwells," Canción said, trying to sound official. "We had some reports of—"

And right on cue, the lights flickered out, because Empa had activated the UHF radio transmitter that detonated the EMP bomb in their van.

"What the hell?" the security guard spat as the battery-powered emergency lighting clicked on.

The two receptionists' owlish eyes reflected in the diffuse light, the guard equally wide-eyed. Muffled shouts sounded from behind closed doors.

"Check your comms!" Canción strode for the nearest of the building's four stairwells with the others close behind. "They've cut the power!"

"Cut the power? How the hell could they cut the power?" The guard sounded incredulous, as if the laws of radio telecommunications and electricity wouldn't dare to ruin his day by being so rude as to fail.

"That's why you're getting on your radio, numb-nuts! Find out what the hell happened and report it!" They were through the double doors and around the nearest corner before the guy even tried to call.

"Well, the EMP didn't get this far," Gippy offered, which was obvious with the emergency lighting still working.

"Let's hope it disabled the door locks," Jeri said.

She sounded steadier than Canción felt. "How long do you think before they start evacuating?"

"A while. Elevators will be down. They'll have to send someone down the stairs, then back up with any information. That's maybe fifty floors, depending on—" Empa fell silent as people began coming out of doors along the hallway, shouting questions, some fully panicked.

Canción began shouting for calm, ordering people back in their offices. "We're trying to figure out what happened! Just calm down and talk to your supervisors!"

That didn't calm anyone, but it at least cleared the hallway. They ignored the grumbling employees and picked up the pace. They reached the nearest stairwell and hurried through the door. Emergency lights glowed at every other corner, so they started up. The security guard's helmet radio began squawking before they reached the next floor, a cacophony of voices demanding answers that nobody had.

"The security guards aren't much calmer than the workers." Gippy turned the volume down but kept it on, just in case they heard something interesting.

"Confusion to our enemies," Empa said. "There is no greater gift."

Canción waited at the landing for the others to form up, then tried the latch. It rotated, but the door wouldn't open no matter how hard he pulled. "It's locked."

"I thought they were supposed to unlock when the power went out," Jeri said.

"They are, which means they either have some kind of backup power, or the builders violated construction codes." Empa tried the latch but had no better luck.

"Should we try the next one up?" Gippy asked.

"They're probably the same. Safety protocols require no more than four floors between unlocked doors for emergency reentry, but there are only three high-security floors, so they could keep them all locked and still be legal." She peered at the edge of the door, top and bottom, and frowned. "They have electric strike locks, but the mechanism's on the other side. We'll have to blow the hinges."

"What in the name of…" Miaka's monitors and every indicator on his desk's elaborate comm system went out with the lights. Only the emergency strobes continued working.

Cursing in half a dozen dead languages, he pulled his phone, which had a signal, and tapped Sikal's icon. Her face came up, but a shaky hand view instead of her desk monitor. "What's happened?"

"I don't know yet, sir. No comms below the sixtieth floor. Even cell phones and radios are out. The emergency generators should—"

The lights flicked back on, and his desk began to reboot.

"Emergency power has been restored to secure floors, sir. The battery backup for the servers protected them, but the network's rebooting. I'm sending security personnel down to find out what's happened."

"Elevators?"

"Except for three that were above sixty, they're non-functional." Her eyes flicked away from the phone, obviously checking her monitors, which must have been on a battery backup. "Numbers six, four, and number two freight elevator are still working. The others aren't responding to the system reboot."

That didn't sound right. Even if someone cut power to the entire building, the emergency generators would reboot critical systems, including elevators. And what could affect hand-held radios, cell phones, and computers on every floor below sixty? Electronic warfare wasn't his bailiwick, but this was more than a bunch of rowdy bikers firing guns at the building and shouting slogans. This was sophisticated.

"Get me information. This is more than a simple extremist attack. I'm on the move." He rose and strode for the door. Halfway there, he stopped, then changed direction to an impressive wet bar set into a black marble credenza. Pulling open a drawer, he lifted the inset rack of silver swizzle sticks and slipped the custom Walther PPK/S from its velvet bed. He dropped it in the pocket of his jacket. Two magazines went in the other pocket, which balanced the hang of his suit nicely. He checked his appearance in the mirror behind the bar, straightened his lapels, and headed for the door.

Two guards stationed outside—standard operating procedure during any emergency—fell in at his heels without him having to say a word. As he barged through the double doors to the private residence, four more at the security station snapped to attention.

"Call me an elevator."

"Yes, sir." A man tapped the console. "The system's still reinitializing. It'll be up in less than five minutes."

Five minutes... Hell could fall from the sky in five minutes. His phone vibrated again, but it was that prick Son of Armaros. He ignored it. "Stairs. I need to get to one forty-nine."

"This way, sir." One of his personal guards gestured to the left of the bank of elevators.

He spotted the emergency exit sign and followed. The man held the stairwell door for him, and his Gucci loafers echoed off the steel steps as he descended one floor, the rumble of combat boots following close behind. The door was secured, but his watch ID unlocked it as he reached for the handle. A squad of security guards on patrol lowered their weapons and snapped to attention, spouting apologies for aiming guns at the CEO.

He ignored them and strode toward the lab situated on the south side of the building. There was another security station with four more guards stationed at the lab entrance, but they recognized him and stepped aside.

"Stay here," he told his escort, not breaking stride as he barged through the doors.

The Daughter of Yomyael looked up at him as if surprised. "Yes? What is it?"

"There's an emergency in the building, and something's knocked out all electronics below the sixtieth floor, so we don't know exactly what happened yet." He glanced around, but everything seemed completely normal; computer systems and medical monitors functioning perfectly. "Don't tell me you didn't *notice* the power outage."

She shrugged. "There *was* no power outage here. We're on centralized battery backup. I noticed that silly yellow strobe flashing, but..." Her brow knitted. "You said something knocked out *electronics*, not just power?"

"Yes, throughout the lower third of the building." He looked at Terpsichore, strapped into her zero-feedback cushion sarcophagus, her head immobilized in a halo brace and VR system that covered her eyes and ears. Her mouth was filled with a black rubber block, a tube inserted through it to supply nutrients. Monitors displayed an array of wavy lines and numbers, most of which meant nothing to him. "How is she progressing?"

"Getting there." The daughter of madness smiled like a ghoul over a fresh corpse. "Implantation was fully successful, hormone levels are changing accordingly, and the combination of drugs and direct neuro-stimulus coupled with virtual visual and auditory augmentation has pushed her very close to a psychotic break. Her EEGs are becoming erratic. We've established the perfect balance of mental trauma without physical damage. Once she breaks, she'll tell us anything we ask for."

The last sentence was the only thing that made sense to him and told him everything he needed to know. "Good. Keep at it. We'll get this cleared up and—" His phone vibrated again, this time his assistant, Sikal. "Yes?"

"We have radio contact with our security team on the ground floor. The assault from outside has ended, and the militants have fled. NAFAS police are on the scene. Everything electronic is dead down there, and there are reports of some kind of explosion on the loading dock, but no sign of blast damage. They've found people bound and gagged, and security cameras painted black. Someone's gotten into the building and *apparently* fired some kind of EMP."

"EMP?" He remembered the reports from Trenton's house, all electronics destroyed, four kidnappers posing as talent scouts hauling Trenton out after he collapsed. Authorities had reported that the electronic surveillance and storage drives were destroyed without any signs of external damage, and even cell phones didn't work. Analysis had concluded that some kind of electromagnetic pulse had fried everything, even destroying video records of the perpetrators. There had been speculation about militant anti-pornography terrorists, which wouldn't have been the first assassination attempt on his incubus conduit, but nothing had been corroborated.

First Trenton, now here, and both use EMPs. This couldn't be a coincidence. "There are terrorists in the building. All security on high alert." Then another piece of the puzzle clicked into his mind. "They're coming *here*, probably to interfere in our special project. Lock down the top three floors."

"Security is already organizing an evacuation, as per standard protocol when there's a bomb involved, sir," she informed him.

The Son of Samyaza gritted his teeth. "Cancel that for all security personnel! Send everything we've got to cover the top three floors. Let the local cops deal with evacuating non-security personnel. Do it now!"

"There aren't enough elevators functioning to bring all of our security up to—"

"Then bring up all you can and let the rest climb the fucking *stairs*! Now!"

"Yes, sir." The call ended.

He turned back to the Daughter of Yomyael, but she was already back to her monitors, immersed in a single-minded assault on the mind of Terpsichore. He left her to her work. Someone was coming here, and he had to organize a defense.

"It'll be noisy." Jeri stepped forward to place a plastic-wrapped shaped charge on the lowest hinge, pleased that her hands weren't shaking, then reached into her bag for another. The ride up the elevator had been the worst part, trapped in a box in a tower full of naffies. Blowing the door hinges would bring them all running like rats to rotten meat.

They'd all read the manuals on the little charges, just in case she couldn't do her job, which really meant injured or dead. Empa's little euphemisms that avoided stating the grim truth were more irritating than helpful, but she couldn't exactly tell her she was full of shit. Each charge had peel-and-stick adhesive for easy application to virtually any surface, and the plastique could be molded to fit any shape. The glue would stick your fingers to the explosive permanently if you touched it, so she pressed it to the hinge with the palm of her hand, and pulled the tiny string that solidified the polymer that lined the back of the charge, directing the blast forward. They were shaped to cut through metal with minimal collateral damage, which meant they shouldn't blow scraps of shredded steel back at them. They'd tested one on a burned-out car's engine block, and Jeri thought they were the coolest thing since the double-ended dildo.

"And there may be guards right on the other side," Gippy said, as if they needed more to worry about.

"No choice." Empa took a step back and drew her pistol as Jeri placed the second charge. "We need to find out where Cora's being kept, and to do that, we need to interrogate someone who knows."

That meant delving into someone's mind, which also meant a live prisoner, but Jeri doubted the guards on these floors would know anything more than the one she'd interrogated on the loading dock. As she finished with the third charge, they all took their assigned positions beside the door, weapons at the ready. Empa and Gippy would go through first, which was fine with her.

Jeri flicked the shielded detonator activation switches on all three charges and stepped around Canción. "Fire in the hole!" She pressed a button on a little transmitter at her belt, used the three-second delay to cup her hands over her ears, and the charges blew the hinges to bits.

Before the deafening echo even died, Empa and Gippy kicked the door at the same time. The bottom of the door swung inward, and the striker bar at the top slipped out of the lock, allowing the heavy slab of double-walled steel to slam against the floor. Secrecy was now a moot point.

"The fuck?" Gippy hissed, and the reason for his expletive needed no explanation.

Light shone through the smoking doorway from long LED ceiling panels. Unlike those below, this floor had power.

"They must have backup power. Move!" Empa snapped, and she and Gippy advanced with guns raised, Empa high, Gippy low, covering both sides.

"Clear!" Empa announced.

"Clear!" Gippy echoed, and they went through.

Jeri and Canción followed, and he holstered his pistol in favor of the carbine. Jeri pulled her pistol, but also reached over her shoulder to unzip the top of her pack, allowing easy access to Empa's katana.

The stairwell came out in an L of two hallways, one straight toward where the freight elevator would be, and another to their right. Also, unlike the lower floors, they had no maps for these levels. Even construction blueprints had been blank, the victim of Joseph Miaka's multi-billion NAD security measures. They had no information on these floors except for a few photos of his personal living space posted on Lifestyles of the Ridiculously Wealthy websites and Walker Trenton's memories. The positions of elevators, stairwells, plumbing, and the void for the building's earthquake counterweight, which took up the center of the five floors below 150, would be the same as below, but they had no idea what else these floors were allocated to.

At least the halls aren't full of guards pointing guns at us, Jeri thought, but the noise of the door charges would undoubtedly draw attention.

Gippy's stolen radio crackled as if to emphasize that last point. "Loud noise from the southwest corner. Sounded like an explosion or gunfire. Sending a team."

"Heard that on one forty-nine," another voice confirmed. "Sounded like the stairwell."

"Secure the southwest stairwell," the first voice ordered.

"Go right." Empa holstered her pistol and waved Canción forward to the point position. They all followed suit, and he took the lead. "Follow the plan. We're investigating the noise, just like every other goon on the floor. We find someone to interrogate, locate Cora, get her, and get the *fuck* out."

That sounded good to Jeri, so she kept her mouth closed and followed along.

They hadn't gone far when a door opened and a woman in a corporate power suit stepped out. "You! What was that noise?"

"An explosion in the stairwell. We're investigating." Canción had practiced long and hard to sound like a security guard, and seemed to be pulling it off. "Have you seen anything unusual?"

"No, other than the power going out and costing us a day's worth of work! What's going on?"

"You didn't get the evacuation order?" He spared a glance to Empa, raising an eyebrow in a silent question, but she shook her head.

"Well, yes, but then it was canceled, which you well know." She looked him up and down. "You *should* know that."

"I do, ma'am, but I had no idea if *you* did." Canción put a little steel into his tone, which elicited an almost comical frown from the woman. "Return to your work and follow any announcements that come over the network."

"Well!" She retreated into the office, and Jeri glimpsed a dim interior, rows of desks with monitors, and a huge split screen displaying dozens of images of people and places. The door slammed, and they continued on.

"Why not interrogate her?" Canción asked in a low voice.

"She was in data manipulation, not anything to do with Cora that I could see," Empa replied. "We need someone who knows what's going on *here*, not in China."

"Fine." He continued along, his volatile temper intact, at least until they blundered around a corner into another security detail.

As Miaka barged through the doors from the lab, a tremor shook the building, and the guards' radios all began squawking about an explosion.

"Where? What floor?" Miaka asked the chief of the security station.

"Not sure yet, sir, but it sounded like the southwest stairwell, opposite side of the building. We're sending teams to check it."

"We don't have enough security personnel to—"

With a "Ding!" the elevator right in front of the security station opened, and every guard raised a weapon. That included the nine guards in the elevator.

"Stand down!" the chief barked, and rifles were lowered. "Three of you newcomers in each direction. Check the stairwells. The rest of you reinforce this station. Did you leave any people on one forty-eight?"

"Yes, sir. Three." The officer in charge of the detail gave orders, and trios of guards clattered off in both directions.

"Hold the elevator!" Miaka commanded, striding forward, his personal guards close behind. "I'm taking it up." He wanted nothing to do with stairs if there were explosions. "And find out how the hell someone got past our security!"

19

FROM HELL'S HEART

Fucking hell!" The leader of the guard detail's hand relaxes on the grip of his carbine. "You scared the shit out of me. Where did you come from?"

I lower my pistol and holster it, thanking my father's mother that I didn't put a bullet in the guard's forehead out of reflex. I'm in combat mode, which is dangerous when we should still be in deception mode. *Steady state, Empa...*

"Up from one forty-seven," Canción says, defaulting to the truth. "Heard a hell of a bang and came up. The stairwell door's fragged."

"Why didn't you report it?" another of the three asks, clearly still suspicious at the arrival of four guards they don't recognize, two of them women, which are rare in Grand Hope's security force.

"Radios are out." Canción doesn't sound as convincing this time. "You didn't hear about that?"

"That's only below sixty." The leader's hand returns to his carbine. "Who's your section chief?"

I see this going bad and move to Canción's right, my hands relaxed, watching the barrels of their weapons. All three are handling their carbines, which isn't smart this close, but typical of the average soldier to rely on the more powerful primary weapon.

"We *were* below sixty," Canción responds tersely. "We were sent up here on orders. Don't get your panties in a wad!"

"You said you were up from one forty-seven!" the leader takes a step back, and I can sense Gippy tensing. "And who's your fucking section chief?"

Canción raises both hands. "Everyone just calm down."

I feel it this time, the thrill of his gift up my spine like a strain of music in my head. All three of the guards faces suddenly change, apprehension, fear, anger, suspicion all gone in a blink. Their hands relax on their weapons again.

"Our chief's name is Howard," Canción tells the leader. "We were on the fiftieth when—"

Canción's pulse of energy hits them like a linebacker, staggering all three. I wasn't expecting that, but I learned a long time ago to take any opportunity given to me. I'm moving more quickly than they can recover, stepping up to the guard on the leader's right. One hand blocks him from raising his rifle while the other jams the muzzle of my Colt into him just below his body army, angled up. The muzzle blast is muffled against him and sounds like someone dropping a heavy book. His eyes bulge, mouth gaping, and he goes down. Gippy uses a K-bar I didn't even see him pull, stabbing twice in the groin, then again into the man's throat as his legs fold. Canción goes old-school, slamming a fist into the leader's nose. Already dazed, the blow's enough to knock him down, if not out. My foot comes down on the man's carbine before he can recover, and my pistol's at his neck.

"Wait!" Canción's hand is on my shoulder. "We need information."

He's right, and I hate that he's thinking more clearly than I am. Combat mode took over once again, the reflexes of ten thousand fights, a thousand battles, hundreds of wars blinding me to everything but kill or be killed. *Northern Syria, house-to-house combat, men, women, and children forced by ISIL to wear explosives and act as human shields. My crosshairs on tear-streaked faces...* But he's right; we need a prisoner.

"One word and your brains go bye-bye." I press the muzzle of my pistol under his chin, and he nods frantically, blood dribbling from his smashed nose.

Gippy disarms him, while Canción shakes his injured hand. His blow did almost as much damage to his knuckles as it did to the man's face. I should teach him not to strike with a closed fist, but now's hardly the time.

"We're gonna have company soon." Jeri applies duct tape to the guard's mouth and zip-ties to his wrists. "Someone's found the stairwell door."

Shouts from behind us confirm her claim. I look for an exit, but there isn't one, and we need time, at least a minute or so. There are, however, many locked doors, and each one has an ID scanner. "Get IDs. Help me get him up."

Gippy snatches the chip cards from the guards' belts, and Canción and I hoist the man up. The other two are bleeding all over the Transmedia logo carpet, but there's nothing we can do about that.

I nod to a nearby door. "There. If they find the bodies, they'll assume we kept going. Don't track any blood. This should give us a minute."

Gippy taps the guard's ID and the door lock blinks green. We're through the door in a rush. The lighting is dim, and six astonished Transmedia technicians stare at us in terror. One draws a breath to scream.

"Everyone just relax," Canción says, and I feel the trickle of his gift once again.

The fear drains from their faces, and I feel only calm curiosity, which I find *really* creepy. "Just stay seated and keep your hands away from your keyboards." They sit in an arc of workstations, each with two curved screens. "Jer, cut the cabling and destroy their phones and IDs. Gip, watch them. Can, close the door and help me put this heavy asshole in a chair."

Everyone complies, Jeri taking great pleasure in putting her sword to use on the network cables. The screens go dark, and the workers' fear slowly returns as she rifles them for electronics, katana still in her other hand. We prop up the guard, and I bend over to fix his eyes with mine.

"We're not going to hurt you unless you give us a reason to. Do you understand?"

He nods so frantically it looks like a seizure.

"Now, I need you to tell me about a woman who was brought here. A special woman who they probably called a terrorist. They'll be holding her in some sort of medical facility. Where is she?"

The man mumbles something behind the duct tape, but I don't need him to speak. All I need is for him to think about my questions. I dive into the pool of his mind and see his life in a flash: military, brush wars, atrocities, payment under the table, and a promised career with Transmedia to keep him quiet, a husband and mother he's support-ing... And there, right on the surface, is all he knows about Cora, and all the rumors circulating among the security personnel about her, Miaka's interest, and the creepy Dr. Feriday conducting the medical procedures.

"She's one floor up in a medical lab." I pull out of his mind, and notice that Jeri's been liberal with the duct tape and cable ties. The workers won't be spreading any rumors about us until we're long gone. "Gip, check the hall. When it's clear, we head for the southeast stairwell and go up."

"Excellent!" Gippy cracks the door just wide enough to see what's going on, and we form up behind him. "Clear! Go, go, go!"

We exit and race on down the hall. The bodies of the guards have been moved, and there are bloody footprints heading the same direc-tion we're going. We miraculously reach the stairwell without running into another patrol, though a bank of elevators and a security checkpoint loom around the corner. I glimpse black-clad guards, but their attention is on the checkpoint, accusations and epithets flying back and forth. They don't notice us as we slip into the stairwell, but as the door closes quietly behind us, I know our luck won't last much longer.

Flames surround me, then ice, then nothing but the screams and discordant laughter of tortured souls. Heat, cold, pain, pleasure, and ceaseless noise. I know it's not real, just electrodes they've inserted into my brain, VR images, and sounds, but I can't make it not feel real, not *sound* real, even smell real, and the horrific images playing before my eyes are all too real.

I'm in Hell.

Demons play with the souls of the damned in ways that make me physically ill. The souls can't die, but they can be shredded, roasted, devoured, violated in ten thousand ways, then reconstituted to be tortured again. As can mine.

I haven't slept in days. For all I know, this *is* real, some technological connection through the mind of a demon into a window to the dark realm. I know for certain, or at least the shred of sanity I cling to knows, that I'm not really there. I can't be. I am the daughter of Israfal, Angel of Music, who plays at God's right hand. I'll be called to Heaven when I die. I'm more certain of that than anything else in my existence.

When I die... That moment replays in my sleep-deprived mind: *the revolver in my hand raising, then the gunshot and my arm jerking, bone shattering.* I was denied that escape. Such an easy trap, the bait so convincing, an unknowing pawn sacrificed for the opponent's queen... me.

Pain again, and the leering face of a demon feasting on my flesh and laughing.

Not real, not real... And yet, I can't tell anymore what's real and what isn't. I cling to that tattered shred of my sanity and plead, *Please, Father, take me home. Your daughter has spread your love through millions of human souls. I am deserving of release. Please...*

Deliverance.

The booming voice isn't real, or it is and I'm really damned and Hell is reading my thoughts. A figure appears amid the sea of tortured souls, beautiful and terrible, wings black as night spanning the sky, eyes like stars in a tapestry of samite. The sound of those wings is a hurricane at sea—*a flash memory, 1715 aboard the* Gryphon, *the sole surviving ship as the storm drove the others ashore on the unforgiving Florida coast... Delivered from the jaws of death...* This time, I see no deliverance, for I know this creature, the fallen star, Lucifer.

God's brightest angel looms down, grinning a forest of gleaming sabers, Morningstar eyes glowing like beacons in a midnight sky. He reaches for me, and I am torn from my chains. The maw of the Lord of the Fallen gapes, and I am plunged into that cavern of darkness...

Nothingness engulfs me.

No pain, no vision, no sound, no sensation whatsoever... I am nothing. I am gone. Oblivion... and my tattered mind reaches for something, anything to grasp.

But there is nothing.

I can't even scream as my soul shatters into a million-million irreparable shards.

Then, from the nothingness, a strain of music, sweet and simple, a child's voice humming a tune no human could ever have contrived. Heartbreaking and lonely, but joyful and loving all at once. I know that song... that voice... but from where?

I grasp at the song like a lifeline thrown from a ship with the only thing I have left, the only thing I ever had, my love for music, and that voice, the voice I know so well. My very own song. *Mi Canción...* The simple, loving, lonely tune plays over me like rippling crystalline water in a stream, soothing my torment, massaging my soul, taking all the shattered pieces of me downstream into a calm pool of love.

20

SONG OF INSANITY

Far below, down the zigzagging stairwell, boots rumbled on metal, voices echoing, a *lot* of them.

Canción looked to Empa. "I thought you said they would evacuate."

"The civilians," she explains. "Evidently, our presence has drawn reinforcements. With luck, the backup generators will boot up the elevators, at least the ones that were above sixty, so we'll have a way down."

"Lucky, lucky," Gippy muttered.

Canción could feel their bridled tension, the tight control, Empa's steady spirit, and it calmed him slightly. "Then we go up."

"We gotta *move*, E," Gippy added, taking the lead. "We got maybe ten minutes before we up to our dicks in naffies."

"I took the layout from the guard," Empa said as they reached the door. "There's a checkpoint by the elevator bank to our right. If they're calling reinforcements from below, there may be more than we bargained for. The entrance to the lab is across from the other elevator bank on the other side of the building."

"The lab doesn't have a back door?" Jeri asked.

"No, the center of the building's taken up by a pendulum damper

181

to stabilize the building during earthquakes. We have to go around, and the checkpoint's in our way."

"It doesn't matter." Impatience gnawed at Canción like a dog worrying a bone, the energy from the emotions he'd absorbed begging to be released. They were too close now for anything to get in their way. "We go through them. This is taking too long."

"I'm just saying that this will get ugly. There's no chance to be subtle or bluff our way past. We get close and hit them hard." She nodded to him and swiped her stolen ID card. "Canción, you're on point."

He nodded and flipped the fire selector on his carbine from semi to auto. Empa turned the handle, and he went through first, his hands open and empty at his sides, as unthreatening as possible. Empa and Gippy flanked him on both sides, and Jeri walked right behind him.

Music ran through his mind, the thrill of a twelve-string guitar picked by a virtuoso, the tune unmistakable. *Mother... She's here!*

The checkpoint took up the entire hallway, two Armorglass-protected stations with a turnstile between them. They would pass three elevators before they reached it, and there were eight guards at the station, two in the open and three on each side behind the glass. Their eyes were already on him.

He banished the melody from his mind and nodded amiably to the guards. "We're up from sixty. Comms are out down there. What the hell's going on?"

"Terrorists in the building. Miaka thinks they're coming here to steal his special project." One of the two guards in the open gestured to the card reader turnstile. "Protocols have been opened for all GHS personnel. Just scan in and take up positions."

"Just don't tell me to climb any more fucking stairs." The quip elicited smiles, but the moment he swiped his stolen ID, the system bleeped a discordant note.

Their smiles vanished. "What's wrong with—"

"ID mismatch!" A guard to the right snapped, and all eight reached for weapons.

Standing at the turnstile, he was beyond the Armorglass barrier, so

Canción drew in all their fear, anger, and hostility in one quick breath, and blasted the entire right-hand station. The wave of energy caught the nearest man square in the face, snapping his head back so hard that vertebrae shattered and his helmet flew off. The other three were smashed back into the wall, the one who'd been sitting flying off his chair.

Gippy unloaded from his left, catching the man standing at the turnstile before he could draw his pistol. Slugs impacted his groin, stomach, chest, and head, only the first and last penetrating the body armor, but more than enough to put him down. Empa flew over the gate to his right, firing into the other three before she hit the ground in a roll. Jeri dodged far left and sprayed bullets into the Armorglass with her M4. The salvo didn't penetrate, but it sure got the attention of the guards. Those who weren't hit by Empa's fire dropped to the floor.

As Canción whirled left, bringing his own M4 to bear, something slammed into his body armor. His ears rang in E-flat, and he staggered back. His finger slipped on the grip of the carbine and the weapon discharged through the desk of the security station, three rounds before he could get his finger off the trigger. Pain lanced through his left bicep, but his knees didn't fold.

Empa stopped firing and reloaded, and Gippy grabbed the collar of Canción's armored jacket to pull him back. By the time Canción's ass hit the floor, both Gippy and Empa were firing on the guards he'd knocked senseless. Before he could get back up, it was over.

"Reload and move! Cameras have us, and my face is probably setting off every alarm in the building." Empa snatched a magazine from a fallen guard to replace her own. "Canción, how bad are you hit?"

"Not bad. I—" He touched his left bicep and his fingers came away bloody, but he could move his arm, albeit painfully. "A graze, and my ribs hurt."

"Let me stop the bleeding." She stepped over to place a hand on his, and the pain in his arm eased. "You were lucky. Jeri, you okay?" She moved past him to Jeri's side.

"Uh, yeah, but…" She was trying to reload her carbine, but couldn't fit the magazine in. "Can't stop shaking, and my ears are ringing. I don't know why… I was fine, and then…"

"You're okay. You did well." Empa touched her cheek, and Jeri seemed to calm. "Come on. They know who we are, where we are, and where we're going. It's going to get harder from here."

Jeri nodded, managed to fit the magazine in, and chambered a round.

"And thank you," Canción added. "Your distraction ruined their aim and probably saved my life." He didn't know if it was true or not, but she smiled and nodded, and he felt her emotions lift, steadying. She was afraid, but he knew better than to ask if she wanted him to take it away. They were in this together, and fear was a necessary survival instinct.

He followed Empa, relying on her to take the lead now. His ears were still ringing, but he could hear the music through the tinnitus, flawless improvisation, unmistakably his mother's. He paused and put a hand on Empa's shoulder. "I can… *hear* her."

"Cora?" Empa looked at him dubiously. "Her voice?"

"No, her music." He cocked his head and pointed at the left-hand wall. "That way."

<hr>

The Son of Samyaza stopped pacing the priceless Asian rug to tatters at the chime from his desk. He stabbed the tab on his chair's armrest that opened the live call from Sikal without sitting down. "Talk to me."

"There's… a disturbance on one forty-nine, sir. Gunfire. One of the security stations was attacked by four people wearing Grand Hope Security uniforms." She was pale, and her voice shook. "They're… all dead, sir."

"They *who*? The terrorists or the guards?"

"The guards, sir. They…" She swallowed, and he saw her terror.

"The video shows one of the terrorists, a tall man, doing something that knocked several men flat. I don't know how, but..."

"Show me!"

"Yes, sir." Her distraught face vanished and a video without sound came up, or rather four videos in four windows on one screen, each showing the same security station from a different angle.

Four uniformed guards came into view, a tall man in the fore, then two slimmer figures, a man and woman, and an even smaller woman behind with a satchel over her shoulders. The tall one scanned an ID, and the other guards reacted as if something's wrong, hands on weapons. In response, the leader raised his hands, and the others seemed to relax, then he turned to his right and the view in front of him distorted, as if some kind of shockwave distorted the air. The nearest guard's head snapped back like he was hit in the face with a baseball bat, and the other three were flung against the wall.

"What the..." The force of the shockwave came from nowhere, and there was no recoil, as if the man had simply shouted them to death.

Then all hell broke loose, multiple people firing. One woman dove over the turnstile with the grace of a gymnast, firing a pistol as she flew. The other woman sprayed an entire magazine into the Armor-glass barrier. The tall man in the fore was hit, but the other man pulled him back. It was over in seconds, all the guards down, the four terrorists regrouping. Then the nimble woman's face came into one of the camera's fields.

"Freeze that!" the Nephilim barked.

The image froze, slightly blurry but clear enough. He'd seen that face too many times not to recognize her immediately. "Empa!"

"Yes, sir," Sikal confirmed. "Facial recognition has verified that this is the terrorist fugitive responsible for the rebellion in St. Louis, the attack in Manhattan, and probably the one in Cartagena. Two of the others match descriptions given to authorities after the assault on Walker Trenton's home two weeks ago. The other woman isn't in our database."

The Nephilim's mind spun. Empa and Terpsichore, the last two living Ageless on Earth, were both in the building. He pulled up the best frame of the man who had blasted the guards with a shout: chiseled features, blue eyes, fair completion... *Terpsichore!* The resemblance couldn't be denied. This was the anomaly, the son of Heaven and Hell, who could destroy demons and Nephilim utterly. This was Canción.

Something he had not felt in five thousand years surged through the Son of Samyaza. Fear was an emotion Nephilim weren't accustomed to; immortality had wiped it from their psyches. But this was the sole creature in the universe who could reputedly send his very essence to oblivion; no exile to Hell, no respawning into another human host, just... forever nothingness. He knew that fear now, and his indomitable pride quailed in the face of obliteration.

He ended the call and pulled his phone from his inside jacket pocket, activating an application that he never thought he would use. It was theatrically named the "Armageddon Protocol." The app opened and displayed three fingerprint locked options: "Disable" "Arm" and "Exit." He tapped "Arm", which opened a new window with only three more options: "Disarm" "Detonate" and "Exit." His finger hovered over the middle option.

One tap would detonate charges on the suspension struts that supported a six-hundred-ton earthquake pendulum occupying the center of the building beneath him. The weight would fall straight down through the entire building and into the foundations of the building, impacting on a solid block of reinforced concrete set into bedrock. With nowhere else to go, the impact would blast outward, creating a half-mile diameter crater into which the Grand Hope Tower would collapse.

He and the two other Nephilim would die, but he would take Terpsichore, Empa, and Canción with them. He and his Hell-spawned cousins would respawn, and the War of Souls would be over.

You could win it all, he thought, his finger trembling, *but you would only see your victory through the eyes of a child.*

He tapped "Disarm" and exited the app. It wasn't cowardice, just the opposite in fact. He would face this creature, Canción, and destroy him, then spawn an army from both Terpsichore and Empa. His reward in Hell would be eternal and glorious.

He tapped a sequence on his desk, activating a monitor in the lab. "Dr. Feriday, the terrorists are on your floor. They're coming after Terpsichore. Pull the plug and bundle her—"

"Not now!" the daughter of the mad angel snapped. "She's in sense-dep, and her EEGs are highly erratic. She's breaking. We'll have everything we need from her in a matter of *minutes!*"

"You'll be up to your ass in gunfire in minutes! Pull the plug and evac her to the roof. I'm calling in my helicopter." His fingers danced on the keyboard, executing the evacuation protocol. The hilo would carry a dozen besides the flight crew. He and his prize could be in the air in fifteen minutes. *Maybe two prizes*, he considered, *if we get lucky with Empa.* But a bird in hand was worth two in the bush, and he could blow the building to smithereens the moment they took off. "Do it now!"

"You don't understand! If I pull her out of the simulation now, she could go catatonic!"

"I don't fucking *care!*" He could hear the staccato pop-pop of gunfire over the laboratory audio feed. If that wouldn't get this insane idiot moving, he knew what would. "Terpsichore's *son* is here!"

"Canción?" The Daughter of Yomyael's eyes widened with fear and madness, then narrowed in cold calculation. "We have them all! Institute the Armageddon Protocol!"

Armageddon... The option loomed once again, but two decades before he could reap his rewards, versus two decades to create an army that would corrupt the rest of mankind with the progeny of Terpsichore. This coward wanted to throw it all away.

Pride reasserted itself, supplanting his fear. "Not yet! Get Terpsichore to the roof, now. She's the key; she's carrying the weapons Hell will use to corrupt all of mankind! If we institute the protocol, it'll be *centuries* before we succeed without them!"

"Your *pride* will be our annihilation, Son of—"

The building shuddered, thunder echoing through the hallways. There could be only one reason: The Son of Terpsichore had come for vengeance. He ended the call and stabbed his desk monitors to life. He needed data to mount an effective defense against this menace.

"Time to raise some Hell, Jeri." I duck back from the spray of gunfire coming from the security troops. There's about sixty feet between the corner I'm hiding behind and the corner they're hiding behind, too far to run it without being riddled with bullets, and even a grenade won't silence their weapons long enough. We need a big bang, and Jeri's carrying it in her pack.

"Really?" She looks at me as if I just dropped my pants. "Like, *seriously?*"

"Seriously." I trade places with Gippy, who has donned his VR laser sight headset. He props his M4 around the corner and stares into space, firing single rounds with deadly accuracy. They fire back, but blindly, and with only his weapon visible, the worst they could do was hit the electronic scope. "We've got to clear the road before they can get anyone behind us, and you're our bulldozer."

"Fuckin' A!" Jeri doffs her pack and unzips it with shaking hands.

She might be freaked out by gunfire, but she does love to blow things up and has learned a lot about demolitions. Besides the door charges, we've brought along one specialty antipersonnel device for use in confined spaces. She pulls out a disk about the size and thickness of a Roomba, with a short antenna atop, and six wide rubber wheels beneath. Inside, there is nothing but explosives, fragmentation, a battery, and six electric motors. Designed strictly for indoor use, the ingenious little bomb will skitter along on any reasonably smooth surface until it reaches its designated target distance, then explode. Upon detonation it acts like a 360° Claymore mine, though with a shorter kill radius.

"How far?" She pulls a controller from the pack and flips up the safety cover.

"Seventy feet." I watch her tap in the range, marveling in horror at the ingenuity humans have applied to slaughtering one another. From the moment ninth-century Chinese monks discovered gunpowder, explosives changed the course of warfare. Ironic that they were searching for a life-extending elixir and discovered something that resulted in the massacre of billions. *Better dying through chemistry...*

"Ready." She activates the range fuse, orients the deadly disk toward the enemy, and sidles up behind Gippy. "Gip?"

"Careful. I think we pissed them off." He trades places with her, dumping a partially spent mag and reaching for another.

"This should calm them down." She kneels at the corner, places the device on the floor, and nudges it into the hallway with the muzzle of her rifle. Gunfire blasts sheetrock from the corner, inches from her face before she can flip the activation toggle. The bomb races off down the corridor in a zig-zag pattern, bouncing off walls to evade incoming fire. "Cover!"

We all take her advice, flattening ourselves and covering our ears. Shouts and gunfire ring out from the enemy as death rolls down the carpeted hallway toward them.

A mind-numbing blast numbs my senses in the confined space, shrapnel ripping through hallways and curtain walls in an expanding radius, deadly to about fifty feet. A deadly hail of ball bearings flies outward at a slightly upward angle, shredding the legs of anyone within twenty feet, and cutting through thin partition walls like paper. The Armorglass of the security station is undercut, shrapnel scything through the desks and the soldiers behind them.

Memories of mines blasting through human flesh, blowing the tracks off tanks, throwing white phosphorus rain in incinerating arcs... As the ringing in my ears eases, I can't differentiate the screams of my memories from those of our current enemies.

I'm up and around the corner before the last of the debris stops rattling to the floor. Gippy and Canción aren't far behind, and Jeri watches our backs as we quick-step up to the site of the explosion. Paradoxically, the blast point is clean, the base of the mine still lying there relatively undamaged. Around it is a ring of utter destruction. The elevator door is riddled to knee height, and the entire security station cut down, as are most of the soldiers. Some are miraculously only stunned by the blast, sheltered by the body armor of others. A few even reach for their weapons, but we shoot anything that moves. I don't count, but there must be two dozen casualties, more Hounds of Hell cast into the fray by those who spend human lives like currency.

Jeri throws up.

"Steady now." I go to her, feeling her anguish and disgust like waves of the blood we walk through. "This isn't your fault. It's war, Jeri. Soldiers aren't evil for killing other soldiers."

She wipes the vomit from her chin and stares into my soul. "Aren't we?"

"If we are, I'm doomed," I admit, but I know it isn't so.

"Can we stop philosophizing and rescue my mother?" Canción's intensity hasn't diminished with the battle. He's a stallion in the traces, fighting for his head.

"Let God sort 'em out, Jer." Gippy fishes a couple of magazines from a dead soldier's kit, steady as stone. "They may not know they're on the wrong side, but talkin' 'em out of killin' us wasn't an option."

Jeri nods, holding her weapon a little more firmly. "I'm okay. Let's get Cora and get the *hell* out of here. I'll freak out later."

"Good girl!" I nod to Canción. "Which way?"

He points his weapon at a pair of heavy steel doors some thirty feet down a wide hallway, only dented by the recent barrage of shrapnel. "Through there. She's close."

How he knows this, I have no idea, but I trust his intuition. After all, he knew the body they buried in

Boquete wasn't Cora's. It stands to reason that he will know when she's near.

"Alright, form up." They do, for which I give thanks, and I stalk toward the barrier.

The portal is labeled "Laboratory" and "Authorized Personnel Only," along with biohazard and radiation warnings. Whether the caution placards are real or just to dissuade inquisitive employees, I don't know or care. My cousin is within, and we're going through. There are no windows, and the doors open toward us, but I'll bet my very last bank account that they're locked. We split into two pairs: Gippy and Jeri, me and Canción.

"Pull slowly, Gip," I tell him.

He tries, shaking his head once. "Locked."

"We don't have time to screw around!" Canción growls, and he's not wrong.

"Hinges, Jeri. Quickly. Just one side."

"Sure." She pulls door charges from her pack, applying them with remarkably steady hands. She's found her steady spirit.

I glance at Canción, wondering if he's taken her fear and disgust, but I can't read him at the moment, at least not past his burning intensity.

"Ready!" Jeri steps back, and we huddle as far away from the explosives as we can in the confined space.

"Blow it, and we go through in formation. You see a gun, don't hesitate." They all nod.

"Fire in the hole!" Jeri pushes the detonator's switch, and the steel hinges are reduced to scrap metal.

Gippy and I kick the door low, and it swings inward and falls flat. I'm greeted by maniacal laughter and a wave of hatred; there's a Nephilim inside.

We go through, sweeping the interior of the large space left, right, and center; a medical facility, with bays for patients—or subjects— benches cluttered with lab equipment. Two scrub-clad technicians or nurses huddle to one side, their hands raised. An older woman with wild hair and deep-set eyes, wearing a lab coat over a rumpled fractal-printed blouse, stands beside a hospital bed, laughing. A slim pistol in her hand is nestled against the shaven head of a woman on a bed, barely visible for all the apparatus.

Cora...

I can't see her body at all, entombed in a sarcophagus-like case. A cranial brace with earphones and visor covers most of her head, festooned with electrodes and some kind of neural probes. Several IVs hang on poles beside the bed, roller pumps administering who knows what. A bank of monitors displays vitals, as well as a number of para-meters I'm not familiar with. What they're doing to her, I have no idea, and I shudder to speculate.

Visions of Auschwitz, Dachau, Kraków... The atrocities and those who committed them at the behest of their Nephilim Fuhrer and the very one who orchestrated it all, Heinrich Himmler, aka the Son of Samyaza... My finger trembles on the trigger of my rifle as I center the reticle of my weapon on the Nephilim's face and growl through gritted teeth. "Drop the gun."

"Or *what*, Ageless? You'll *kill* me? Ha! One twitch and I—" Her wild eyes go suddenly blank, her features drooping, and she drops to the floor like a ragdoll, the pistol falling from her limp hand to clatter on the hard surface. The waves of hate that radiated from her vanish as if they never existed.

Canción walks past me without a word, the energy of the Nephilim's absorbed soul buzzing in him like a dynamo.

"Holy fuck-a-rolly!" Gippy, as usual, is a step ahead of me in vocalizing his incredulity.

"Cover them!" I point to the two techs and stalk after Canción to Cora's side. "Jeri, blank the cameras and watch our six!"

I pause long enough to kick the pistol away and check the Nephilim, but there's no consciousness behind her wide eyes. The body's alive, but not for long without a mind. Cora... that's another story.

Canción has the earphones and visor off before I can intervene. He's humming a tune to her, complex and beautiful, but her face remains slack, her eyes darting around unseeing. I glance at the medications they're administering and cringe. Psychotropics, hallucinogens, and a mish-mash of neurochemicals. I don't know what will happen if we simply stop the infusions, but we have no choice. First, however, I place a hand on her shaven head and peer into her ravaged mind.

Chaos... terror... hopelessness... sadness... images of Hell, torment, then nothing. Oblivion...

And yet, under the layers of trauma, I hear the same strain of music Canción is humming. I can't tell if she's hearing it or he's mirroring it, but they're in perfect harmony. I ease myself around her psychological trauma and pull it away. I can't destroy her memories, but I can alleviate some of the damage. She draws a deeper, ragged breath and sighs it out, somewhat calmer, but still near-catatonic. And still, there is music beneath it all.

I remove the cranial implants carefully, healing the damage as I go. I receive a blinding headache without the drugs she has on board to block the pain, but it starts to fade quickly. I laboriously remove the cranial brace, disconnect electrodes, remove her feeding tube, and start on the fasteners of the sarcophagus.

"What *is* this thing?" I ask one of the techs, but he just stares at me in terror.

"Answer, or I decorate the wall with your fuckin' *brains*, asshole!" Gippy's threat—backed up by the barrel of an assault rifle a foot from the tech's face—elicits an immediate if somewhat shaky answer.

"Sa...sensory deprivation, artificial neural stimuli, neurochemical...um..."

"Torture," Canción growls. "They tortured her mind because they needed her *body* undamaged." His emotions, I realize, are boiling with more sorrow than I felt from him when he thought Cora had died, but that simmers on a blazing bed of rage. "Oh, mom... I'm so sorry." Tears, the first I've ever seen him shed, drip from his cheeks to her face.

"Let's get her out of here and see what we can do for her." I succeed with the last fastener, and the lid rises like peeling Velcro apart. "Mother of..."

I stare at her bent left arm, her malformed legs, and swallow a curse. I knew she was injured, of course, but I never considered that the Nephilim wouldn't at least set the broken bones. I've healed badly from severe fractures before, and had to have the bones rebroken and set straight. The way we Ageless heal, setting the fractures would have been a simple affair, but these monsters hadn't cared enough to do it. Or, I realize, they let her legs heal awry intentionally to keep her crippled, as slave owners once did to keep their property from running away.

My teeth grind as I struggle to calm my tumultuous spirit. *Triage... Treat what is risking her life and deal with the rest later, Empa!*

The interior of the sarcophagus is like barely solidified gelatin, perfect body temperature for sensory deprivation. I start pulling catheters, and she shivers, an autonomic response, but a response. She's feeling something genuine for the first time in weeks. The last IV is out, and I heal the needle punctures and insignificant damage of the catheters, which doesn't improve my headache. Finally, I delve into her physiology, looking for drugs, of which there are many. I can't take them all at once, or I'd pass out, but I remove what I can. My head swims with chaotic emotions but nothing specific. I grab a warm blanket and a robe, and we lift her from the cradle to a nearby stretcher.

She becomes more responsive, humming that same tune that she and Canción are sharing, and her eyes are darting around, seeing what, I don't hazard to guess. I feel her confusion, fear, borderline panic. I hope I didn't do more damage than good removing the drugs, but I couldn't see all the psychological trauma through the pharmacological fog. I see it now, and it terrifies me. She's very near a psychotic break, which I realize is exactly what they were trying to do, either to make her compliant or corrupt her soul. The latter doesn't seem likely. The former, yes; they would ply her damaged mind for information about us. Again, I take what I can encompass, and she calms, but the shivering terror is still there. The fear of nothingness beyond death, that all her faith was a lie, her very *origin* a lie. That panic is building, and there's nothing I can do to prevent it.

Then I realize that there's someone who can.

"Canción!" I grasp him by his vest, shaking him from the trancelike music he's sharing with Cora. "I need you to take her fear."

"But..." His eyes focus on me, his face streaked with tears. "But you said..."

"This is different! She's near a psychotic break, an emotional cliff. If she goes over the edge, there's no coming back. This is an *emergency*. Take her fear! Save her from plunging into oblivion!" I've seen that oblivion in her mind, looming to swallow her. "Do it now! And fill the void with music, with *love*! Let her know you're here!"

"Okay. I'll do what I can for—"

"Empa!" The urgency in Jeri's tone snaps me from our current emergency to another. She stands with her back to the wall beside the gaping doorway, fear writ large on her face. "We're in deep shit!

I hear the rumble of boots and shouting from beyond the wreckage and slaughter we wreaked. Reinforcements have arrived, and we have no other way out. "Gippy, cover the door with Jeri. Use whatever you have to hold them off."

"On it." Gippy leaves the two bound techs to help Jeri, taking up a position behind the remaining door, his VR laser sight in place.

"Canción, we have to move out of the line of fire."

Canción helps me wheel the stretcher out of view. "I did it. She's calmer."

"Excellent!" I touch Cora's forehead and feel her ease, the melody they're sharing now in the fore, the fear, anxiety, dread all gone. Only love remains. I hear her thoughts, *Canción...Canción... my Canción... my song...* and it gives me hope for her. "Good. Keep her mind stable. She's been through Hell and back, literally. I'll take more of the drugs and trauma when I have—"

Gunfire tears through the open doorway, shredding the equipment that so tortured my cousin. Gippy and Jeri try to return fire, but the intensity of the barrage keeps them pinned, and the remaining door is taking a beating. As I join them, Jeri pulls a door charge from her pack and hurls it down the hallway, slapping the detonator before it even hits the ground. The explosion is nothing compared to the antipersonnel mine, but we only had one of those.

"Sure wish we had some *grenades*!" Gippy dumps a mag and loads another. "They're usin' Armorglass riot shields!"

"Just be glad *they* don't have grenades!" Jeri has dumped her pack and transferred everything she has left into her pockets. Musashi's sword now rides at her belt.

"If they advance, aim for their legs," I advise. "When they try to recover the wounded, shoot *them* in the legs! Pile them up. Save the door charges! We may need them to get out of here!"

"Ain't no way out of here, E," Gippy says with a sardonic smirk. "We boxed in like sardines in a can. That earthquake pendulum thing is behind us, and the walls are reinforced concrete. They've got more people and ammo than us. It's all over but the cryin'.'"

"It's not over 'till it's over," I counter, but the words of my long-lost squad leader, Sergeant Getash, ring hollow. Gippy's already done the math and he's not exaggerating. We're in a box, and there are wolves at the door. My mind races for a solution, all the battles I've been through, five *thousand* years of memories, and I come up blank. We're outnumbered, outgunned, and have no avenue of retreat. Musashi would admonish me for my folly. We were fools for coming here in the first place.

So much for our daring rescue...

21

MELODY OF TEARS

For the first time in his life, Canción allowed himself to cry. Always before, he'd either bottled in his sorrow or expelled it with the emotions he'd absorbed from others. Now, with the energy from the soul of a Nephilim seething within him, he caressed his poor mother's shaven head and wept unashamedly.

All my fault... She was safe, and I led her right into a trap. Selfish... stupid... wanting to be a family in the middle of a war.

"Canción."

The whisper, barely audible above the roar of gunfire, snapped him out of his misery. "Mom?"

Her eyes were focused on him, her lips curved in a sweet smile. "You're... really here? Not another delusion?"

"I'm *here*, Mom." He kissed her brow and squeezed her hand, gazing into her beautiful eyes, hearing her song in his mind. "I came for you. I'm sorry. I should have let you be. You were safe."

"No." Her head moved back and forth weakly in denial. "Not... your fault. Worth the risk. My choice." Her free hand rose to grip his arm. "My sweet song, you're so beautiful. I'm so proud of you."

"You shouldn't be, mother. I'm... not like you. I don't know if—"

"Shhh, my song." Her fingers brushed his cheek. "None of us

knows the mind of God, but She loves you. She made you for a reason. You're Her sword."

"Her *sword*?" The statement caught him flat-footed. Was she delusional, still under the influence of the drugs they'd given her?

"Yes. You... saved me, my sweet song. Now let... the hand... of God *wield* you." Her eyes sagged closed, and her hand fell to the stretcher.

Asleep or unconscious, he didn't know, but he felt her fear rising again and took it away. He wondered if her mind was utterly shattered, for she wasn't making sense. *The sword of God? Let the hand of God wield you?* What could it mean, if anything?

"Canción!"

Empa's bellow jerked him away from his confused sorrow to the reality of their plight. She and Gippy hunkered beside the now bullet-riddled steel door, unable to fire back without being shot. Jeri crouched with her back to the wall, her rifle at her feet, empty, her pistol in her hand, her other gripping the hilt of Empa's sword.

"We need you!" Empa shouted. "They're advancing! We're cut off! There are too many! We need a way out!"

A way out. He looked around, realizing that there were no other exits. No way out but through the dozens of soldiers sending a hail of lead down the hallway at them.

Through them... like a sword.

Canción checked his mother once more, took her smoldering fear, and left her to follow her final wish. He was God's sword. It was time to let Her wield him.

"Back away from the door!" His voice sounded strange, quiet in his own ears, or maybe it was the gunfire. He saw the fear in their eyes as he stepped forward, standing tall, relaxed, to face the bullet-ravaged door. Muzzle flashes lit the hallway from beyond it, and he saw shadows of soldiers creeping forward. The door shuddered, shards of steel and lead spalling across the room. They sang like hornets past his ears, tugging at his clothing, his flesh, his soul...

"Canción! Be careful! You're in the line of fire!"

He locked eyes with Empa, and took her fear, took all of their fear, and his own sorrow, his own guilt, his own anguish. He took it all and destroyed it within himself, adding it to the bridled furnace of energy from the Nephilim's soul.

"No, I'm not," he said, facing the riddled door. "*They* are in mine."

He breathed in, held it, and shouted it all out in a focused maelstrom of force.

The steel door disintegrated, blown into razor-edged shards by his voice. Paint, sheetrock, wiring, carpeting, and the steel studs of curtain walls peeled back with the force of the shockwave. Soldiers vanished in the storm of shredded metal, plastic, and pulped building. Bulletproof vests held together by fabric fasteners came apart with their wearers, Kevlar, carbon fiber, and ceramic panels ripping through the fragile flesh they were made to protect. Rifles and ammo became scythes, tearing through hands and limbs. The entire hallway disintegrated into a storm of demolished building materials, weapons, armor, and human flesh and bone.

The storm struck the bank of elevators, collapsing the fragile doors inward, warping the steel girders and rails that held them in place, and blasted out the back wall into the offices and workspaces beyond, a freight train plowing through a grove of trees.

Evacuating personnel below heard the storm pass overhead as they struggled past even more soldiers heading up the stairwells and increased their pace. Those on lower floors staggered as the entire structure shuddered like a gigantic tuning fork struck with a hammer. The people who were being escorted out of the building's ground floor stared up in awe as the blast sent debris through the hurricane-proof windows. Desks, computers, workstations, glass, and shredded soldiers rained down onto nearby buildings and the street half a mile below.

Canción stared at the channel of destruction he had wrought. *The sword of God...*

"Holy *shit* balls!" Gippy stood from his crouch and peered around the corner into the demolished hallway. A ragged hole had been blasted all the way through and out the side of the building, the cityscape visible through the dust and debris.

"Move!" Empa barked. "We've got a chance! Get Cora and *move!*"

Grand Hope Tower shook as if a 6.5 quake had taken it in its teeth like a colossal Pitbull shaking a chewy toy. Half of Miaka's security feeds from the two floors below went blank, and thousands of NADs worth of Waterford crystal rattled musically on the wet bar. The floor actually swayed beneath him, the superstructure groaning, but Grand Hope Tower was built to withstand a category nine quake. Eventually, the movement steadied, and the strange vibration subsided.

The Son of Samyaza stabbed a button on his desk so hard he cracked a manicured fingernail, and Sikal's terrified features appeared on a monitor. "What the *hell* is going on?"

"Sir, I..." Her eyes widened further, darting left and right, obviously taking in other monitors that he couldn't see. "It must have been some kind of explosion, but there was no blast as such. Not like the previous one. The troops that arrived at the lab reported that some kind of... antipersonnel bomb had wiped out the guard station. They set up a line to advance on the lab. I have only glimpses of the assailants."

"I've already seen all that!" He snapped, but she had no way to know. For once, he'd pulled down the feeds himself instead of going through Sakal. Now she was telling him what he already knew. "I need to know what shook this building like a fucking earthquake. Half of my feeds have gone dark. What's going on right *now*!"

"Right now..." her eyes blinked in disbelief. "Sir, *debris* is falling from the north side of the building! Elevator bank two is out. None of the security personnel sent to secure the lab are responding. Most of the monitors on one forty-nine are nonfunctional."

The last part he had just told her. Sikal either wasn't thinking clearly or she was overloaded with information. "Debris? What are you talking about?"

A flash of exasperation crossed her features. "Sending you the street feeds, *sir*!

His monitors came alive with video of all manner of garbage falling from the sky. Some of it hit neighboring buildings, but most impacted the street itself, where police were urging people to take shelter. Much of the debris was pieces of the building, office equipment, furniture, but also a number of mutilated human remains. Strangely, none of it was burned, even though many of the bodies had been utterly shredded. This didn't garner any sympathy, of course, just curiosity.

This told him what had happened to his security forces, but not *how* it had happened. These were results, not causes, which meant she had no data at all. He'd replayed the laboratory feeds after the previous explosion and had seen the glimpses of the four blowing half the door off the hinges and entering. Only seconds after they stepped inside—before the skinny young woman had blanked out the security cameras with a paintball gun—he'd watched the Daughter of Yomyael collapse as if she'd fainted.

I should have blown the whole fucking building right then! He'd announced an all-out emergency, and troops from below had swarmed up the stairwells in answer. Sixty heavily armed security guards had initially responded, more on the way, and there was no way out of the lab. He'd had them like bugs in a bottle.

Then the camera feeds at the security station had gone blank, and the building had shaken. *But how?*

"I need real-time data on what did this!" he snapped to Sikal. "Show me the last few seconds of the cameras on one forty-nine; slow motion and as high a resolution as you can get!"

"Yes, sir." She worked for a few moments, her face contorted in concentration, then, "Coming to your desk, sir."

Six of his monitors lit up with scenes of the hallway, the demolished security station, the bodies of the dead guards, and the living ones all aiming weapons toward the lab. Some hid behind triple-layered Armorglass salvaged from the wreckage, those behind them firing from shelter. They were taking fire, but returning it tenfold. The footage advanced frame by frame, one image per second. Then something catastrophic happened.

The bullet-riddled door disintegrated, pieces of shredded metal flung down the corridor with tremendous force. One frame caught the image of a door push bar still attached to a torn piece of steel. The troops were cut to pieces, and the two camera feeds in the hall went blank. The one over the elevator showed the approaching wave of destruction, only three frames filmed at 60 frames per second. Nothing stood against the onslaught. The walls were peeled off the steel studs as soldiers vanished in sprays of flesh, blood, and bone pulped by the debris-filled shockwave. The last monitor froze on the final image, a horrified guard's face, mouth open, screaming.

"What could cause a blast like that?"

The question had been rhetorical, but Sikal answered anyway. "Unknown sir. Nothing conventional; not without a significant explosive charge to propel the shockwave, and there was no such explosion. The blast was focused and directional, like the force from an artillery round at close range."

All that told him nothing, but it certainly gave him pause. He recalled the video of Canción destroying half of a security station with some type of energy he'd conjured out of thin air. Could this blast be the same, but infinitely more powerful?

The get of Israfal and Azkeel... music and destruction... The son of Heaven and Hell evidently had powers they had not yet witnessed.

The question, he realized, wasn't what had caused the blast, but what to do about it. The answer was simple.

"Seal off the stairwells and shut down all elevators! We have them boxed in on one forty-nine. They got what they came for and will try to leave with the evacuating civilians. Block off all avenues of escape and give orders to shoot anyone trying to leave that floor. *Anyone!*"

"Yes, sir."

"And where's my helicopter?"

"On approach, sir. ETA, three minutes."

"Good! You'll evacuate with me and the VIPs. How many troops do we—"

The doors to his office burst open, and the Son of Samyaza had his pistol out and aimed at the intruder before he realized who it was. "*Fuck,* Renquist!" He took his finger off the trigger and glared at the Son of Armaros. "*Knock* for Hell's sake! You just about earned a bullet for your rudeness!" He turned his attention back to Sikal. "How many troops do I have on one fifty?"

"Thirty, counting those assigned to you and Mr. Renquist."

"Send them all to defend the stairwells!" That should be more than enough to keep them safe while they got the hell out. "Secure all essential systems, dump data and encrypted access codes to our portable server, and evacuate with us."

"Yes, sir!" The screen went blank.

While he tied up loose ends, the Son of Armaros strode across the room to the wet bar. The four personal guards touched their earpieces and headed off toward the nearest stairwell, following Sikal's orders to defend the floor.

"What in the name of the Prince of Darkness is going on in this place? Have you seen the news? *Wreckage* is falling from the building!" He poured three fingers of ridiculously expensive whiskey into a tumbler.

"*Seen* the news?" He sneered contemptuously. "I *create* the news. Now, calm the hell down. We're arranging evacuation." The Nephilim saw no need to inform his subordinate that the one creature on the planet who could destroy their kind utterly and forever was only one floor below, or that they seemed to have rescued Terpsichore and blasted dozens of armed guards right out the side of the building. "My helicopter will be here in less than three minutes, and we'll be on it. Then I push the button that will win the war, and we clean up the mess."

"Win the *war*? What are you talking about?" The liquor was halfway to his mouth when the Son of Samyaza unloaded at least part of the truth.

"*Empa* is in the building. She killed the Daughter of Yomyael to rescue Terpsichore."

"The hell?" His eyes went wide with the ramifications. "Tell me you can destroy them *both*, Miaka."

"I can." He stood, shot his cuffs, and straightened his lapels. "As I said, with the push of a button, but I'd like to *be* here after I deal the winning stroke."

"Then let's get the fuck out of here!" He downed his drink and tossed the crystal tumbler onto the wet bar. The two-hundred-year-old glass didn't break, being Waterford, but it wouldn't matter. The entire building and much of the surrounding real estate would be reduced to rubble the moment they were in the air.

22

VENGEANCE IS MINE

The distinctive hornet-nest howl of a coaxial helicopter roars past the gaping maw of destruction as we struggle through the wreckage of the former security station.

"They've called in *air* support," Gippy growls, helping to lift one end of Cora's gurney over shredded flooring. "All we fucking need!"

I cock my head to listen, decades of experience identifying aircraft by sound kicking in. "Just one, and not a gunship. It's a heavy, which means troop transport."

"How many do they carry?" Gip asks.

"About a dozen, which doesn't make sense." We make it past the worst of the wreckage, walls and floor stripped down to support struts, exposing wiring, plumbing, and HVAC ducts, and roll the gurney toward the stairwell.

"Why not?" Jeri asks as we near the stairwell door.

"Because they already have an army. There's no sense in bringing in more."

Canción isn't paying attention to me, but cups his mother's face in his hands, soothing her. Cora's conscious, but disoriented, as if her son is the only thing in the universe that matters. Right now, for her, maybe he is.

Jeri opens the door wide enough to peer through, her pistol ready. "Landing's clear."

As we unstrap Cora in preparation to carry her down a hundred forty-eight flights of stairs, Jeri steps out. Gunfire erupts from above and below, deafening in the echoing column of steel. She staggers back, swearing, and loses her balance.

Gippy's there to steady her. "You hit?"

"I think..." She grips her left arm, and her hand comes away bloody; then shock turns to pain on her face. "Fuck!"

"Steady, Jeri." I touch her and feel the damage, a through-and-through puncture to the bicep, but it missed the bone and the brachial artery. I seal the blood vessels and feel the dizziness of sudden shock and blood loss. Without the surface wound, her bleeding will subside quickly, and mine will stop in minutes, but I can't afford the weakness. I shake a bandanna out of a pocket—essential combat field dressings—and wrap it around my arm. "Tie this tight!"

Gippy complies and pulls another for Jeri's arm, talking as he works. "We're boxed in again, E, high and low. And you can bet your very favorite gun that the other stairwells are the same. Unless you can sprout some angel wings, or Canción can do his BFG-9000 trick again, we're hosed."

Aside from the pop culture references, he's not wrong. "We could check the freight elevator, but they're probably shut down." But something's nagging at me worse than my aching arm. "Why box us in? And why bring in a helicopter that can transport..." Realization dawns, and I look up. "*Pride!*"

"What?" Jeri and Gippy say in perfect unison.

"Miaka is the Son of Samyaza, the fallen angel of *pride*. This is his fortress, and he's got Cora, me, *and* Canción all in one place. He can win the War of Souls in one stroke. All he's got to do is destroy his own fortress with us in it. He would respawn, but his *pride* won't let him miss his own victory. He wants to take credit, reap his reward..." I point up. "*That's* what the helicopter's for."

"He's going to evacuate?" Gippy's eyebrows arch. "And then..."

"Probably call in a drone strike." I shrug. "Or even a hit from

NORAD, if his network still has connections to the nuclear defense system."

"Nuke LA?" Jeri gapes. "They wouldn't!"

"Not a nuke, but nuclear *defense*," I explain. "A cruise missile or MOAB drop would be more likely. For all we know, the deployment aircraft could already be in the air."

"No." This is the first word from Canción in minutes, and now his icy blue eyes fix mine with a cold intensity I've never felt from him before. "No, he's *not* going to escape."

"Fuck *him* escaping," Gippy counters. "How do *we* escape?"

"We go up there, I destroy him, and we take his ride." He touches his mother's face, and I feel the burning need for revenge growing within him. Then he points back the way we came. "Up the elevator shaft."

"The *elevator* shaft?" Jeri's voice cracks into a squeak. "It's a half-mile drop!"

"But only *fifteen* feet up!" I latch onto the idea like a lifeboat in a storm, urging everyone to wheel Cora back to the demolished elevator bank. "They won't have soldiers at the doors, and we can jimmy the door release from inside the shaft."

"Then what?" Gippy helps push. "And how do we get Cora up there?"

"We can rig a harness from wiring." Canción gestures to the denuded walls and the bundled yellow and blue strands of fiber-optic cabling. "But we have to get up there before Miaka escapes! If we don't, we'll have to fight through more soldiers to get to the roof." He nods to Gippy. "We get him, and we have another BFG 9000."

I'm surprised he was listening, and even more so that he understood the video game reference. "He's right. Come on!"

We work our way through the mess to the gaping maw of the elevator shaft. There are three to the bank, and only one was on this floor. The car is completely gone, but the cables of the other two are intact. The I-beam frame holding them in place is warped from the intensity of Canción's blast, but the bolted connections appear solid. "We move. Get your harness rigged, Canción. I'm going up."

"Not without a harness!" Gippy insists. "And you're hurt. I should go."

I grit my teeth, unwilling to put him on point simply because I could be wrong and there could be a dozen soldiers at the egress to the next floor. But once again, he's not wrong. "Fine, but you be fucking quiet, scope out the hallway and secure a beachhead. Canción goes next because we need his muscle to pull Cora up. Once she's up, Jeri and I follow."

Canción's already stripping wire from the walls, using a combat knife to cut through the finger-thick cable. He cuts three strands about twenty feet long, fashioning one into a surprisingly good harness in a matter of seconds, his knot work as good as any sailor's. I get the most incongruous flash memory of John Rackham teaching me how to tie a bowline, and can't help but smile. *The little brown eel comes out of his hole, swims around the anchor rode, then swims back down into his hole. Aye, Lass! On the first try, too, but then yer likely an expert with eels and holes, then.*

Jeri stares at me aghast. "What's funny?"

"Nothing. Memories of a bygone day, lassie. Now let's get a move on. Time and tide wait for no one!"

Canción secures the makeshift harness to Gippy and ties the other end to an exposed curtain wall stud. "If you fall, it should hold you, but it'll hurt. Don't fall." His cold, matter-of-fact tone concerns me. His emotions are all gone, expelled with the blast that saved us, except for the burning need to destroy those responsible for Cora's torment. That's all that he is at the moment, which is dangerous.

"Steady now." I check the knots. "And remember. *Quiet!*"

Gippy nods and steps out into space, gripping a steel I-beam, then stops. "So, if we have to take the helicopter by force, can you fly it?"

Another flash memory, *jungle coming up at us as I fight controls slick with the pilot's blood.* "I... um... had a crash course once."

Gippy's not having any of my bullshit. "Define *crash* course."

"The pilot was killed, I took the controls, and we crashed, but *most* of us survived."

"Marvelous." Gippy gains a foothold on one of the cross beams and starts up.

Jeri bites her lip watching him climb up, and I offer a supportive touch. She's shaking.

"Steady spirit, Jeri."

"Right. And *that's* likely."

"You can. Just breathe." I lend her a little of what I am, and feel her accept it, take it in, and hold onto it like it's the last thing in the world that makes sense. I squeeze her hand. "I gotcha."

She nods and squeezes back, and we peer up into the darkness where the young man we both love has vanished.

"Okay," comes a whisper from above. "I'm set. The release looks simple."

Something clanks softly, and light pours into the shaft from the hallway above, illuminating him as he levers the doors open with a combat knife. He leans out to peer through the crack as best he can, then pulls the doors wide enough to poke his head through.

"We're clear. The security station's empty. I hear voices, though. Hurry!" The harness falls past us, and Canción pulls it up.

He works his arms and legs through the loops and pulls the central knot tight. I can feel his eagerness, more dangerous than the enemy at this point.

"Easy now. Take your time."

He shoots me a glare. "We *have* no time. If they escape, *everything* is lost." Before I realize what he means, he clambers up the inside of the shaft toward the light from above, more agile than I would have thought possible for someone his size.

As he climbs, the meaning of what he said takes form in my mind. *Everything...*

Five thousand years of struggle, war, torment, and loss have come to this. If they escape, the Son of Samyaza calls in a missile strike, and the last Ageless on Earth perish. *Hell wins...* I go to Cora, touch her, feel her music, but little else. Her son has stripped her terror away like amputating a gangrenous limb, invasive but necessary. Another more recent memory, *Canción video chatting to Cora from the car, taking her worry by simply making eye contact.* I realize where we are, who is at the reins of this nightmare, and my mind reels.

Telecommunications... Holy shit! I can't breathe with the epiphany.

"You okay?" Jeri asks, obviously sensing my sudden distress.

I manage to nod and start unfastening the straps of my body armor. *Steady spirit...* "Help me put this on Cora. It'll be better than a harness for her."

"Sure." Jeri helps me fit the heavy vest onto Cora, snugging the Velcro straps.

I find Cora's eyes open and on me, her features peaceful, her fear gone. "Hey, cuz. You okay?"

"Canción?" she asks, and I know it's not mistaken identity. She's asking if he's okay.

"Just upstairs. We'll be with him soon."

Her eyes focus more closely. "I... know..." She blinks, and I feel her recognition; the music within her wavering. "Empa?"

"That's right. Now just relax. What was that tune you were humming?" We can't have her regressing at this point.

"Tune?" Her eyes close, and the music resurges, steadier, complex, and beautiful beyond measure. "Canción..."

"I'm up!" Canción whispers down from above.

We secure the end of the cable to Cora's vest, and I give it a tug. "Okay! Up."

The cable comes tight, and they pull my dear cousin up through the wreckage toward the light and music of her son.

A fire had ignited within Canción that he wasn't sure he could ever quench, his mind racing with his mother's music and the longing for retribution. The sight of her twisted limbs, her blank eyes, and the feel of her terror had set that blaze, and it was growing, consuming him with every passing moment. The song of destruction, his father's legacy, strained for release.

The Sword of God... Let Her wield me...

With distant shouts, curses, and sporadic gunfire coming from the left and right hallways—evidently some of the Nephilim's dogs had mistaken each other for their quarry—the slight noise of pulling Cora up wasn't likely to draw attention. She was limp, however, and getting her over the edge and onto the floor was a struggle. Her eyes were closed, but he could still feel her music, the melody they shared in their souls.

"Help her. I got this," Gippy said, throwing down the harness end of the wire.

"Mom? You okay?" He could feel no more fear from her, only music.

"Canción." Her eyes opened and came alight, her lips curving in a peaceful smile. "My song..."

"I'm here, Mom. Just rest. We're getting you out of here."

She lifted a hand to touch his face. "My most beautiful song..."

He soothed her riven mind, refusing his tears once again. He was the Sword of God. There were no tears left in him. Only vengeance.

Taking in their surroundings, he marveled at the stupendous hubris of the Grand Hope Tower's top floor. A curved mahogany desk sat to one side of ornate gold and ebony doors, the Transmedia corporate logo, and "Joseph Miaka, CEO" in foot-high gold letters on the wall behind it. There was no receptionist at the desk, and all the security guards had been ordered to defend the stairwells. Coming up the elevator shaft had put them behind enemy lines.

Then Jeri was up, struggling out of the harness, her face pale from the climb. She knelt beside him. "Gimmie a mag or two. I'm empty."

"Take whatever you need." He ignored her as she rifled through his ammo pouches. Canción didn't need bullets. He was the Sword of God.

Then he felt something else, and the smoldering vengeance inside him flared. He'd felt it in that horror-show laboratory where the Nephilim had tortured his mother. He'd seen it in her eyes the moment they met—*evil, hatred, madness*. Now he felt even more, and nearby: a burning hatred of all on Earth, all of God's works, of their own creation, the longing to wipe everything away in a storm of annihilation, and also a burning nova of pride, self-assurance, arrogance. He stood and faced that burning beacon of hate as Gippy helped Empa up onto the floor. Through the huge, gaudy doors, he could feel them. More than one. His chance for vengeance.

"They're coming," he growled, taking a step toward the source.

"They?" Jeri knelt and aimed at the doors.

"The Nephilim." Canción stood with his fists balled at his sides, waiting for the door to open.

"Canción!" A hand closed on his arm, Empa's. "Don't destroy the Son of Samyaza! We *need* him!"

"I'm going to destroy them all," he said without looking at her.

"Yes! Them *all*! *Think!*" She squeezed his arm hard. "He's the head of Transmedia, a global *telecommunications* corporation! He'll have direct video comms to every Nephilim on the planet at his fingertips! *All* of them!"

His eyes widened, still not looking at her, but the light of memory dawning; *talking to his mother over video, feeling the worry and fear for him through her eyes, and taking it all away.* "What are you—"

He heard voices on the other side of the door, and it opened. As a dark-skinned woman carrying a metal briefcase emerged, Empa and Jeri raised their carbines. Two men followed, one tall, older, and broad-shouldered, the other Joseph Miaka—even if he hadn't known the man by sight, Canción knew that both men were Nephilim. He could *feel* them now.

Three more people followed behind them, all carrying cases. Two wore white coats over black pants, and one a black jacket, white shirt, and ascot tie. The woman in the fore was speaking, but Canción wasn't listening. The music from his mother was all he could hear, the blinding hate from the two Nephilim all he could feel.

They all froze at the sight of people in guard uniforms aiming weapons at them. The dark woman squeaked in alarm and dropped her briefcase, but a chain from the handle to her wrist came up short.

Recognition flashed in the eyes of the two suit-clad men: they knew Empa, and by association, him. The broader Nephilim reached into his suit jacket, probably for a gun, while Miaka sidestepped behind the other. As the one in the fore drew a pistol from his pocket, Canción locked gazes with him. The unending desire to lay waste to the entire world burned behind those dark orbs, until Canción ripped it away, encircled it, and crushed it to death within himself.

The big man dropped like a steer in a slaughterhouse, his pistol still gripped in his hand, pinned beneath his soulless body.

As he fell, the bystanders gasped and stepped back. Miaka drew not a weapon, but a phone from his sleek jacket pocket, his thumb poised over the lit screen. Somehow, that phone looked more deadly than any gun could have been. Canción could have destroyed him before he touched the screen, but the man's eyes were averted, or maybe just fixed upon Empa. Without the window into the man's soul, he couldn't destroy the Nephilim. With the energy from the other one, he could kill the entire group, but not before the man's thumb touched the screen. Not even a bullet through the brain would stay his hand in time.

"Stop!"

The simultaneous shout from both Miaka and Empa froze everyone, including Canción. Empa and Jeri were poised, weapons trained on the small group. Gippy crouched behind them at Cora's side, out of Canción's view, maybe watching the hallways. One gunshot would bring dozens of soldiers running, and they'd be trapped once again, but Canción could clear a path as he'd done before.

"You've *lost*, Ageless daughter of Raphael!" the Nephilim crowed in triumph. "One tap, and Grand Hope Tower comes tumbling down, and *all* of you with it."

Canción could see the truth in the man's face, the victory, the triumphant ego, and wondered, *So why not do it? Why tell us? He could have pushed the button while his phone was still in his pocket!*

The people around him stared at Miaka in unbridled horror, backing away, clearly thinking he was insane. They didn't know what he truly was, that if he died, he would respawn in another newborn human, living again to savor his victory. But something was keeping him from doing exactly that. Canción glared at the man's averted eyes and opened his mouth to ask what that something was, but Empa answered the question for him.

2 3

DEAL WITH THE DEVIL

ot before Canción destroys you utterly, Son of Samyaza."

My voice is steadier than I would have thought possible, but the inevitability of this moment has gripped me. *Steady spirit, cold calculation, always look for the advantage, consider options, assess your opponent, and never show your enemy your spirit.* The lessons of Miyamoto Musashi visit me as if his ghost's hand rests on my shoulder. He gave my struggle focus, but even before I met him, I knew in my bones how this war would end. *My entire life, eons of war, only one inevitability: death, failure, loss, and the end of mankind.*

Unless...

I see in the Nephilim's eyes that he knows I'm not lying. Even before I said it, he knew that if he blew the building out from under us, it would take time to come down, and that in those last few moments of his life, Canción would destroy him utterly. *The Son of Samyaza, the fallen Angel of Pride, will not let that happen; his hubris won't allow it.* I see the truth in the Nephilim's eyes. He knows, like me, that this is the end of our eons-long struggle. And yet, his pride won't let him sacrifice himself for the victory he holds in his hand.

"You suggest I let you *go?*" the Nephilim sneers at me, a fog of hate and hubris radiating from him.

"You have two choices," I reply. "Activate whatever bomb you have planted, and perish, or make a deal with us."

His thumb twitches over the face of the phone, his sneer intensifying. "A *deal?*"

"Yes, a *deal.*" I struggle for calm, disallowing the truth from registering on my face. *Never show your enemy your spirit.*

There is a third option, one that will change everything, but I can't let him realize what it is. He knows what I am, what I can do if he gives me a peek into his mind. If he realizes that he holds the key to our victory in there, he'll blow the building and accept oblivion as his reward. I have to give him a better option, an escape of sorts.

"We can banish you without destroying you, and your brethren still have a chance to win the war. We're outnumbered a hundred to one, after all. Your soul survives, and you can gloat over our loss in the future."

"Or I press the button and we win the war instantly." His hubris is still intact.

I need to quench that fire of defiance, so I show him a glimpse of oblivion. "Yes, and you perish forever... *instantly.*"

"Unless I blow my brains out before he can destroy me."

The woman with the metal briefcase backs away further, her eyes wide. She clearly thinks her boss is crazy.

"Pull a gun and I'll blast your arm off," Jeri says between clenched teeth, not hiding her nerves as well as the rest of us. She's not that good a shot, and knows it, but the bluff is a good one.

And I *am* that good a shot.

"Oblivion is too high a price to pay, Son of Samyaza. Banished, your soul survives. Destroy us, and you never see your victory. Your pride perishes with you."

"The thing about oblivion, Daughter of Raphael, is that nobody can say it's the *worse* choice." He grins, and I can see he's made his decision. "In the end, we're all—"

A rifle barks a single round, and the bullet blasts a hole through the Nephilim's phone. His thumb stabs the shattered screen, and his eyes fling wide in realization: he's been had.

Oh, Gifford, my sweet, brilliant son... His scope made the shot easy, and he's given me the third option.

The moment of inevitability shatters, and everything happens at once.

The Nephilim moves, pulling a shiny pistol from his pocket. Jeri unloads, her salvo cutting his knees to shreds. The bystanders sprawl screaming to the floor. As the Son of Samyaza falls, I put a burst through his right shoulder. He hits the floor in a bloody heap, thrashing to reach the fallen pistol with his uninjured hand. Canción barrels forward, fearless, careless.

I lunge to grab his shoulder before he can destroy the Nephilim's soul and our one chance. I feel his burning need for vengeance, his stolen childhood, his shattered life in Cartagena, the lie of Cora's death, betrayed by the one person he trusted most in the world, and lastly, his own insurmountable guilt for his mother's suffering. He *really* needs to learn some self-control.

"Wait, goddamn it!"

"No!" He whirls to glare at me, and I feel his power swelling. As our eyes meet, I know in my gut that he can rip my Ageless soul from my body in an instant, just as he did the Nephilim. "I'm going to—"

"Not *yet!*" I pour myself into him, show him for the first time my *own* power, the grace of Raphael, Angel of Healing and Empathy, my love of all humankind, and all the losses I've ever experienced over my *very* long life. I also show him my plan, the information that the Nephilim holds in his mind, and what we can do with it. The revelation hits him like a slap in the face. "Give me thirty seconds with him and you'll *have* your revenge, Canción. More than you can imagine! I *promise!*"

I hear his teeth chirp as he grinds them, but he doesn't rip my soul from my body. Maybe he *is* growing up a little.

"Can we stop pissing each other off and figure out what the fuck we're doing?" Gippy is dragging Cora out of the hallway into the private residence foyer. "We gonna have very unwelcome company in about ten seconds!"

"And how do we deal with *these* assholes?" Jeri is standing on the Nephilim's wrist, her carbine pointed at the bystanders.

"Cover the hallway, Canción. *Please.* You'll have your vengeance a *hundred*-fold, and we'll *all* get out of here alive."

"Fine!" He whirls away to help Gippy with Cora.

I join Jeri, relieving the Nephilim of his shiny Walther and kneeling beside him. "I've got this one, Jeri. Make sure the rest aren't armed but don't hurt them."

"Take *all* my fun away, why don'cha?" I think she's joking, but I'm not sure. I've seen the most mild-mannered people in the world transform into brutal killers under battle conditions. "You all line up over there and drop all that shit! You, what's in the bondage case?"

"A mobile server." The dark woman cowers back with the others. "Mr. Miaka's personal backup drive, financial information, *everything*!"

"Excellent! You keep being nice and you'll get out of here alive. Fuck with me and I'll take that case off with your hand." She draws Musashi's sword for emphasis, and the four back up against the wall, hands up and empty.

"And *you...*" I lean close to the thrashing Nephilim's face, but his eyes are tightly closed, and he won't meet my gaze. I feel his terror, the fear of oblivion, or worse, an eternity of torment for failure when we send him to Hell forever. "Time for a little *chat*, Son of Samyaza." I pry his eyes open and dive into a sea of hubris and hatred.

I've done this before and regretted it every time. I once thought I could change them, heal them, show them that there is love and kindness in the universe. All I ever got back for my effort was loathing and spite. This time, I have a specific goal worth the maelstrom of vileness I must plunge into.

I wade through the horrors of a truly depraved soul: eons of cruelty, mountains of orchestrated atrocities, carefully plotted genocides, sowing hatred, bigotry, mistrust, and suffering with every step of his millennia-long existence. I sift through the heaps of information sequestered behind a wall of a burningly narcissistic ego, a mountainous database of vileness, and take what I need: Passwords, access codes, names, connections... the entire network of Hell's minions on Earth. As I rip the information away, he gets a peek into my mind and sees what I plan to do. With that realization, a new terror rises in him, and he begins to struggle even harder.

I can't help but feel a twinge of satisfaction. "Payback's a *bitch*, ain't it?" I stand and realize there's gunfire from the hallway.

Gippy's lying flat behind the curved desk, his rifle braced along the floor around the corner. Canción has a pistol in hand, facing the other direction. He leans out, and I feel the surge of his power expelling the energy from the Nephilim soul he's destroyed. The sound is like a sudden tornado ripping down the hallway, and the guns from that direction are silenced.

"Canción!" He turns to me and I wave to the crippled Nephilim behind me. "He's all—"

A pistol fires right behind me, and I know my momentary lack of vigilance has betrayed me. The Son of Samyaza has crawled to the destroyed Nephilim's empty body and pulled the pistol from under it. The first bullet catches me in the hip, twisting me like being struck with a mace. The next misses me but hits Canción square in the chest. He staggers, but his body armor absorbs the impact. If the Nephilim's aim had been better, we'd both be dead, and our victory transformed to failure.

Never waste the mistakes of your enemies, Emiko. They are priceless gifts...

Musashi's voice ringing in my ears, I use the momentum of the bullet to whirl on my good leg and bring my rifle to bear, but there is no third shot. Jeri is closer, bared katana in hand. One swift stroke, straight out of her training and perfect, separates the Nephilim's gun hand from his arm. Then I'm falling, for the bullet struck bone, and my left leg doesn't want to support me.

"Empa!" Jeri drops the blade and catches me before I topple. "No, no, no!"

I feel her sudden panic, her fear that I'm going to die, and I steady myself on my good leg.

"It's all right." It's really not, and my hand comes away from my hip painted bright red, but I'm not going to die. Still, it hurts like the devil, which seems ridiculously ironic since the son of a devil actually shot me. "I'm not going to die." I press my bloody hand to the wound and feel the iliac crest move independently from the rest of my pelvis. "Broken bone, but I can walk... sort of."

"If you don't bleed out!" Jeri's pulling first aid supplies from a pocket. "Take off your pants!"

"Always trying to get my pants off..." Shock is hitting me hard, and I feel like I might pass out, but strong hands grasp my shoulders, and I hear music.

"Let's get her into that chair before she faints."

"Good idea. I could use a sit down... and maybe a cuppa." The edges of my vision are turning gray.

Canción helps Jeri move me, and she lowers my pants to my knees before I can protest. There's a lot of blood. I sit on my right butt cheek and my vision stops swimming.

"The bullet put a hole in your belt." Jeri gingerly teases my under-wear out of the wound, sending stabs of pain through me. "Some pieces of bone in there, and I can't see the bullet."

"Just stop the bleeding." I've got an inordinate number of bullets floating around inside me, some centuries old. It's a good thing I'm not susceptible to lead poisoning. Someday, when the war's over, I'll have them all taken out and make a necklace or mount them on a wooden plaque. *When the war's over...* I never thought I would consider that, but now it's a real possibility.

As she squirts something into the bullet wound—an emergency coagulant mixed with lidocaine that stings going in, but will numb the injury in moments and stop the bleeding—the barrage of hate that I've been feeling since the doors to the private residence opened suddenly vanishes. I glance over to where Canción kneels beside the former Son of Samyaza, whose soul is now being destroyed, rendered down to energy by the offspring of Heaven and Hell. The bystanders stare on in horror as their former lord and master stops struggling, eyes fixed wide, staring at the ceiling while his body slowly bleeds out.

Canción stands and stares at me in passing. "Did you get what you needed?"

"Yes. The keys to everything." I wince as Jeri slaps a dressing on my hip.

"Good." He walks to the corner where Gippy lies prone, leans out, and sends the energy of the destroyed Nephilim blasting down the hall. The shockwave rips a new hole in the side of the skyscraper and silences the guns.

I feel no emotion from him now, not even the burning thirst for revenge. I consider, not for the first time, what a monster he might have become if not for the love of Cora. I examine my poor cousin, lying oblivious to the surrounding mayhem, and wonder if the Nephilim have already started their plan for creating a race of weapons for Hell. I didn't feel an incipient pregnancy in her, but I wasn't looking for one, and microscopic blastulae are almost impossible to spot at such an early stage.

"You're good for now." Jeri helps me back to my feet—my vision blurs for a moment but steadies—and pulls up my pants. "Try not to get shot again, huh?"

"Top on my list of things *not* to do. Thanks." The hip hurts less already with a syringe full of painkiller in it, and I can put some pressure on my left leg without lightning shooting up my spine. "And nice cut with your sword, badass bitch with a blade."

My praise brings a blush that I find incongruous and adorable. "Thanks. Can we get the *hell* out of here now?"

"Just one more thing to do." The unaccustomed quiet is unnerving. I fix the woman with the briefcase with a hard stare and feel her terror of me and Canción. I can use that. "Tell me where Miaka's office is."

She points a shaking finger. "Through the doors and left. End of the hall. N...name on the door."

"Perfect." I turn back to Jeri. "You need to secure our ride. Canción and I have something to do, then we'll join you."

Her flushed features go pale. "No way. I'm staying with *you!*"

"Jeri." I grip her shoulders tightly. "We *need* that helicopter. With no word from Miaka, the pilot won't hang around forever, and if I'm with you, they may shoot us on sight. If they leave without us, we'll be trapped up here. We won't be long."

"If Canción didn't just blow the shit out of the only way to the roof." Gippy stabs a thumb down the hallway. "Looks like a wrecking ball paid a visit."

"The roof stairs are separate," the woman with the briefcase offers before I can speak. "I can take you up. I am... *was* Mr. Miaka's personal assistant. The pilot will know me and follow my orders." She glances at the other bystanders. "We'll help you get away if you take us with you."

I don't know if she knows what Miaka truly was without delving into her mind, but I can see in her eyes that she's done the math. Her boss is dead, and we're not the monsters he probably painted us out to be. If we were, they'd all be dead. We're her only way out of here, and she's carrying access to a trillionaire's financial empire in that case, one hell of a negotiating bonus.

"Best deal I've had all day." I nudge Jeri. "Get going. They can help carry Cora up. Don't let them leave without us."

Her resolve steadies, and I'm proud of her. "You better not get killed while I'm up there, woman."

"I *told* you." I kiss her. "Top of my list. Now go."

Gippy and Jeri order the three servants into motion, and they drop their packages and comply.

"Take *care* of her," Canción growls as they lift Cora.

They stare at him in abject terror, nodding compliance.

They bundle up Cora and head off. When they're gone, I face the man who could have been a monster and is instead a weapon for God. "Come on. We've got a war to win."

24

THE SWORD OF GOD

Miaka's office disgusted Canción. Growing up in Boquete and then Cartagena, he helped the homeless and impoverished victims of the rising sea struggling to survive. He'd helped his mother bring joy to their lives, and later, built homes for those who had none. This lifeless, soulless room probably cost more than a dozen homes, and the entire building, perhaps hundreds of thousands.

All in the name of pride.

Burn it down... he thought, nurturing that thirst for revenge that had been so suddenly quenched by exterminating that sanctimonious horror, the Son of Samyaza. Canción had felt the beast's confidence, arrogance, and the smug certainty that he had won the War of Souls single-handedly as he'd pulled the creature's soul from his body. In that instant, his pride had transformed to horror, then it had been quenched like a candle dropped into the sea.

Now, for the rest of them...

He followed Empa as she limped over to the expansive desk, unclipped her carbine to prop it nearby, and sat carefully down. The chair slid forward into the crescent-shaped array of ergonomically arranged controls, keyboards, trackballs, and small touch screens.

With one tap, the entire desk's glossy black surface rose up and unfolded into a huge curved multi-screen. One more touch, and a lower central window lit up with a standard log-in page.

"This might take a minute. Watch the hall. We may get visitors."

"Right." He picked up her carbine—he'd left his empty and abandoned at the foyer—and faced the open doors of the office. With two of the four main stairwells destroyed, soldiers might investigate, but they might also choose to stay put. After Canción destroyed half of their force, Gippy's stolen radio had lit up with enough expletives to make a hardcore porn star blush. The vaunted Grand Hope Security was on the verge of mutiny, and the lack of response from the upper echelon didn't help. So far, the hallway seemed quiet.

Outside the building, however, was anything but quiet. Dozens of drones and a few media helicopters flew distant orbits around the tower, cameras undoubtedly trained on them. He could imagine the talking heads giving their accounts of the "terrorist attack." Empa and Canción were the villains here, as far as the public consumer of information would be considered. No one knew the war they fought, the prices they'd paid, the monsters behind the world's decline, and the despair of humanity. They couldn't change that.

But now, if Empa's plan worked, they could change the endgame.

"I'm in!" She moved the chair back, stood shakily, and beckoned him over. "Come here and sit down."

He complied, handing over her carbine. The chair conformed automatically to his heavier, taller frame—a little creepy—and slid forward until every control on the station lay at his fingertips. The central screen displayed a list of contacts not unlike a cellphone's directory; a very long list of names, and after each, a title, location, local time zone, and, lastly, the name of the fallen angel who sired them.

"How many?" he asked, awed by the list.

"A hundred and sixty-seven, not including the Son of Samyaza. One of those is lying in the foyer, and another in the lab. There are several who are too young to be part of the network yet, but this is the lion's share of the worldwide Nephilim network." She lifted her carbine and stepped away from the desk. "It's time to see if that trick you pulled with Cora over the phone will work on a Nephilim, Canción. There's a trackball at the tip of your right armrest. Just click on a name, and you'll get a detailed display on another monitor with options for contacting them."

He moved the little ball, centering the selector icon on the top name: Julio Guterez, Head of Marketing, Petróleos de Venezuela. Caracas, Venezuela. GMT-4. Son of Tauriel. He clicked on the high-lighted entry, and a full page of information popped up on another monitor, including personal details, family, home address, financial information, and current projects. At the top of the display, also like a phone, were the options to text, call, or video call, and the local time, 0417.

Time to wake up and die, pendejo. Canción clicked "video call," and the screen changed to a blank panel with a blinking green icon labeled "calling."

The man who answered was young, dark-haired, and in bed. "Hola?" He blinked, and his eyes focused. "Quien diablos eres tú?"

Canción sensed the Nephilim the moment those dark eyes met his —the cold desire for solitude, to wipe the Earth clean of all life, simply to be alone and above it all—the Son of Tauriel, the fallen angel of mountains and solitude.

He couldn't resist answering, "Soy la espada de Dios." Then he smashed through the window of the man's eyes into the Nephilim's soul, wrenched it free of the human body, and crushed it. A moment of horror registered on the empty body's face, then the eyes rolled up, and the view jostled and spun. A woman's voice in the back-ground asked what was wrong in Spanish. With the seething ball of energy of the Nephilim's destroyed soul glowing within him, Canción ended the call and moved the trackball over the next entry on the list.

"Did it work?" Empa asked.

"Yes." He clicked on the entry: Zahra Hamidi, Egyptian security analyst, Gihaz El Mukhabarat El 'Amma. Cairo, Egypt. GMT+2 Daughter of Penemue. "One down; one hundred sixty-four to go."

Gippy didn't like this. Leaving Empa behind with Canción—who was frankly acting bat-shit crazier by the moment—felt like pulling his own teeth out with a pair of rusty pliers. The Indian woman seemed compliant and stable, but the other three were too terrified to be predictably reliable. He led the way with the assistant, while Jeri brought up the rear, her carbine steady on the others. She had really come through this like a pro, and he was so proud of her he could barely contain it, but the praise and adoration would come later. Right now, they had to secure the helicopter at all costs, and to do that, he needed every advantage he could get.

One possible advantage was walking right next to him carrying a case that might be worth billions, if not trillions of NADs. He had assessed her as an intelligent, competent—albeit terrified—professional, but she could also be playing them, leading them into a trap.

"So, you were Miaka's assistant? What did you do for him?"

She glanced at him with narrowed eyes. "Everything business related."

"The telecom business, or was there more?"

"Mr. Miaka had hundreds of contacts all around the world, many of whom had nothing to do with telecommunications or information technologies. It wasn't my place to judge his... personal life, but he had powerful associates across all industries and in many governments." She led them to a heavy steel door in the center of the building labeled, 'Roof Access Authorized Personnel Only', and swiped the black band she wore on her right wrist over the ID plate. It beeped, flashed green, and the door popped open.

"And did you know what he *really* was, besides a telecom trillionaire?"

She started up the stairs. "I don't know what you mean."

Even Gippy could tell she was lying and called her on it. "Bullshit."

She stopped and glared back at him. "What I knew about him is none of your business."

He grinned at her attitude. "*Everything* you know about him is my business, lady. You said you'd help us, but I need to know if you really will, or if you'll fuck us over the first opportunity you get."

"I have absolutely nothing to gain by fucking you over," she said, and might even be telling the truth to a certain degree.

He nodded to the case chained to her wrist. "You've got *trillions* of reasons to fuck us over, and only one reason not to."

"If I betray you, you'll kill me." She stated it like a fact etched in stone, which, of course, it was.

"That's the one reason," he agreed. "I just need to know if you think risking your life is worth what's in that case, but before you make a decision that could change both of our lives for the worse, know this." He nodded to the case again. "We don't need what's in there. You help us out of here, you and your friends can keep it."

Her eyes widened, perfectly manicured brows arching. "Bullshit. You'll just kill me and take it."

He shook his head. "That's your former boss's style, not ours. Besides, we probably can't access half of what's in that case without your help. You're our ticket out of here, lady. We need you. But you need *us* as well."

"Why?" She asked, clearly not buying his line.

"Because our ride out of here hinges on you talking us aboard that helicopter, but there are going to be a lot of questions about where your boss is. If they investigate and find him dead, and you literally holding the bag," he nodded to the case, "you're fucked. With us, you're safe as a baby in their momma's arms."

"Until we're on the ground. Then I'm not so safe."

He shook his head again. "What's your name?"

Her eyes narrowed again. "Why do you want to know?"

"Because I'm tired of calling you 'lady' and my hands are full of weapons, so I can't Google the name of Joseph Miaka's personal assistant."

Her lips crinkled into a moue of disapproval. "Dema Sikal."

"Great, Dema, so this is all you need to know: We came here for her," he pointed to Cora. "She's important to us. We have her. Help us get her out, and you win our undying appreciation, your freedom, and whatever's in that case. Do whatever you want after that. We don't care. We have absolutely *no* reason to hurt you unless you hurt us."

"I could tell the authorities about you," she said.

Gippy snorted a laugh. "The naffies already got our faces, so you telling them about us will only get that case taken away from you."

She just stared at him, and he could see her doing the math again.

"So, we got a deal, or what, Dema?"

She nodded once. "Deal."

"Fucking awesome! Let's go." He motioned her up the stairs.

She continued up, and he followed her, sparing a glance back at Jeri.

She just rolled her eyes and kept her weapon trained on the others. Good, she still didn't trust them. Neither did he, but he thought he might have just upped their odds of getting out of here in one piece by a significant margin.

2 5

ARMAGEDDON SONG

I'm seriously concerned for Canción. In the span of a minute, he's taken the souls of ten Nephilim, and I can feel the energy of their essences burning within him like the melting down core of a nuclear reactor. Number eleven—Bruce Lockland, Senior Advertising Consultant, Arrotex-CSL Pharmaceuticals, New Sydney, Australia—perishes in his car, the view careening out of control as the vehicle smashes into a bridge abutment. The power within him grows, but he clicks the next without hesitation.

"Canción." I place a hand on his shoulder. Cora's music within him is gone, silenced by distance or obliterated by the incipient nova of energy he's holding within himself. I can't feel his thoughts through the haze of power; it's like trying to read newsprint while staring into the sun. "You have to expel it. Let it go."

"Where?" he asks through clenched teeth. "If I destroy any more of the building, the electrical system might fail, and we lose our connection." He pulls up another call—Dae Mao Phong, CEO Mitsubishi Heavy Industries. Seoul, Unified Korea, Daughter of Saraknyal—and destroys the woman before she even fully wakes up. "Out the window, and I could kill innocent people. Up and I risk mom and the others."

"But you can't hold it all within yourself. Not *all* of them."

He stares at me, a cauldron of energy burning behind his eyes. "You don't know what I can or can't do, Empa. I'm the sword of God."

"The *what?*" The statement takes me aback. The last person I knew who said that was Achilles, the Son of Archangel Michael, the day before he died at Troy. A haunting déjà-vu visits me, as if I'm looking into the soul of Achilles as the fatal arrow flies.

"Mother said it. She told me to let God wield me. This is what I was *made* for."

He's delusional... or not. If not, I should shut the hell up, but he's my cousin's son. Cora would never forgive me if I let him destroy himself, even if it was to win the war.

"Canción, please. Expel the energy out there, into the sky." I wave a hand at the window, the swarming drones and helicopters.

"No." He pulls up another—Enrico Mateo, Brazilian Agriculture Minister. Brasilia, Brazil. Son of Shamsiel—and destroys him. The primordial nova of energy within him grows. "I blow the window out, and they see us. Police helicopters will shoot us."

I shade my eyes and see that, yes, there are more than one NAFAS police helicopter orbiting the building at a distance. Damn him for being right. "Canción, think of Cora! She'll waste away if you're not there to take away her pain." It's a low blow, but he doesn't even respond, pulling up yet another Nephilim, then another before the first one even answers.

They both perish in an instant. How many now, I don't know. He's pulling up two more before I can say another word.

"You should go," he says as another Nephilim's eyes roll up, their soul feeding the sword of God. "Get mom out of here."

"I *can't*, Canción!" I feel the energy growing. His skin feels warm, like he's spiking a fever. I consider knocking him out, but the bridled power within him would probably escape, killing us both, and likely Gippy, Cora, and Jeri as well.

"Then you'll die here, and Gippy won't leave without you, so he and Jeri and Mom will die too. The Nephilim will win by default." His eyes bore into me, and now I'm sure they're glowing with a pale inner light. "Don't do that."

I can't, and he knows it. "But, Canción..." I feel tears on my face, and realize I've broken Musashi's first rule. My spirit isn't steady, it's shattering within me. "We fought through Hell and high water to save you! I'm not going to let you blow yourself to smithereens!"

"This was *your* idea," he growls through clenched teeth, pulling up three more connections in quick succession. "Hundreds of *millions* have died opposing the Nephilim, Empa! What is one more if I can *truly* tip the balance! Get out of here! I'll win the war for you, but you have to survive! I can't contain this much energy for long!"

Dying at his side would have been easier, but he's right, there are others to think of, and the war... the *goddamn* war that has consumed my entire life. "Fucking hell!" I whirl away without another word and limp to the door, my vision a blur of tears I can't afford to feel.

Steady spirit, Emiko, Musashi tells me as we walk through the garden of blossoming cherry trees, petals falling around us like the tears of angels. *Do not cry for the dead. Cry for the living.*

I remember my response to Musashi's final lesson. "I *am*, Musashi-san." I turned and left him there, dying of a disease he wouldn't let me heal, unwilling to allow decrepitude to make him less of a warrior, and too skilled a warrior to have died in combat, at peace with his fate. His honor and spirit humble me still.

I stagger through the halls to the roof stairwell. The door's propped open by an unexploded door charge, Jeri making sure I can follow. I step through and let the door close fully, for I know in my heart that Canción won't be coming. I wipe the fog of sorrow from my eyes and begin laboriously climbing the stairs one at a time, because my hip is fucking killing me.

Gippy opened the door to the roof, momentarily blinded by the blazing sunlight and the hornet-like howl of the helicopter's rotors. The aircraft sat a hundred feet away, exactly like the two they'd seen in New Mexico—flat black with no markings, weapons pods in front of the side door—the ones that had gunned down Chaki and taken

Cora away. The tail rotor turned lazily, and the side door stood wide open. In the middle of that door crouched a single soldier... behind a deck-mounted gun aimed right at them.

Gippy clenched back the sudden urge to urinate and raised a hand, hopefully in a friendly gesture. His helmet radio squawked something he could barely hear over the howl of the rotors. He rapped the side of his helmet with his left hand, indicating a poor connection.

"Where is Miaka?" his radio howled.

"He's coming!" Doubtful, but it seemed like a good opener. The promise that the boss was on the way would keep the aircraft on the pad, at least for now. "He sent us ahead with the package! Dema Sikal is with us!" He gestured to her as the others emerged from the doorway.

"It's true!" Sikal screamed into her watch/comm device. She held up the case. "Check my comm signature! I'm Dema Sikal! We have the package and Miaka's secure portable server! We need evac!"

The door gunner turned and said something to the cockpit crew, then turned back and raised the muzzle of the gun to aim over their heads. "Get aboard!"

"Fuckin' A!" Gippy waved them forward, leaning close to Jeri as they passed. "Whatever happens, don't shoot the hilo's controls. It's our only ride outa here."

She nodded once, her eyes on the aircraft. "I've never flown before."

"Me either." He trotted past the bystanders carrying Cora to take the lead with Sikal. "Chalk up one more new and terrifying experience."

With him and Sikal in the lead, the two valets and butler helping Cora—now walking but not well and muttering about Canción—and Jeri bringing up the rear, they hardly looked official, but Sikal's cred must have been enough to get them in the door.

He vaulted up first, helped Sikal aboard, then one of the valets, and they lifted Cora bodily into the aircraft. The crew chief directed them to secure Cora in a stretcher, and Jeri scrambled up last, the sword at her hip drawing a suspicious stare from the crew chief.

"What the hell is *that*?" he yelled over the roar of the rotors, pointing at the sword, his other hand resting on his sidearm.

"It's Miaka's," she answered without a hitch, racking her carbine and taking the farthest seat forward, right behind the pilot. "It's an antique, worth millions. He told me to carry it, so it's not leaving my side. We're waiting on them, so just hold tight."

Gippy racked his rifle and settled into a seat near Cora, impressed with Jeri's quick answer. She might act rattled when the shit wasn't flying at them like hail in a hurricane, but under stress, she rocked. She pulled the sword and laid it across her knees, since the jump seats didn't accommodate someone with three feet of steel at their hip.

The crew chief pressed his hand to the side of his helmet, obviously listening to something over his radio, then turned to Sikal. "Miaka's not responding. What the hell's going on?"

"Some files didn't transfer to the portable server," she responded. "He's in the server room, pulling them down from the mainframe. I have no idea why he's not responding."

"How does *that* happen?" The crew chief seemed more skeptical by the moment.

"Some cabling must have been damaged between his terminal and the mainframe. You *did* notice the huge holes being blasted in the side of the building, didn't you?" Sikal's terse response seemed to settle the guy somewhat.

"Sure, but..." He paused to listen again, then said, "We're sending troops to help Miaka out. Sit tight."

Well, fuck, Gippy thought, casting a glance to Jeri. Her eyes were wide, her knuckles white on the hilt of the sword in her lap. Under the gaze of the crew chief, he dared not even reach for the walkie-talkie in his pocket. *Come on, E... Time to pull out some of that angel-daddy shit.*

Canción sat shaking in Joseph Miaka's ten-thousand-NAD office chair, hands gripping the armrests so hard he could barely move the trackball. Sweat streamed down his face, stinging his eyes. He'd lost track of how many he'd taken, how many Nephilim he'd destroyed. He only knew one thing.

More... more... one more! Click the trackball, open a video call, focus on the eyes, feel the evil, and take it away. Then open another call.

He couldn't hold many more, but he had to go on. *I... am... the sword... of God! This... is what... I was made for!*

Then he heard shouts from beyond the gaudy office doors. Soldiers. They'd discovered Miaka's body. They were coming.

More... faster! Take more! He clicked two more links and opened the calls. An elderly woman and a bright-eyed young man in a private school uniform answered, their eyes widened when they didn't recognize the caller, but before they could speak, he ripped their evil souls from their bodies and destroyed them. The energy building within him howled to be released, but he constrained it, compressed it, and opened two new windows.

"More!" he growled through his gritted teeth.

Something hit the door. Empa must have locked it on her way out.

One of the two contacts answered. The other went to voicemail. Canción destroyed the vile soul inhabiting a black woman in a military uniform and opened three more links. Faces appeared, and he annihilated them as fast as his eyes made contact with theirs.

Gunfire, and bullets ripped through the door. One round punched a hole through the upper right screen on the desk, but didn't hit him. Several more struck the windows behind him, the sound like hail on a tin roof before a tornado.

Canción scrolled down, the cursor hovering over one more name, then his eyes caught the little box to the lower left that said "Open all." *Yes!* He clicked it, the cursor trembling under his quaking finger. "Video / Voice" popped up. He clicked video.

Something smashed into the bullet-riddled door, and it flung wide, but the wall of monitors blocked his view. Voices rang out, demanding, profane, but Canción ignored them.

"Opening conference call," flashed on the central monitor.

Rifles erupted, their muzzle flashes strobing through the room.

The monitors were riddled, bullets zipping past him, spraying shattered plastic and electronic components, and impacting on the windows behind him. One round smashed into his ballistic vest, penetrating the Kevlar laminate, but without much remaining energy. A rib shattered, the slug lodging in his chest wall. Another ripped a track through the meat of his shoulder, punching a hole in the expensive chair. A third bullet punched a hole through the side of Canción's neck, severing the external carotid artery.

Monitors went blank, but not all of them, and the superb computer system re-routed the video images to the two remaining functional displays.

Faces began to appear about the same time that shock and pain arrived in Canción's central nervous system. Nephilim perished one by one as blood pulsed from his neck.

I am the sword of God. Wield me as you will...

The world began to gray at the edges of his vision, but he focused on the faces in the monitor. His control over the raging storm of energy within him began to slip away, but he took more. Faces without names, without love, without kindness, only hate, spite, and vileness... He absorbed their souls like an overfilled balloon strapped to a firehose.

Then he heard something over the roar of gunfire and the bellows of soldiers, the hounds of hell that the Nephilim had sent into the storm to die.

It was music...

I am music... he thought. *I am the song of Terpsichore, daughter of Israfal, God's minstrel... and the sword of God.*

And the sword swept through the Nephilim like a scythe through wheat.

2 6

FLY OR DIE

Gippy heard it over his radio's open channel and knew the shit was going to hit the HVAC. The soldiers sent to help Miaka had found him dead in the residence entry with another man. They were searching for the terrorists.

"What the..." The crew chief's eyes widened, and his hand went to his sidearm again. He'd put two and two together; their story didn't add up. The terrorists were sitting right here in his helicopter.

"Take them down!" the pilot bellowed, galvanizing their response.

And just to complicate everything, the stairwell door opened and Empa stepped out... alone.

"Jeri!" Gippy lunged at the crew chief as the man's pistol cleared the holster. *The weapon! Focus! That's all that matters!*

The weapon rose, the muzzle pointing at his center mass, the man's finger moving as if in slow motion from the trigger guard to the safety.

Click.

Unlike the Glock Gippy was familiar with, the Colts they carried were single-action, so they kept the hammer back in the holster, and the safety on. Safety now off, one pull of the trigger would fire the weapon.

As the crew chief's finger moved from the safety to the trigger, Gippy's hand closed on the barrel, pushing the muzzle away. The weapon fired, the bullet passing to his left side. The weapon's slide recoiled, and the forward sight tore the skin of his palm. He held on, pinning the slide back. His momentum undiminished, Gippy slammed into the man, bowling him over.

Another gunshot in the close confines of the helicopter; Jeri's or the copilot's weapon, he didn't know, and he didn't have time to look. The pistol was pinned between his chest and the crew chief's, so Gippy reached for his combat knife with his left hand. Before the knife cleared the sheath, the crew chief cracked the lip of his helmet into the bridge of Gippy's nose. Stars exploded in his eyes and his head snapped back, his grip on the pistol turning to water.

The crew chief heaved, and Gippy felt himself lifted, tumbling back. Through the stars and swimming vision, he glimpsed a splash of red on the copilot's window, Jeri surging to her feet, whirling, redirecting her weapon toward the pilot.

Atta girl! He hit the deck, his helmet cracking the edge of the seat, sending more stars exploding through his head.

The bystanders were screaming, one of them hit by the crew chief's shot, but again, Gippy was too busy to see which one.

The crew chief lurched up, pistol in hand, the muzzle centering in Gippy's blurry vision. Behind him, Jeri stood with her pistol nuzzled under the pilot's right ear.

"Freeze!" Jeri's bellow sounded nothing like her, and both the pilot and the crew chief complied.

The chief couldn't see her but knew she was right behind him. The pilot, however, could feel her gun's hot barrel pressed to his skin and dropped the weapon he'd half-pulled from his vest.

Gippy couldn't take his eyes off the gun pointing right at his forehead, the man's finger on the trigger. He could see in the crew chief's eyes that he knew if he killed Gippy, the next shot would be in his own back, but he wore both a helmet and a vest, so there was a chance he'd survive. That she hadn't already pulled the trigger meant that her gun was trained elsewhere, and there had been only one shot from forward, so that must be either the pilot or the copilot. She'd been sitting behind the pilot, with a clear view of the copilot's seat.

"Shoot the pilot and your friend dies," he growled.

"Shoot me and you *and* the pilot die," Gippy countered.

The man grinned. "She can't get us both, and you need the pilot."

"Never tell a woman she can't multi-task." Jeri's left thumb flicked the scabbard loose from her katana. She slashed, the black scabbard sliding down the blade as it swept in a flat arc. The polished bronze koiguchi cleared the tip of the blade as the black lacquered scabbard passed over the crew chief's shoulder. The movement past his shoulder caught his attention for an instant. That instant was his last, for the blade swept on, the tip slicing through the man's spine like a chef's knife through a carrot.

Snick.

The chief blinked, his mouth gaping, trying to form words, but the nerve impulses his brain was sending to his lungs, vocal cords, and his finger resting on the trigger of his pistol never arrived. The weapon dropped, and his head lolled forward, knees folding like a ragdoll's. He landed in a heap, still alive but utterly paralyzed.

Before Gippy could even stand, Empa arrived, the muzzle of her carbine sweeping the interior of the aircraft. "Sweet Jesus of Nazareth..." Her stunned look was priceless.

"You're *late*, woman!" Gippy wobbled as he struggled to his feet. "What, were you *shot* again or something?"

"Sorry. I can't quite run yet." She accepted his help into the aircraft, scanning the carnage. The copilot was dead, his brains decorating the starboard side cockpit window. The crew chief would be dead in moments, unable to breathe. The one bystander hit by the stray bullet was being tended to by the other two, the wound evidently superficial but painful, if the stream of imaginative profanity was any clue.

Gippy's eyes focused upon the empty roof behind Empa. "Where's Canción?"

"He chose to stay, and I couldn't make him leave." She took a seat, pain lancing across her features. "We need to get out of here *now*."

"But..." Gippy's mind fogged in confusion, and he wondered if he was concussed. "*Stayed?*"

"*Now*, before all hell... or heaven breaks loose." Empa nodded to Jeri, still standing with her gun pressed against the pilot's neck, her hand gripping the naked Katana. "Take off!"

"You heard her, buddy." Jeri prodded the pilot with her pistol. "Two choices: fly or die."

"Flying! We're flying!" The pilot's hands moved on the controls, and the howl of the rotors intensified. "Everyone, strap in!"

Canción... Gippy sat and affixed his lap belt, memories of Cora's son flashing through him. He turned to the Daughter of Israfal lying still on her stretcher, her face peaceful, eyes open, lips moving slightly as if singing or carrying on a conversation with someone who wasn't there. Someone who she loved, who would never be there ever again. Then he thought of Emil, the finest man he'd ever known, never to see his son again.

Gippy's heart broke for them both as the helicopter lurched off the roof.

A CHORUS OF ANGELS

So many souls destroyed... Canción ripped another evil soul from its human shell, his eyes flicking to the next face on the display. *Gone... another... gone...* One after another, taking them all in as fast as his eyes could make the connections. *Gone... gone... gone.*

Some part of his mind strayed, wondering if he'd be judged harshly for obliterating the grandchildren of God. But if not this, what was he made for? He was the sword of God. A sword is made to kill.

Soldiers bellowed, advancing around the desk, weapons trained on him, but it was too late. Their bullets could do nothing to stop the song building within him; *Armageddon Song...*

But maybe it wasn't. Maybe the song within him was only the beginning, the *prevention* of the Armageddon that Hell's minions sought to bring about. Maybe he was turning the tide of humankind from the influence of the Nephilim to something else.

Let them determine their own destiny, he thought, ripping another Nephilim from its human shell. *Let love, life, and happiness prevail over hate and greed.* Another... another... and there were no more. The screen was blank, only a few of them hadn't answered. The balance was tipped. It was done.

And his hold on the seething nova of the hate he'd destroyed slipped away.

Rough hands grabbed him, voices growling hard questions, but he paid no attention. Someone pressed a hand to his neck, but blood loss wasn't going to kill him.

Mother...

He prayed that she had gotten away, that the cataclysm within him wouldn't catch her in its wave of destruction, but the end was inevitable now. He couldn't hold it back any longer.

The notion struck him that all he'd ever done was destroy. People's emotions, their lives, their hope... But then he heard his mother's music, his own voice singing along, and saw the beaming faces of the people of Boquete whose lives they'd touched with their love, the poor farmers in Las Brisas as they moved their children into their new homes.

It wasn't all bad, then...

The energy within him soared outward, too much for him to expel in any kind of directed assault. Canción incandesced like the filament of an old-fashioned lightbulb receiving too much current, the terror-stricken faces of the surrounding soldiers alight with the glow. It consumed him, the office, the soldiers, the building around him in an expanding wave of light.

And he heard music more beautiful than any he'd ever heard before, yet familiar. A chorus of angels—his grandfather's music of which Terpsichore was only a part, of which he was only a tiny splinter—expanded within his soul.

We're barely a mile away when the top of Grand Hope Tower ceases to exist.

"Mother of God..." I don't know what I expected. I've seen a lot of explosions; daisy cutters, fuel-air bombs, even one nuclear blast from a safe distance. This is like none of those.

A strobe-bright impulse shines for an instant, a perfectly spherical wave of light expanding in the blink of an eye. There is no fire, just a shockwave of material so pulverized that it glows with energy. The dust sphere slows as it expands, thinning to a haze, and the top of the building—at least thirty floors—simply aren't there.

I draw a breath, remembering the fall of the World Trade Center towers, expecting the 600-ton counterweight suspended at the building's apex against earthquake motion to fall down through the building, but that, too, is simply gone. Drones and a few helicopters flying near the building are caught in the blast, falling like birds caught by a shotgun's spray. The shockwave of sound rattles our own helicopter, drawing a stream of expletives from the pilot. Debris as fine as beach sand falls in a half-mile radius, and as the air clears, the building still stands, or at least most of it.

"Mother*fuck!*" Gippy cranes around to gape at the spectacle.

Jeri just sits there, tears streaming down her cheeks, her gun still firmly pressed against the pilot's neck.

The top of Grand Hope Tower looks like it's been bitten off by a very hungry Godzilla. Girders stick up, some bent, others appearing as if metal-eating termites have gnawed them down. The glass of the next twenty or so floors is shattered, along with that of a few nearby buildings. I mumble a silent prayer that everyone was evacuated from those floors in time.

"Less than if Miaka had hit that button," Dema Sikal says, her voice emotionless. "It would have collapsed the entire building, taking out several city blocks."

"You *knew* about it?" Gippy glares at her. "How could you work for a monster like that?"

She shrugs infinitesimally. "Like the pilot. Fly or die. None of us were given much of a choice."

The other bystanders nod, and I understand. Just like so many who fought for the wrong side in wars all around the world, knowing their commanders were monsters, they had no other choice.

"Where to?" The pilot's question snaps me out of my reverie.

I haven't considered a destination, since we had planned to escape in our own vehicle. Not the best strategy in hindsight. I glance at Gippy with a raised eyebrow.

"Griffith Park, east side, near the freeway. Just put us down and you can go."

His choice is a good one, only a few blocks from our storage unit and vehicles.

"All of us," Sikal adds, turning to me. "I hope you can give us a ride to a hospital."

"Call an ambulance." I nod to the case she's carrying. "I think you can afford it."

She gapes down at the case in her lap as if she forgot it was there, then back up at me. "You'd really let us keep it?"

I sigh, lean back, and close my eyes, nurturing my broken heart with the knowledge of our victory. "I need money like I need another bullet in my ass."

EPILOGUE

SOULS TO SAVE

Gippy drove through the winding highways of Washington State with Jeri riding shotgun, destination British Columbia and the megacity of Vancouver. They were quiet, Gip watching the road, Jeri monitoring NAFAS police, DHS, and half a dozen other feeds on her tablet. They were in hunting mode, their prey, an investment banker named Wallenger, one of the few Nephilim lucky enough not to answer their phone on that fateful day eight months ago.

He glanced at Jeri, her brow furrowed in concentration, and nudged her leg with his hand. "Okay?"

"All clear." She responded without looking up. "Decoys are working like a brand-new vibrator."

He snorted a laugh at her euphemism. They'd learned a trick from the new CEO of Transmedia, sowing the nets with misinformation about sightings of the terrorist cell responsible for the explosion of Grand Hope Tower. NAFAS was searching Des Moines, Iowa for them. Even if they were pulled over by a cruiser, their IDs and disguises should pass close inspection. For the first time in his life, Gippy had a genuine NAFAS citizen identity, though false. Even the car they drove was legit, right down to the lease. But that wasn't what he'd meant.

"Excellent! So, how are *you?*"

"Oh, fine for now." She flashed him a smile, then returned to her work. "Stressed, but I'm focused. On the job."

"Good."

After their harrowing escape from the doomed Grand Hope Tower, they settled in their covert workshop/shipping container, Cora resting comfortably, injuries stabilized, Jeri had broken down. Not as badly as he had after Manhattan, but bad enough. He and Empa had held her until it passed, and she'd been embarrassed, but they both assured her she'd done well, what she had to do, and held it together under fire, which was all that mattered. He'd also told her of his own breakdown, which he had before, but she seemed to have forgotten. She was still scared and hated violence, but that, too, was good; scared kept you alive, and people who loved violence weren't the people Gippy wanted to get into deep shit with.

"About two hundred miles. You hungry, or you wanna wait until we get there?"

"Let's wait. The hotel has a good restaurant."

"Fine by me." He pulled an energy bar from a pocket and tore it open with his teeth. "We're doin' the good job, Jer. Never forget that."

"Oh, I know." She sighed and shrugged. "Just wish we were there for Cora's big day."

"Me, too, but when the opportunity arises, you gotta grab it by the balls."

"True that," she agreed, flashing him another smile. "War's a bitch, but she's *our* bitch."

"True that." He patted her leg and focused on the road, their goal, and all the souls they were going to save by sending this Nephilim to Hell.

In a picturesque ranch house east of Roseburg, Oregon, nestled in the foothills of the Cascades, I help Sister Janice bring the three fussy little newborn bundles of joy to their mother. The triple birth was hard on Cora, but she bore it well, being in excellent health and no stranger to motherhood. She played Carmina Burana for the last thirty minutes of the ordeal, which seemed odd to me, but inspired her. She even timed her final contractions to the sequential crescendos, which made me laugh.

At first, Sister Janice was concerned with the births, for none of the babies cried as normal newborns do, but they were breathing, eyes open, and I felt their souls take up residence as they entered the world.

Cora is sitting up in bed, still drenched in sweat. Mozart plays low now in the background, soothing and playful. and Emil sits on the side of the bed, stroking her sodden hair and praising her. Both the music and his touch calm her, and her eyes glow with delight as we lay the two girls and one boy down with her.

As one, their eyes lock onto her, wide and rapt, fascinated, loving... I've never seen newborns so absolutely focused.

"They're *beautiful*, Cora," Emil praises, stroking her hair. "You did so well!"

"I did?" She blinks down at her children, truly meeting them for the first time. "*Three*? I don't... They *are* beautiful, aren't they?"

Her memory still isn't completely back to normal; she's known for months that she was pregnant with triplets. In fact, we had many hard conversations regarding her pregnancy. She understood fully, even without remembering all the horrors perpetrated upon her, that the father of her multiple conception was a Nephilim, the Son of Armoros, Angel of Unmaking. I have no idea what a mixture of music and unmaking will result in, but the decision to continue or terminate her pregnancy was Cora's alone, and she chose to continue. With her son gone, which she understands but still sometimes forgets, her instinct is to bring more hybrid souls into the world, for we both know that this has been God's secret intent for a very long time.

"They are indeed, and healthy and *clearly* happy to see their mom."

Janice helps her situate the trio, who are much more interested in Cora's face than anything else.

I've birthed a lot of babies in my time, and Janice is no rookie at midwifery, and we exchange a knowing glance: the newborns are unusually attentive, alert, and even-tempered. Emil marvels at them, his face glowing with adoration for mother and all three babies.

"They're so... *amazing*," he says, brushing one pudgy cheek without disturbing the little girl's rapt attention.

"So like Canción." Cora coos to them and hums along with Mozart's Magic Flute Overture. Their already rapt attention intensifies at the sound of her voice and the music.

"Well, let's let mother and children get acquainted." Emil gets up slowly and shoots me a meaningful look. I follow him out of the bedroom into the kitchen where we have food and coffee.

"Cuppa?" I ask, pouring one from the urn for myself.

"Please." His back pops audibly as he stretches. "I honestly don't know how women do it. That was exhausting for *me*, and I wasn't doing any of the work."

"Comes with the territory." I pour and hand him a cup. "I'm envious, actually."

"I can't imagine..." He sips and changes the subject abruptly. "So, how is she doing?"

"Physically? She's fine, of course. Healthy as ever; living in the country suits her." I know what he's getting at, but I don't feel like going there. It's a joyous day, and I don't want to dwell on what Cora has lost. In the end, she's still Terpsichore, and her music still lives within her.

Emil obviously does. "And the rest?"

I suppress an exasperated sigh. "She's not improving, and I don't think she ever will. I was never a psychologist, but..." I'm not going to tell him all that I suspect they put her through, but direct neural stimulation coupled with sensory deprivation and virtual sensory input would have put anyone over the edge. "She's recovered as much as she will, I think, but still suffers from short-term memory lapses. Long-term... I can't tell exactly how much she's lost. Who knows. The babies might help her in time, and the mind is an amazing thing. I've seen people recover from serious brain trauma with proper therapy."

"Mmm." He looks sad, and I put a hand on his shoulder for comfort.

"She's happy and cognizant of her surroundings, Emil. She knows who and what she is, and who we are." He and Janice visited to help us get settled in the new house, but Cora hadn't recovered much by then. When we confirmed her pregnancy, they returned to Colorado but promised to come back for the birth, even though they had to drive through deep spring snows to get here in time. "She still takes joy in music and plays every instrument we put in front of her. She understands what happened, but doesn't remember much of it, or at least buried it deep enough that it doesn't give her nightmares. She even helps with the vineyard. She has a knack for gardening, and her legs mended well after the corrective surgery."

"I just wish..." He sighs and shakes his head.

"So do I, Emil, but that never makes it so." I know he's thinking of Canción. I've told him what happened, how his son destroyed more Nephilim in ten minutes than I could have exorcised in a century. "He changed the *world*, Emil. You should be proud."

"Oh, I am, I just wish I could have spent more time with him and seen him with Cora."

"She asks about him every so often, has to be reminded that he's gone, but she doesn't dwell on it much." Truth be told, Cora doesn't dwell on anything much, even the war, the remaining Nephilim, or our safety. That's my job, and one I'm taking seriously.

"How many are left, do you think?" he asks, evidently reading my pensive look. "Nephilim, I mean."

I shrug. "Impossible to say exactly, but at least twenty-five or thirty. We can account for eleven, banished or destroyed prior to the Grand Hope event." That's what the media is calling the terrorist attack culminating in the mysterious explosion. In all, one hundred and six people were killed or went missing, most of them security guards, and their deaths haunt me, more hounds of hell sent into the inferno. "And there were a hundred sixty-five more in Miaka's contact list. Of those, some simply didn't answer the phone. We've found and banished two of those, but some may have gone into hiding. I don't know how many Canción destroyed before..."

"Before he blew up." Emil frowns and shakes his head. "I saw it on the news. Half the *world* saw it in real time. They must know what happened."

"The surviving Nephilim? Yes, I'm sure they figured it out, which is why some of them have vanished." I finish my coffee, steadying my spirit with a long, slow breath. "I'm guessing twenty or so were too young to be part of the network. Gippy and Jeri are out hunting the ones we missed. Or at least the adult ones who were on Miaka's list and didn't mysteriously die with no apparent cause. That's nine more that we know of, but we may have missed a few."

"You *memorized* Miaka's list?" He arches a dubious eyebrow.

"Not really." I smile and tap my head. "I took what I needed from him to access the network. When I do that, it's... kind of like a copy and paste into my brain."

He blinks and raises his eyebrows. "Handy."

"Yes, except for the five thousand years of atrocities he committed that are now *also* up there." Talk about nightmares.

Emil looks distressed. "That's horrible."

"You're not wrong, but I'm dealing with it." I shrug and pour more coffee. "I never knew he was Heinrich Himmler in a previous incarnation."

His eyes widen again. "The engineer of the holocaust? Good God!"

"Right? And a hundred other really horrible people, most of whom history didn't even record." I put a hand on his shoulder again. "But he's gone. Forever."

"Thank you." He tries to smile but fails, then takes on an introspective mien. "If you'd like, Janice and I can stay here as long as is necessary to settle the babies. Maybe a year?"

"Of course, and I'll welcome the help!" I'm not looking forward to being the primary caretaker of three growing babies and don't even want to think about toddlers yet.

"It'll give you time to concentrate on the war."

"Yes, there is that..." I consider the possibility of actually winning the War of Souls, and my spirits lift. Gippy and Jeri are a good team, and we also have an unexpected ally in Dema Sikal, who managed to take Miaka's position at Transmedia. How much of his fortune she embezzled, I have no idea, but billions, certainly. She's changed the global media environment in less than a year, though the powers that be in NAFAS are gunning for her. "We're making progress, Emil. Maybe, one day, we'll find and destroy the last of them, but I honestly don't know what will happen when we do."

His brow furrows. "What do you mean?"

"I mean, even *I* don't know the mind of God. She may let humanity determine their own future or take everyone to Heaven for just rewards. Or maybe something else entirely." I smile at his consternation. "Not our problem, Emil. We win, then it's *Her* decision."

"*Their* decision," he corrects. "I'm changing my pronoun for God, since everyone has a different perception of Them anyway."

"Fair point." Funny that I haven't done the same in all my centuries, but it seems appropriate. Even as Their granddaughter, I don't know exactly what God is, but I know one thing: They love all mankind.

Emil's mood shifts to introspection. "Do you think that... when I die, I'll see him again?"

I know he's referring to his son, and I nod. "Yes, Emil, I *know* you will." I pull him into an embrace and squeeze tightly. "We'll all see each other there, and Cora and her children will play music for all of us."

The End

ACKNOWLEDGMENTS

Thanks once again to all the people at Falstaff who make dreams come true. We are the Misfits, and we are legion.

Keep up the fight!

ABOUT THE AUTHOR

Professional sailor, SFF fan, career biologist, gamer, and author, Chris has a diverse bibliography of science thrillers, nautical fantasy, epic fantasy, science fiction, horror, post-apocalyptic fantasy, and RPG tie-in stories. His game tie-in work includes Pathfinder, Iron Kingdoms, Shadowrun, Arkham Horror, and Traveller RPGs. He has over 30 novels in print and has won numerous awards, including the 2020 Scribe Award for best tie-in short story. His most recent releases are from Falstaff Books (Book Three of the War of Souls post-apocalyptic fantasy trilogy) and the new Asian-themed high fantasy Seeds of Darkness Trilogy. A new Pathfinder Tales novel, "Operation Hell-mouth" is slated to release in November 2025.

ALSO BY CHRIS A. JACKSON

(* with Anne L. McMillen-Jackson)

<u>From Jaxbooks</u>
A Soul for Tsing
Deathmask

<u>The Blood Sea Tales</u>
The Pirate's Scourge
The Pirate's Truth
The Pirate's Bane
Ash Walker
Blood Walker
Death Walker

<u>Weapon of Flesh Series</u>
Weapon of Flesh (also on Audible)
Weapon of Blood (also on Audible)
Weapon of Vengeance (also on Audible)
Weapon of Fear *(also on Audible)
Weapon of Pain *
Weapon of Mercy *

<u>The Cornerstones Trilogy</u>
(with Anne L. McMillen-Jackson)
Zellohar *
Nekdukarr *
Jundag *

The Cheese Runners Trilogy (novellas – also on Audible)

Cheese Runners

Cheese Rustlers

Cheese Lords

The Seeds of Darkness Trilogy

Man of Peace

Daughter of Horses

Son of War (Summer 2025)

The Scimitar Seas Novels

Scimitar Moon

Scimitar Sun

Scimitar's Heir

Scimitar War

From Shadow Alley Press

Pacifica

Stratos

Vesuvia

From Falstaff Books

The Dragons of Boston Trilogy

Dragon Dreams

Dragon's Nemesis

Dragon's Legacy

The War of Souls Trilogy

The Last

The First

The Eternal

<u>From Paizo Publishing</u> (also on Audible)

Pirate's Honor

Pirate's Promise

Pirate's Prophecy

Operation Hellmouth (November 2025)

<u>From Privateer Press</u>

Blood & Iron (ebook novella)

Watery Graves

<u>From Fantasy Flight Games</u>

The Deep Gate (hardcover novella)

<u>From Catalyst Game Labs</u>

Crocodile Tears (ebook novella)

FRIENDS OF FALSTAFF

Thank You to All our Falstaff Books Patrons, who get extra digital content each month! To be featured here and see what other great rewards we offer, go to www.patreon.com/falstaffbooks.

PATRONS

Dino Hicks
John Hooks
John Kilgallon
Larissa Lichty
Travis & Casey Schilling
Staci-Leigh Santore
Sheryl R. Hayes
Scott Norris
Samuel Montgomery-Blinn
Junkle
Vickie DeSantos
Quincy J. Allen
Allison Charlesworth

Thank You for Supporting Independent Publishing!

We believe that you should be able
to read your books, your way.
That's why this Falstaff Books
print edition includes a digital copy
at no additional cost!

Just scan the QR code with your device,
follow the directions on Prolific Works,
and enjoy!
You can also join our newsletter when prompted,
and never miss an awesome Falstaff Release!